I0603333

REDEMPTION

A REALM OF FLAME AND SHADOW NOVEL

CHRISTINA PHILLIPS

PHOENIX 18 PUBLISHING

CHAPTER 1

GABE

The last thing the Archangel Gabriel wanted was to mingle with a bunch of mortals, but it couldn't be helped. Whenever he finished one of his covert missions, he made a point of returning to the place where his client had first approached him. A symbolic gesture for anyone who might be tempted to solicit him for a favor.

A warning to stay away.

Five minutes was all it would take. He was meeting his fellow archangel, Mephisto, in ten.

He teleported to Zega, an exclusive club on one of the pleasure planets in the Andromeda Galaxy. It was a frequent hang out among half-blood immortals and excessively wealthy mortals looking for expensive thrills and interspecies sex.

As soon as he materialized, the effect of his archangelic radiance was instantaneous. The crowd pulled back, mesmerized, and a couple of mortals fainted. The music thundered, the floor vibrated, and he strode through the club, raking his gaze across the myriad faces focused on him.

A few would recall his previous visit and, combined with the alleged disappearance of his client, the whispers would spread, reinforcing his reputation as a mercenary who demanded a fee only the desperate would pay.

"My Lord Gabriel."

The voice came from behind him, and Gabe swallowed a groan as he swung around. He was too damn tired to interact with presumptuous mortals. All he really wanted was to get blind drunk and crash for a week. Unfortunately, the likelihood of doing either was remote.

He gave the tall male who had accosted him a withering glance, but the man didn't back away or apologize for his impudence.

"A moment of your time, my lord. That's all I ask."

"No." He turned away, but the man grasped his arm, and Gabe stopped dead. What the hell? Mortals didn't grab at him like this. Ever. Especially when they were obviously hoping for a favor.

"I've been searching for you for the last three Medan moon cycles."

Gabe slowly turned, and after a couple of seconds of eye-contact, the man finally appeared to realize his error and released him.

"Forgive me." He bowed his head in respect and kept his eyes trained on the floor. "Lord Gabriel, you're the only one who can help me. I beg you to consider my request."

Gabe made a cursory scan of the man's aura. A faint trace of immortal heritage glinted, which wasn't a surprise, considering the man's attitude. But there was something else entwined with those faded threads. An elusive glimmer that he'd never before encountered.

Reluctant interest stirred. It wouldn't take long to hear his request.

He gave a brief nod.

"You have two minutes." He strode to a darkened alcove where a couple was entwined. "Move." His voice was low, and the couple instantly leaped to their feet and sidled past him, clearly eager not to raise the wrath of an archangel.

He sprawled on the seat and propped one booted foot on the table. Without waiting to be invited, the man sat opposite.

"My name is Jaylar. I come from the planet Medana, in a solar system in the Beta Spiral of Andromeda," he said, although Gabe didn't know why he felt it necessary to give his address. "My daughter, Evalyne, is missing. We believe she's been taken off the planet."

Damn. He'd hoped for something far more complex.

"Maybe she took off by herself."

"You misunderstand, Lord Gabriel." Jaylar swallowed, clearly struggling to compose himself. "Although the blood of the gods flows in my veins, my lineage is diluted and Evalyne's mother is a pureblood mortal. Evalyne didn't inherit my ability to teleport. She's never left Medana in her life."

This is a waste of time.

"So, she found herself a lover who gave her something she lacked. I don't track runaway lovers."

Jaylar leaned across the table. His eyes glowed with a hint of madness. "She's four years old, Lord Gabriel."

Fuck.

The jagged rip in his heart, that would never fully heal, burned like acid, as long buried memories clawed for release.

Not now. Ruthlessly, he pushed the haunting echoes of another life back into the abyss. It was the only way he could function.

The only way he'd managed to survive.

A four-year old child was missing. Of course he'd take on the mission.

He kept his expression impassive. If word got out that he was a sucker for a missing child, he'd be inundated by frantic parents. His reputation was such that right now, only those on the verge of insanity dared to approach him.

He would help them, and in return he demanded a client's soul. Rumor had it he claimed their life, as well.

Either way, it was a fair exchange for hiring the services of an archangel. Even if the rumors were little more than a smoke-screen for what he really exacted as payment.

He slung his arm over the back of the seat and rapped his fingers on the leather upholstery. "Give me the details. I'll let you know what I decide."

Jaylar slid a small package across the table. "The information on this disc documents Evalyne's life. We'll pay anything. My life is yours. My wife wants you to know—"

"Stop." Gabe said. Jaylar had already given him all the information he needed, and he picked up the package and dropped it into his pocket. "I require access, so I can contact you."

Jaylar bowed his head in assent for the mind probe. It took barely a heartbeat for Gabe to gather the information he required to initiate a telepathic link in case of emergency.

He stood. "I'll be in touch."

Jaylar also stood. "How long before you decide? Is there a way I can contact you in the meantime?"

"When I've had time to access the information, I'll let you know whether the assignment appeals."

Jaylar's hands fisted, but he kept his mouth shut.

"And no. You can't contact me. The link is strictly one way."

"But my lord, you must understand the urgency of—"

"Those are my terms." His voice was deadly, and Jaylar backed up a step, appearing to belatedly realize he was seriously pushing his luck.

Gabe wasn't known for his benevolence. If anyone else requesting his services had spoken to him with such disrespect, there was no way he'd even consider the assignment.

But there had never been a choice. A child was involved.

He already knew he was going to take on the case.

Aurora

"You're going to have a lovely time." Aurora gave her mum an encouraging smile as they stood by the front door of their small cottage on the coast of Cornwall. The late July breeze was warm and the scent of honeysuckle filled the air. "You haven't been to London in ages."

"But I want to be here, with you, before you go back to university."

Aurora exchanged a glance with her dad. The pain in her heart was reflected in his eyes. Although it had been years since her mum remembered the past, just lately she'd been forgetting the present, too.

Time is running out.

And that's why she had to make sure her parents went on their annual weekend getaway, so she could put her plan into action.

"Aurora's finished Uni," her dad said as he wrapped his arm around her mum's shoulders. "She's moved back home for a while. She'll be here when we get back."

Her mum gave her the strangest look, and shivers raced over her arms. It was almost as though she knew about Aurora's plans.

But she couldn't. It had been years since she and her mother had been able to communicate telepathically, and besides, that wasn't the same as mind-reading.

There was no way her parents had guessed what she was going to do.

"That's right." She kissed her mum's cheek. "It's only for a couple of days. Go and enjoy your anniversary break."

"Anniversary…" There was a faraway note in her mum's voice. And although her dad quickly recovered, she caught the stricken expression on his face. It didn't matter how often it happened. He was always devastated with every reminder of just how much her mum had lost.

"Tomorrow it's twenty-five years since you arrived here, Aria," he said softly, and there was so much love in his voice tears prickled in Aurora's eyes. "We celebrate every year."

Her mum's eyes clouded, and it was hard to keep smiling when all she wanted to do was rage to the uncaring universe. *Why has mum forgotten so much?*

Agonizing didn't help anyone. But her experiment just might.

There was a long silence before her mum turned to her dad. Aurora held her breath. Had she remembered?

"But I've always been here, Tom," she said, and Aurora's fragile hope shattered.

Early the following morning, Aurora sat cross-legged on her bed as she did a final read of her checklist on her laptop. Her room, set under the eaves of the cottage, might be messy, but her data was meticulous.

Today she was going to find, and enter, the world where her beloved mother came from.

A world in an alternate dimension.

Just because her parents had never tried to cross dimensions again, didn't mean she had to accept their word that it had been a once-only, never to be repeated miracle.

For eight years, since she'd turned sixteen, it had been her driving focus. And not just because she was desperate to find answers to so many questions she had about her own unique heritage, and to finally meet her mum's beloved sister, Aurora. Her namesake.

Or the deep, secret fear that had haunted her for as long as she could remember that she was a freak who shouldn't exist.

It was because she realized how tenuous her mum's grasp on reality really was.

With every passing year her memories became more faded

and confused. And on the rare occasions she *did* speak of her old life, it was as though it was nothing more than a childhood dream. But the more she denied her past, the more fragile her health became.

If Aurora could bring back proof of the parallel world, she was convinced that everything would go back to the way it used to be. All her mum needed was a rock-solid reminder of her own world.

And Aurora knew exactly what she needed to find.

She picked up a silver photo frame that usually took pride of place in the living room. The delicate, ethereal flower that had been lovingly pressed and preserved so many years ago never failed to send trickles of awe along her spine.

Her mother had worn this exotic bloom in her hair the day she and her father had finally met for real, instead of in their shared dreams. She'd been in a meadow and had picked the flower just moments before walking into her dad's arms. It was the only link they had to her mum's world.

And it was this link that would open the gateway.

THE SUN WAS STILL low on the horizon as Aurora made her way through the village to the woodlands on the far side. The scientific part of her, that had got her through four years of university, didn't see what difference it made *where* she was when she put her theories into practice.

But in her heart, she knew being in the exact spot where her mother had stepped into this world was her only chance of success.

She sat on the ground, facing the woods. The summer sun warmed her shoulders, and the faint rustling of the countryside sank into the beat of her heart.

Everything revolved around the strength of her psychic grip

on the flower in the frame and the image she had in her mind of the meadow where the flower had once grown. There was no logical reason why she needed to enter the astral planes before conducting her experiment. It was a spiritual realm, and in theory could be accessed by anyone who went into trance or deep meditation.

Except she'd loved the astral planes since the first time she had ascended as a child. And, just as importantly, it was the place where the idea to link to her mum's world had come to her.

I can do this.

It would work. It had to.

With practiced ease, she slipped into trance, and within seconds the vibrant landscape of the astral planes shimmered, as though a gossamer veil had fallen across the realm. She focused her psychic energy on the flower and her own trans-dimensional heritage.

Her instincts were right. It would be enough to allow her to open a gateway from the dimension of her birth into the dimension where her mother had been born.

A spiderweb of glittering raindrops materialized in front of her. It pulsed like a living entity and gently cocooned her in a breathtaking, ethereal sphere.

Yes ...

From nowhere, a silent roar thundered, an anomaly that shouldn't even exist here. Waves of discordant energy vibrated through her and terror spiked as countless levels within the astral planes tumbled into chaos around her.

And then she slammed back into her body with such force she couldn't breathe, and an imprint of distorted, violet lightning flashed through her reeling mind.

What just happened?

CHAPTER 2

GABE

Gabe tossed back his fourth whiskey in as many minutes, but it might as well have been water for all the effect it had. That was the trouble with Earth. Even in the worst dives on the planet, the alcohol was never potent enough to numb his brain.

Not that this exclusive club in the heart of London was a dive, with its celebrity and wannabe-famous clientele. But Mephisto, the oldest archangel of them all, had contacted him just before he'd visited Zega. And since it had been at least a couple of decades since they'd last seen each other, he'd agreed to meet him here.

Even though he'd been late, Meph still hadn't arrived. Any other time Gabe would have left already, but after his meeting with Jaylar, the prospect of hanging out with another immortal and getting blind drunk seemed like a good idea.

Not going to happen here. It didn't stop him ordering a fifth whiskey.

He leaned his back against the bar and eyed the humans as they drank and flirted with each other, oblivious to his presence. His glamour was barely a level one, but it was more than enough to blur their perceptions if they glanced in his direction. He'd had enough of mortal adoration for one day.

Mephisto obviously didn't care who saw his mesmeric glory. Like a cursed god, he strolled across the club toward Gabe, and the humans parted before him like a subservient wave.

"You look worse than shit," Mephisto greeted him as his besotted entourage edged closer. "I should've checked in with you years ago."

"Call your lapdogs off." Gabe glanced at the crowd. Humans were among his least favorite lifeform in the universe, and while he could tolerate them from a distance, this was pushing his limits.

"You're still an antisocial bastard." Mephisto grinned, and a faint shimmer radiated from him across the club. The humans blinked, disoriented, before stumbling away and leaving the two of them alone at the bar.

Gabe ignored the comment, since it was true. But although they hadn't seen each other in years, the other archangel had already ruffled his long-destroyed feathers. "What do you mean, you should've checked in with me? I'm not your fucking responsibility."

"Ego's still intact, though." Mephisto snapped his fingers and the bartender placed a glass in front of him. "You're *all* my fucking responsibility."

Right. It was only the mocking gleam in the other archangel's eyes that reminded him Mephisto didn't do serious. Ever.

Except one time.

A shudder inched along his spine, burning the livid scars that even after millennia still distorted the flesh on his back. Sometimes he could go years—okay, weeks—when the searing loss of his wings didn't scorch his soul.

Let it go, already. That wasn't going to happen, but it didn't stop him wishing for it.

He didn't like being in anyone's debt. Especially Mephisto's. But some things could never be repaid.

The other archangel pulled a squat, black bottle from the pocket of his long trench coat and topped up both their glasses. "Tonight, you're getting laid. Get that down you."

Gabe scoffed. "If you wanted to get me drunk, why are we here?" Even if the bottle contained some wild off-world spirit, he'd need more than a few shots to get wasted. And he wasn't going to touch the *getting laid* comment. While Mephisto lived to fuck, Gabe couldn't even remember the last time *he'd* had sex.

There was nothing in the universe that would get him to confess that to anyone.

To prove his point, he tipped the sparkling yellow liquid down his throat. Fire blazed, incinerating his tongue, mouth, and whole fucking GI tract. Supernovas exploded in front of his eyes and a primal drumbeat throbbed through his brain. The glass shattered in his hand, and through an orange mist, Mephisto smirked.

"Lightweight."

"What the fuck?" The words were a strangulated wheeze, and it was a struggle to focus. In the past, he'd tried every alcoholic blend in creation. None of them were this potent with just one gulp.

"A gift from the Demonic Council in gratitude for my phenomenal diplomatic skills. I don't share this shit with just anyone."

Gabe coughed, and blood splatted across his fingers. While archangels and demons were deadly enemies from the dawn of their existence, there was no active war between them. Most of the time they kept out of each other's jurisdiction. At least, in theory. "You mean you stole it."

"Whatever." Mephisto took a swallow of the lethal drink, and his eyes blazed crimson. "Tonight, you're having a woman from Earth. It's my mission."

"Not going to happen." And it had nothing to do with his unintentional, self-imposed celibacy. Even when he'd screwed around, he hadn't touched women from Earth. The idea curdled his guts.

"It's time, Gabe." Mephisto procured another glass, slammed it on the bar, and filled it to the brim. "You need to move on."

He laughed. Not that it was funny. Obviously, the demon drink was starting to take effect. He drained the second one, and this time managed not to crush the glass when the alcohol splintered his sanity.

Damn, that was good. A mellow benevolence warmed his blood, and through a swirling orange haze he contemplated the club's occupants.

Still way too human for his liking. He'd forego mindless sex and stick to the booze tonight.

A discordant bleep drilled through his brain, and Mephisto pulled a phone from his pocket. Interesting. Why did he need a phone? And one that originated, of all places, from Earth? There were countless more advanced civilizations who had similar devices. He had a couple himself that were useful for contacting non-telepathic races.

Mephisto checked his message and a frown slashed his brow. "Fucking unbelievable." There was no hint of his usual mockery. "It worked."

It wasn't like Mephisto to be enigmatic. Genuinely intrigued now, Gabe placed the glass on the bar and attempted to banish the swirling fog that was trying to penetrate his eyes.

"You need some help?" Fuck, had he said that out loud? First, Mephisto never needed help. Second, Gabe would never offer it. It was the way things were between archangels. Assistance was only ever given in the direst of circumstances, and it was never spoken of.

His reluctant admiration for the inventor of the demon drink increased another notch. It was mind-rot at its finest.

Mephisto shoved the phone back in his pocket. There was a familiar, maniacal gleam in his eyes. "No. But you, my friend, do."

As Mephisto teleported from the club, a couple of women draped themselves over Gabe. He froze, glaring at the spot where Mephisto had been just a second before. Since his glamour was enough to render him all but invisible to humans, it was obvious the other archangel had bedazzled the women who were now stroking his chest and gazing at him in adoration.

"I haven't seen you here before," one of the women said in a breathy voice as her friend sighed and rubbed her head against his biceps. "But you look *soooo* familiar. Are you an actor?"

"Let's go back to my place," whispered the other one. "It's not far."

I'm going to fucking kill him.

"Not tonight."

His feral growl had no effect. They continued to gyrate against him and drop reverential kisses over his shoulders.

The demon drink might have lowered some of his inhibitions, but it sure hadn't corrupted his libido. The women could be marble statues as far as his body was concerned.

Was it because they were from Earth? *Or has my sex drive died?*

Shit, that hadn't occurred to him before. Mephisto was right about one thing. He did need to get laid. But not here. And never with humans.

He peeled their arms from him, gritting his teeth against the distaste that roiled through his chest at the touch of their naked skin. Some things never changed. Not that he wanted them to. Armageddon could annihilate the entire planet before he found a human from Earth appealing.

He needed to leave. Right now. It would be easy enough to crash a party on a half-civilized planet and find a willing female. Or three. Why the hell not? It had been eons since he'd enjoyed an orgy. Just because the thought wasn't getting him hard didn't mean it was a bad idea.

Twenty-four hours of hedonistic pleasure, and then he'd focus on his next mission.

From nowhere, a blast of icy terror ripped through his brain, freezing his blood and sending eerie prickles of inexplicable menace along his spine. Paralyzed, he didn't even care when the two women fell onto him again, like vampiric succubi.

Danger.

Raw dread scraped through his synapses. A primal fear dredged from the depraved soul of creation. Alien, skeletal fingers clawed over his heart as an ancient horror seeped from his deepest memories.

This isn't real. It had been millennia since those nightmares had haunted him. *I'm not going back.*

Blackness tumbled around him, and the world winked out of existence.

Aurora

CAN'T BREATHE.

Everything hurt, and vertigo spun through Aurora's mind.

What's wrong with my chest?

The spinning slowed, and with a jolt, reality slammed into her.

A heavy weight pinned her to the ground.

What the hell?

Panic flared, a molten wave that licked through her blood and liquified her nerves. She was flat on her back, her arms by her sides, and her fingers splayed against the ground. Grass?

Open your eyes.

She couldn't just lie here. For a start, she didn't even know where *here* was. Suppose she'd succeeded in her mission?

Suppose she hadn't?

I'm afraid of what I might see.

Was it just her imagination that the weight crushing the life out of her was shaped like a hard, muscular, body? An *unmoving* body. A bolt of terror scorched through her as fireworks sparked inside her brain, like she'd short-circuited her memory.

God, I hope not.

And having a one-sided conversation with herself wasn't going to help get her out of whatever *this* was. The most likely explanation for her predicament was she'd somehow given herself an electrically charged shock from the astral planes.

Was that even possible?

It was better than the alternative.

She screwed up her cowering courage and tentatively forced open her eyes.

A muscled shoulder, encased in a dark blue shirt, greeted her.

Shock slammed through her, shredding the lingering fog that clouded her brain. It wasn't a figment of her imagination. *There's an unconscious man on top of me.* His face was buried in the curve of her shoulder and neck, and tangled dark blond hair teased her cheek.

Her fingers dug into the grass and adrenaline flooded her. Except she couldn't fight or flee because *there was a strange man sprawled across her.*

He hadn't attacked her. He wasn't trying to assault her. Calm down and think.

Maybe they'd collided when she had crossed from one dimension into another?

That was the danger of undertaking a cutting-edge experiment like this. There were so many unknown variables involved.

She hitched in a shallow breath, but it didn't help much. At least he wasn't dead. His breathing was warm against her throat, and his heartbeat was strong.

She needed to escape before she suffocated.

Gingerly, she tried to push him off her. It was like trying to move a mountain.

Concentrate. Her lack of oxygen was affecting her sense of reality. Maybe she should say something?

"Hello?" Her voice was hoarse. And seriously, was *hello* the best she could do? But what else could you say to a comatose stranger who was in danger of asphyxiating you without even knowing it?

He didn't move, but something stirred. Her face burned as the unmistakable length of his cock thickened against her jeans-covered thigh, and her fingers froze in his hair. *Why am I twisting his gorgeous hair around my fingers?*

She had no idea. But she couldn't pull free.

His weight shifted, a slow realignment of heavy limbs, as though he was becoming aware of his surroundings. With languid grace, he raised his head, and, for one eternal moment, an overwhelming sensation of déjà vu quivered through her. His perfectly sculpted face, enhanced by an irresistibly sexy stubble, seemed as familiar as her own reflection.

That was crazy. She'd never seen him before in her life. And he wasn't the type of guy anyone could forget in a hurry. *Stop staring at him.*

She might as well tell her heart to stop beating. Because his eyes were a swirling kaleidoscope of blues, greens, and silvers. *Am I hallucinating?* But she wasn't. They were captivatingly beautiful, unique. And yet threaded through her awe was a faint echo of haunting recognition.

"Hello?" he repeated. His voice was low, sexy, and sent a needy thrum vibrating through her blood. She licked her lips, and his gaze dropped to her mouth. *Help.* "Were you at the club?"

What club? Why wasn't he freaking out? There had clearly been a cosmological fuck-up. It was the only thing that made any sense.

That doesn't make any sense at all.

"No." It came out as an undignified croak. He braced his weight on his forearm, and she sucked in a jagged breath as she caught sight of the familiar trees she'd known all her life. *My experiment failed.* Right now, that was the least of her concerns. "You just suddenly appeared from nowhere."

How dumb did that sound? But it was true. She was on the outskirts of the village where she'd grown up, and the sun was still low in the sky. If she'd been knocked out, it hadn't been for long.

Still didn't explain anything about the arrival of this breathtaking guy. Or why he was behaving as though he did this kind of thing on a regular basis.

A slow frown creased his brow, and she realized her fingers were still entwined in his hair. What were the chances he hadn't noticed? With a mortifying lack of coordination, she freed them, and then didn't know where to put her hand.

She needed to regain control. Except her initial panic had faded, and although she was in the most vulnerable position she'd ever been in her life, she didn't feel threatened.

If that wasn't a sign of concussion, she didn't know what was.

"Nowhere," he repeated, and a half-smile tilted his lips. *Do not stare at his lips.* "I sure as hell owe Meph one for that demon drink."

Wait. He'd been in a *bar*? How could a guy who'd been drinking in a club somewhere have suddenly materialized on the coast of Cornwall? At least if he had *also* been meditating on the astral planes there would be some kind of connection between them.

His smile was mesmeric. She wanted to run her fingers through his hair again, pull him closer, kiss his delectable mouth.

Heat burned through her, and again she dug her fingers into the grass, in case they did something random like stroke the stubble on his magnificent jaw. *I can't believe I'm thinking this.* What was the *matter* with her?

He might be the most gorgeous man she'd ever met, but she

had far more important things on her mind than caving in to her deprived hormones.

"Could you"—*kiss me*—"get off me?" Before she did something totally embarrassing, such as wrap her arms around his spectacular shoulders.

I've definitely suffered a concussion.

His smile was the epitome of sex and sin and everything in between. She wanted to bask in his glorious splendor and obey his every sensual command.

Get. A. Grip. Was he hypnotizing her?

"Are you sure that's what you want?"

His teasing question whispered across her cheek, a tantalizing promise of unimaginable decadence. How easy it would be to say *no*. Why was she trying to fight the inevitable?

There's nothing inevitable about this.

"Yes." She ignored the regret that fluttered deep in her chest. There was a time, and there was a place, and this was neither.

Shock flashed across his face, as though her response had been completely unexpected. She gritted her teeth before her traitorous tongue overruled her good sense and tried not to melt beneath his irresistible grin.

"Your call." He rolled off her but didn't sit up. Instead, he stretched out next to her, his leg touching hers as he gazed at her with those fantastical eyes. It was glaringly obvious he expected her to protest at his withdrawal. And for an eternal, surreal moment, she almost did.

Not going to happen. *Even though I want to.*

Mephisto

MEPHISTO HAD DONE many things in his long life, but hiding in an oak tree and concealing his presence from another archangel was a novelty. And not one he wanted to repeat anytime soon.

What in the name of the goddess was Gabe doing here? He hadn't arrived voluntarily. He'd literally fallen from the sky. If he hadn't seen it with his own eyes, he never would've believed it. Only the ancient gods and goddesses wielded the power to transport an archangel against their will, and those Immortals had abandoned this sector of the universe millennia ago.

Luckily, Gabe had been unconscious when he'd landed, which gave Mephisto time to throw up a dozen glamours. No way did he want to explain why he was keeping this annoying little human under surveillance.

He'd first come across her a couple of years ago, when he'd attended a university lecture on multiverse theory. Although humans still had a long way to go when it came to understanding quantum mechanics, he ensured he kept up with their advances, pitiful as they were.

Especially when they started theorizing on the possibility of testing for the existence of those parallel universes.

The lecture itself hadn't given him any concern that humans were closer to breaching dimensions than they had been a thousand years ago. But the questions from one particular student had fascinated him.

She queried the use of psychic abilities as the catalyst.

Her views had been brushed aside, but since humans were notoriously unreceptive when it came to the untapped power of their minds, he'd expected that. And while he had no personal experience of crossing into a parallel world, it *was* possible.

And Aurora Robinson's theory intrigued him.

As a precaution he'd tapped her phone so he could monitor her psychic fluctuations. Because if she did somehow come close to succeeding, he planned on shutting down her psychic link and wiping her memory of everything connected to her insane experiment.

Better that than the alternative. Although he didn't often interfere when humans did stupid shit, he made an exception when the outcome involved falling under the jurisdiction of an alien race known as the Guardians.

They had patrolled the dimensional boundaries for millennia. The Dark Matter of the universe, where they lived in ethnocentric isolation, was rumored to hold ancient secrets. Immortals surmised that, when dimensions were breached, it triggered a celestial alarm for the Guardians.

Ten minutes ago, she'd triggered *his* alarm. He'd had milliseconds before she opened a rift and was beyond his help. But when he'd arrived, for a reason he couldn't fathom, she'd ascended into the astral planes to do it.

Like he said, annoying human. But before he had the chance to do a grand rescue that she would never remember, a preternatural ripple shuddered through reality.

Fuck. He was too late. There was no saving her from her fate now. And he had no intention of staying to watch the inevitable fallout.

She'd keeled over—and then Gabe had landed.

Which had stopped Mephisto in his tracks. He didn't believe in coincidence, but it was hard to imagine a possible connection between the two events. And much as he wanted to hang around and see Gabe's response when he discovered he was trying to charm not merely a human from Earth, but one who had metaphorically jumped on the Guardians' hot button, he had shit to sort.

Sometimes, being the Immortals' undisclosed peacekeeper was a fucking pain in the ass.

CHAPTER 3

GABE

I've no idea where I am.

Something dark and primeval gnawed the outer edges of his subconscious, like an elusive warning for his blackened soul. But an alcoholic hum vibrated through his mind, dulling the primitive imperative for answers, and with every passing second, the eerie sense of an unknown terror receded.

Did that demon drink knock me out?

The last thing he remembered was being manhandled by a couple of mesmerized women. The chestnut-haired siren beside him, who possessed a smattering of irresistible freckles across her nose, hadn't been one of them.

She hadn't been in that human-infested club at all.

He needed to find out what had happened, but his usual iron-clad logic drifted just out of reach. There was no rush. Something about this woman intrigued him, and not just because it was the first time in too long that he wanted to get naked, with her.

It was because she'd pushed him away.

Without a glamour, it was the curse of an archangel to bedazzle unsuspecting mortals. His unscheduled side trip had shattered his protective shield, and while this tempting creature appeared shaken, she was far from dazzled.

Her reluctance to melt beneath his archangelic radiance was intoxicating.

"I didn't hurt you, did I?" His full weight had pinned her to the ground. It was a minor miracle he hadn't crushed her ribs when he'd smashed into her. At least, he assumed that was how he'd landed on top of her. *Why can't I remember how I got here?* Wherever *here* was. Not that she appeared injured as she sat up and brushed nonexistent grass from her thighs. Her hair tumbled over her shoulders, and copper highlights glinted in the sun.

She was fucking gorgeous.

"No." She glanced at him, and their gazes locked. She had the prettiest blue eyes he'd ever seen. For an eternity, time stood still as her breathing became uneven and an enticing blush suffused her cheeks. Arousal thrummed in the heated space between them, and the scent of grass and the salty tang of the sea drifted in the warm, early-morning air.

He smiled, aware of the effect it would have on her. Her jagged intake of breath and the way her kissable lips parted, begging for his possession, was everything he expected. He brushed errant strands of her silky hair from her cheek, and primitive need streaked through his blood, straight to his cock.

He leaned closer. It was insane how badly he needed this kiss. Thank fuck no one was around to witness it.

And then she raised her hand between them, her fingers all but grazing his chest, in the universal sign of *stop*.

She's telling me to stop?

Incredulity crawled across his lust-soaked brain. Was this some demon-induced hallucination?

"What happened? How did you get here?" Her voice was breathless, as though she were recovering from a dozen mind-shattering orgasms. He blinked, trying to dislodge the graphic image scorching his reason, but it didn't help.

"I was at a club … and then—" With more reluctance than he'd ever admit, he straightened. "Then I turned up here. What the hell were you doing?"

"I was ascending into trance, in the astral planes."

This was getting more warped by the second. If this was Mephisto's idea of a joke … He left the thought hanging, but only because his brain hurt too much to conjure up suitable retribution.

"The astral planes. Right." It wasn't his area of expertise, but he wasn't about to tell her that. Why was he even having this conversation? If sex was off the agenda, he needed to find his bearings and teleport back to civilization. But something, damned if he knew what, compelled him to remain where he was.

"Yes." Her gaze dropped to his throat, and she gripped her fingers together on her lap.

He narrowed his eyes. Guilt dripped from her, although she was trying hard to hide it. *What aren't you telling me?*

"I can sort of remember this crushing feeling of dread. Like the world was ending or collapsing in on me. It's hard to explain. You didn't get any of that?" she said.

Echoes of an ancient horror skittered across his skull. Except they weren't memories he'd buried so many millennia ago. They were fresh. Recent.

The club.

His phantom feathers burned, an acidic, soul-deep anguish, and he gritted his teeth. *Not now.* Whatever had transported him from the club had nothing to do with the events that had cost him his wings.

And he wasn't about to discuss any of it with this mortal, no matter how intriguing she was. He'd keep the focus on her. Get her to tell him where he was, without having to ask. Although the effects from the demon drink had dimmed, it had screwed with his internal compass, and he didn't have a clue where in the universe he'd landed. "That's never happened to you before while you were in the astral planes?"

"No. The astral planes are tranquil. I can't understand why this was different."

A shadow passed over her face, and the same certainty as a moment ago stabbed through him. *What's she hiding?*

"Can't you?" He meant it as an accusation. It sounded like an invitation to sin. What could he accuse her of, anyway? He didn't care what secrets she kept. She didn't possess the power to render him unconscious or mess with his mind.

No mortal did.

"I don't understand how you can be so *calm* about all of this," she said.

He mentally scanned the area, but it was half-hearted. Sure, he needed to find out where he was, but there was no sense of danger, and damn if he didn't still want her.

To hell with it. It had been too long since a woman had roused his interest. A leisurely fuck and then he'd be ready to leave. He gave her a lethal smile, infused with an additional glimmer of archangelic radiance, and her soft sigh drifted like gossamer on the breeze.

She swayed toward him, and her fingertips brushed his biceps. Such a featherlight touch, and yet even through his shirt sleeve his skin burned at the contact.

This was going to be fucking spectacular. He leaned in for the kiss.

And the unmistakable ring of a phone from behind him splintered the moment.

Fuck that. He sent a blast of psychic energy, and the phone went silent.

"Was that my phone?" She sounded dazed and blinked a couple of times. He traced his finger along the curve of her cheek, and she gave a delicate shiver.

"You don't need your phone."

"Yes, I do. It might be my dad."

It was the *third time* she'd refused him. Even demigoddesses, minor deities in their own right despite their diluted immortal blood, found it hard to resist an archangel. He was so staggered by the phenomenon, he reached for her phone without further protest.

As his fingers touched the device, a distorted, ephemeral image of Mephisto burned through his brain. Mephisto was behind this. Had he ever doubted?

No, but the knowledge that this woman was a creature of Meph's, that willingly or not, she'd agreed to fuck with Gabe's mind, pissed him off more than it should. *I'm only pissed because I still want her.*

He tossed her the phone and she caught it one-handed.

This was his cue to leave. For all he knew, Mephisto had rigged up a remote recording and was watching this whole thing unfold. No way was he hanging around as the main entertainment while the other archangel got his rocks off.

She checked her messages and frowned, and for some reason he couldn't stop himself. "No further orders from Mephisto?"

"What are you talking about?" She transferred her frown to him and sounded so genuine he almost believed her. There was one sure way of discovering the truth, but unless he was on a mission and needed intel, as a rule he didn't probe innocents' minds.

"Big guy. Arrogant as fuck. Hard to forget." Even if he concealed his wings with a glamour.

"Should I know him?" She tilted her head, and a thoughtful expression crossed her face. Now they were getting somewhere. Shame it didn't improve his mood. "Did we all collide on the astral planes, do you think?"

Her obsession with the astral planes grated on his nerves. It had nothing to do with the fact she appeared unmoved their kiss had been interrupted.

"I don't visit the astral planes." He hadn't for years. And he was done playing their games. His navigation system was still out of alignment, but all he needed was a reference point so he could get out of here. "Which planet is this?"

She stared at him as if he'd just spoken in ancient Sumerian. Belatedly it occurred to him she might not have a clue that Mephisto wasn't indigenous to her home world. Fucking great.

"I'm sorry. Did you say *planet?*"

"Or the name of the local star system?" He was never touching that fucking drink again.

"I think I should take you to the hospital. Just so they can check you over, make sure you haven't hit your head or something."

Why couldn't she give him a straight answer? It wasn't that hard. "No."

"It's no trouble. Or I could call for an ambulance." She gripped her phone as though it was a weapon more than a tool of communication. "Why don't you come back to my house? It's not far. I'll make you a cup of tea."

A *cup of tea* wasn't high on his list of priorities at any time, but for some reason he was tempted by her guileless offer. *You're fucking losing it.*

It appeared that agreeing to her terms was the only way to get her to talk. If not for Mephisto's connection to the whole thing, Gabe might have found the incongruity of the situation funny. *Seriously losing it.* "Okay. But first you tell me where I am."

There was no mistaking the alarm that flashed over her face, and he had the crazy urge to reassure her that he hadn't lost his mind. It had been a long time since such a benevolent thought had occurred to him when it came to mortals.

"We're in Cornwall," she said in a soothing tone, and offered him a wary smile. "You really have no idea how you got here?"

His navigation system, that was hardwired into his DNA, kicked into gear, and star systems flooded through his mind like a celestial kaleidoscope. But he didn't need maps of constellations to figure out where he was.

"Earth?" His voice was raw. He should have known from the second she spoke. But the ability to understand any language he encountered was as natural as breathing. He rarely gave it a second thought.

"Uh, yes."

He barely heard her reluctant response. Blood pounded through his brain as fury seared his reason. For the first time in centuries, a woman had sparked his impassive libido. He'd been tempted.

By a woman from Earth.

Set up by Mephisto.

And Gabe had almost fallen for it.

Once, he'd loved the humans of Earth. But that had died millennia ago, and even the ashes that had remained in his heart had long since dissipated to the outer edges of the universe.

Get out of here now. There was no reason to stay. Except for the destructive need to know if this woman was as innocent as she seemed.

There was only one way to learn the depths of Mephisto's manipulation, and if he discovered this blue-eyed mortal was knowingly deceiving him, *the Archangel Gabriel,* he'd make her remaining, fleeting, years of life a living hell.

With minimal effort, as befit her lowly perch on the evolutionary clusterfuck, he scanned the surface of her mind. Looking for answers that weren't turned into riddles. Looking for signs Mephisto had been playing him.

Psychic fire jabbed into his brain and he recoiled, shock reverberating through him.

She had rebuffed him.

How? Only the most advanced, primarily telepathic races should have been aware of such a mild scan.

Her shielding was delicate, beautiful, and would have taken

years to perfect. He'd glimpsed it for less than a nanosecond, but its construct was unique.

"What the *hell?*" She glared at him, which was almost as intriguing as her impressive mental barriers. "Did you just try and get inside my mind?"

He'd never been confronted by an irate victim before. They were either oblivious or, in cases where he really dug in deep, they were in no state to confront anything by the time he'd finished with them. Who could have taught her such a thing? No one native to Earth, that was for sure. Hell, he couldn't think of a *species* with such a sophisticated defense system. He was astounded the under-developed human brain could even master such a thing.

"Well?" Her sharp tone held no trace of the reverence he was used to when dealing with mortals. Nothing about her was what he expected. Even the knowledge that Mephisto's machinations were behind this encounter failed to deaden his twisted fascination with her.

"Are you a telepath?" It was rare for a human, but not unheard of.

"Is that your idea of an apology?"

Was she for *real?* No one, unless they harbored a death wish, spoke to him like this. One quelling glower from him and they were a quivering mess at his feet.

Then again, he wasn't glowering at her, was he?

"I don't do apologies." He gave her a mirthless grin, the one that could fell intergalactic gladiators to their knees. She didn't even twitch. "What's your name?"

She blinked a couple of times, and for an incredulous second, he thought she wasn't going to answer him. "Aurora Robinson."

Silence spun between them. It was obvious she was waiting for him to reciprocate, in which case she could wait forever. He wasn't in the habit of introducing himself.

She slung him a dark frown and snatched up a silver photo frame from the ground.

"It's been very strange meeting you." She stood and brushed grass from her jeans. "If you're sure you're okay, then goodbye and good luck."

With that, she *turned her back on him* and stalked off.

CHAPTER 4

AURORA

Do not look back at him.

He was watching her. She knew it. The urge to glance over her shoulder consumed every thought, but she wasn't about to give him the satisfaction.

He's telepathic.

She stumbled on a hidden rock embedded in the grass. She'd inherited the gift from her mum and had never met anyone else with that talent.

Not that it was something she'd ever asked anyone. The last thing she'd wanted as a kid was to draw any more unwanted attention to herself. It was hard enough being known as the daughter of the village's eccentric environmentalists without her classmates accusing her of being a witch and reading their minds. *Or an alien.* She'd always known of her unique heritage and that she could never share her secret with anyone. And yet she'd always craved to find someone who *understood*.

Like that would ever happen.

Her obsession with genetics had been the driving force for the last four years while she'd been at Uni studying for her BSc in interdisciplinary physics and biochemistry. The lectures analyzing quantum mechanics had been fascinating but ultimately frustrating, since they offered no concrete answers.

But none of her research, either academic or personal, had concluded telepathy actually existed in humans on *this* Earth.

Her mum used to love telling her stories about her own home. A world that seemed so similar to this, and yet at some point during their evolution, their DNA had gone in a different direction. People communicated telepathically as easily as they spoke aloud, and her mum found it strange that on Earth nobody ever did.

It was just one of the many reasons why she'd desperately wanted to find her mother's people. After all, it wasn't as though she was attempting to access a purely theoretical world. Half of her DNA *originated* from that world. Her fingers tightened around the silver photo frame she'd hoped—unscientifically—would be a talisman in her quest today.

Could it really be coincidence that the day she put her years of research into practice, she finally met someone who *was* telepathic? Shouldn't she at least ask him about it, instead of backing off because he was so damn hot and out of her league?

That's not why I left him. Anyone who thought it perfectly acceptable to invade a mind without asking first was a total wanker. She was probably the first person who'd ever called him on it.

Slowly, she turned, and he was still sprawled on the grass, watching her. The sunlight dazzled her, and for an eternal second, she could have sworn he was surrounded by a glowing aura.

Her breath caught in her throat, and she blinked a couple of times to clear her vision. His gaze remained fixed on her, and there was a satisfied smile on his face, as if he'd never doubted she would retrace her steps.

Ego, much? She had the ridiculous urge to turn her back on him again, to prove she wasn't spellbound by his magical eyes, breathtaking body, or lethal sexual magnetism.

Good plan. That would show him.

She took a couple of steps toward him before she even realized.

Whether he was telepathic or not was a side issue. She still had no idea how he'd suddenly appeared from nowhere. But what was more baffling was the fact he didn't seem at all fazed by it.

Any of it.

An uneasy shiver snaked along her arms. Maybe her experiment had somehow dragged him here. The question was—from where?

Was that terrifying shaking on the astral planes my fault?

"Did you forget something?" he said, mockery dripping from each word.

She was standing right next to him. When had *that* happened? His mesmeric eyes ensnared her, and her knees had the alarming urge to wobble. Maybe she'd just sit down beside him and forget about his annoying arrogance. All she really wanted to do was wrap her arms around him and kiss his beautiful mouth.

Focus. She wasn't falling for his deadly charm, remember? Even if her damn feet hadn't got the memo to keep her distance. She'd keep this impersonal and to the point. Who was he and what did he know about telepathy?

"I need to know what happened. You're the first person outside of my family I've met with telepathic ability."

He didn't answer, but his gaze smoldered. The oxygen evaporated from her lungs and she sucked in a ragged breath, which didn't help with the whole breathing thing.

How could he turn her blood to liquid fire with just one look? He must have had plenty of practice. She'd die before she let him know how much he affected her.

He didn't answer her, either. What a surprise. Except she hadn't asked him a question, had she?

Bugger.

She tried again. "Do you know any other telepaths?"

Silence stretched between them, as though he was weighing up options. She held her breath, which was ridiculous, but she couldn't help it. Was she finally going to discover there was a whole secret society of people just like her?

Get real. How likely was that? Then again, how likely was anything that had happened this morning?

And then he spoke. "Is all your family telepathic?"

It was the second time he'd avoided answering her question. But maybe it was because, like her, he'd never talked about it with a stranger before?

Somehow, she found that explanation hard to believe, but she'd give him the benefit of the doubt. "No. Just my mum. What about you?"

His grin was mirthless and didn't reach his eyes, but the feral danger that radiated from him was so damn sexy she almost melted. "I was fostered."

"I'm sorry." Wait, was that the right response? "I mean, you never knew your parents?" *Am I digging this hole deeper, or what?*

"I didn't say that."

It was obvious he didn't want to talk about it. He probably thought she was being a nosy bitch. After all, there was no way he could know how much this meant to her.

"I'm trying to work out if the fact we're both telepathic is the reason you ended up here."

That possibility had sounded *so* much more feasible inside her head. She should've left it there.

Her fingers curled around her butterfly necklace. It had been specially commissioned six years ago, an extravagant eighteenth birthday present from her parents, but for the first time its familiar touch didn't give her any brilliant ideas. The smirk on his face didn't help, either.

"Doubtful." With that dismissive response, he stood, and her mouth dried. He towered over her, and raw, sexual, power charged the air like invisible lightning. He rolled his shoulders, and she tried not to ogle his magnificent biceps as they flexed beneath his shirt.

Fail.

It wouldn't be long before the locals were out, and while she didn't care if they saw her with the most spectacular man in existence, it would also prompt a flood of questions. No way did she want him telling them about the astral planes, or his version of events.

Whatever his version might be, since he still hadn't deigned to tell her anything.

She had to get him back to the house. Maybe he'd be more cooperative there.

And that's the only reason you want to take him back home?

"So, how about that cup of tea?" She took a backward step in the desperate hope it might help clear the lust drenched fog in her brain. It didn't. "We can work out what just happened."

Just shut up. She was making a total prat of herself, and he obviously agreed, since his delicious mouth quirked as though he was trying not to laugh.

She swallowed a defeated groan and walked away from him. Unfortunately, his lethal magnetism was just as strong even when she wasn't looking at him.

"This way." She gave a vague wave of her hand but managed not to glance over her shoulder to see if he was following or not. It was up to him, but at least she'd made the effort to help and not left him stranded.

Stop with the guilt. This wasn't her fault. Coincidences, even inexplicable ones, happened all the time.

Gabe

IT WAS the second time she'd walked away from him. He couldn't figure out why he was watching her cute butt, instead of getting his own ass out of here. Sure, she had a smart mouth he found oddly fascinating, and he conceded it was intriguing that she didn't fall at his feet. And he'd give a lot to study the unique construct of her telepathic web.

But she was only a mortal.

He exhaled an impatient breath and turned his back on her. He appeared to be in a meadow, and an expanse of woodland greeted him. It grated his nerves that he could still see the beauty on Earth. But then, it wasn't the planet he despised.

Just its human inhabitants.

An alien crackling filled his head, sending streaks of fire along his arms. Ancient dread gripped his chest, and he froze as disbelief thudded through his brain.

Not happening. Not here, not now. *Let me be wrong.*

Slowly, he turned, even though it went against every primitive survival instinct. Unholy terror slammed through him as his worst fears were confirmed. Suspended a couple of feet from the ground, a jagged, violet fracture, like static lightning, split reality.

It was the gateway into a hell he never wanted to see again. The twisted realm of the self-styled Guardians, misbegotten creatures whose species went back a billion years to the sunrise of time itself. Their hatred of every lifeform that had evolved after them was absolute.

And Aurora stood in front of the rapidly expanding fissure, mesmerized, unaware of the phenomena's significance, as the grass around the gateway withered and died.

"Get away from there." His voice was harsh, but she didn't move, and the primal imperative to *leave right now* thundered through every atom of his being.

It didn't matter if she ran. The Guardians had singled her out. She would be taken.

He couldn't interfere. It went against ancient protocols, the bedrock of the tenuous peace that existed between every living creature in the universe—and those perverted miscreants of nature. Aberrations, whose only pleasure was to torture their captives in order to satisfy their sick craving to soak in a mortal's terror.

Unease slithered through him. The Guardians were random in their pickings, but was it possible they'd zeroed in on Aurora because they sensed she had been in contact, knowingly or not, with Mephisto?

With me?

He couldn't save her. There was nothing he could do, yet he was by her side before he knew it. "Aurora."

"Stay back." Her voice was hoarse with fear and her arm swung out, hitting his chest, the gesture one of instinctive protectiveness.

Shock slashed through him and he forgot about the Guardians, forgot about the dark energy seeping from the fracture. This fragile human had just attempted to push him from the face of danger.

No one pushed him from the face of danger. It had been millennia since anyone had cared enough to even try.

She had no idea he didn't need her protection, or that even if they wanted to, the Guardians couldn't touch him. She didn't know who he was, and she didn't care about him, but she'd still tried to keep him safe.

A strange, acidic fire scorched his chest. She didn't deserve the fate that awaited her, just because she'd been in the wrong place at the wrong time.

Fuck ancient protocols. He wouldn't stand by and let a mortal who had tried to save *him* be taken by the universe's worst nightmare. Some humans deserved it. But not this one.

He wrapped his arm around her and dragged her against his chest. There was only one place he could be sure that they would never find her.

His sanctuary.

CHAPTER 5

GABE

Gabe held onto her until the shudders wracking her body finally eased. Mortals generally fell apart—no pun intended—after their first taste of teleportation, and the fact he hadn't given Aurora any warning meant she'd likely go into shock.

He wasn't looking forward to it.

Her hair was soft against his jaw, and the faint scent of strawberries teased the air. It was harder than it should have been not to bury his face in those silken curls and breathe in deep.

Her fingers dug into his shoulder, and he swallowed a groan. His brain might not want to have anything to do with her, but her touch was as potent as a siren's call.

Slowly, he released his death grip. Her hand slid from his shoulder and pressed against his chest before she raised her head.

Her eyes were glazed, her lips parted. Grimly, he steeled himself for her inevitable hysterics. *No good deed goes unpunished.*

"What happened?" Her voice was hushed.

"Don't worry. You're safe from them, now."

"Safe?" she echoed, and her brow crinkled as her gaze slipped from his. Her body went rigid as her shocked glance skimmed over his expansive kitchen, and she hitched in a choked breath. The silver frame she'd brought with her clattered to the floor, but she didn't seem to notice.

"Where am I?"

Somewhere you shouldn't be.

He'd acted without thinking it through. How long would she need to stay here before the Guardians forgot her and moved onto another victim?

He already knew the answer to that. An archangel had interfered, snatching their prey from beneath their nonexistent noses. The vindictive little bastards wouldn't let that indignity go lightly.

Curse the gods. This was his sanctuary, his bolt-hole, the headquarters for his black ops ventures. He'd never brought a mortal here. But because of one unguarded second, Aurora was not only here—she could be here for weeks.

Great.

"This is my island. They can't get to you here."

She took a step back and wrapped her arms around her waist as she gave his kitchen another incredulous glance. Why wasn't she freaking out?

She cleared her throat. "Did you just pull me through to another dimension?"

Another dimension? *That* was her first question when her brain registered her surroundings?

It was rare that anyone—let alone a mortal—could leave him speechless, but Aurora came close. "No. Same dimension. But we teleported."

"*Teleported*? How is that even possible?"

How could she panic about teleportation when she'd been unnaturally calm by the fact she'd narrowly escaped being ripped apart by the Guardians?

"Trust me. It's possible."

She let out a ragged breath, and terror flared in her eyes. Not that he wanted her scared, but at least this reaction made more fucking sense.

"Why would you abduct me?" She glanced wildly around as though searching for escape. "Take me back."

He wasn't sure why the word *abduct* ruffled his phantom feathers. He didn't give a shit what anyone said, least of all a mortal. And yet her accusation stung.

"I just saved your ass from the Guardians." What the fuck had happened to his *never explain anything* rule?

"From the what?"

It was terrifying how ignorant humans were of the universe they inhabited. So sure of their position at the top of the food chain, their immature brains would explode if they discovered just how many alien species truly walked among them.

And that wasn't even counting the Guardians, who existed in the Voids, a labyrinth construct within the inhospitable Dark Matter, the vast expanses of space between galaxies, where they reigned supreme in their immense, infernal domains.

"The Guardians," he repeated. "They're not from Earth. They're vicious, and if I hadn't brought you here, *they're* the ones who would've abducted you."

A stricken expression flashed across her face. "I saw something moving in that weird violet light. Like it was trying to come through."

"Hey." Before he could stop himself, he traced his finger along her cheek. Damn, she felt good. He cradled her jaw and her warm breath against his hand was a seductive caress. "You're safe here, remember? They can't penetrate the defenses on my island."

"*I'm* safe? God, do you mean they were coming for *me*?"

They sure as shit hadn't been there for him. "Not you, personally. But you were there, so they would have taken you. They don't need a reason except for the fact you're alive, and you're not one of them."

"Was it something I did?" Her whisper reeked of dread, and he had the insane notion to wrap his arms around her, just so she knew he was there for her.

What the fuck? The only time he pulled a woman into his arms was if he wanted sex. And although he still wanted Aurora, despite her heritage, *sex* hadn't been the overriding factor just now.

Same as it hadn't when he'd snatched her from the jaws of the Guardians.

His hand tensed against her face, but he didn't break contact. Until he'd met her, *sex* hadn't crossed his mind in decades.

Now, he couldn't stop thinking about it.

"It wasn't anything you did." He ground the words between his teeth. And once again guilt ate through him at the possibility the Guardians had singled her out because of him.

He couldn't imagine how, but the ways of the Guardians were shrouded in mystery. He wouldn't put anything past them.

"When can I go home?"

"When it's safe."

"But how long might that be?"

Gods, how many more questions was she going to fire at him? And why was he still touching her? It was harder than it should have been to drop his hand to his side. "When I decide it's safe."

She didn't respond, but he could see the doubt in her beautiful blue eyes. It was a novel phenomenon. No one looked at him with doubt. If anyone had the nerve to disbelieve his word, they at least averted their gaze if they wanted to live.

She attempted to protect me. Even now, he could hardly believe it. But it was the only reason he tolerated her lack of reverence. He inhaled a deep breath. With a few ground rules he'd get through the next few weeks without too much … inconvenience.

"How do you know so much about them?" She didn't try to hide the suspicion in her voice.

"Enough." He didn't raise his voice. Didn't need to. The low, hypnotic note was enough to silence any species, never mind one as primitive as humans. He never explained himself, and he wasn't into charity work. Since meeting Aurora, he was breaking every damn rule in his book.

No more.

He couldn't remember the last time a woman had questioned every word he said.

Yes, I can.

Despair clawed through his chest, interwoven with the guilt that had once all but destroyed him. Would he never find peace?

I don't deserve peace.

He crushed the memory before it consumed him. It was too long ago, and nothing could change the past. Although he'd give everything, just for the chance.

His current headache stood before him, glaring at him as though they were equals. Expecting a reply. With anyone else, he'd let them wait forever. Why couldn't he dismiss Aurora that easily?

"Believe me, I'll return you as soon as possible. I don't want you on my island any longer than necessary."

Without taking her gaze from him, she pulled her phone from the back pocket of her jeans. She jabbed the screen a few times with her thumb. "There's no signal."

Wasn't that the truth. In more ways than she could imagine. "Nothing gets in, and nothing gets out, without my permission."

She shivered, like he'd just threatened her instead of attempting to reassure her—*yet again*—that she was safe.

"Your island." She licked her lips. *Stop looking at her damn lips.* "Are we still on Earth?"

"Yeah." The irony never faded. Earth had become his hell, yet it was still the nearest thing he called home. And now the niceties were out of the way, he'd lay down the ground rules. "While you're here, you can go anywhere. Except my office. Understood?"

"But—"

He cursed violently in the language of the ancients. Would she never simply accept his word? She gazed at him, apparently fascinated. If he didn't get away from her right now, he was going to plunder that disrespectful mouth of hers until she was a mindless wreck at his feet.

The image was so fucking tempting. He clenched his teeth and swung away from her. In all his long existence, only one woman hadn't fallen at his feet and worshipped his immortal existence. He'd been enchanted. Ensnared. Would have torn Earth apart for her and rejected his heritage, if she had asked.

Never again.

And never for a human. Even if Aurora's inexplicable immunity to his archangelic magnetism was intriguing. She wanted him, but pushed him away, and he wasn't going to waste another nanosecond thinking about her.

He marched upstairs and into his bedroom, where his sweeping balcony gave a panoramic view of the subtropical forest surrounding his villa.

His sanctuary. But once, it had been his prison.

He rolled his shoulders, but it didn't stop the ancient need that simmered deep in the ruined tangle of muscle and sinew that gouged his back. A constant reminder of all he had lost.

During those dark years, he hadn't cared. He'd welcomed his deformity, flaunted his scars, and enjoyed a twisted sense of satisfaction in the fact he no longer possessed that which defined his species.

It hadn't lasted long. A few insane decades, and then reality had crashed through his haze of guilt and grief.

The reality that he would never again experience the exhilarating freedom of soaring through the skies.

Razor sharp frustration and unwanted lust pounded through him, and every cell in his body screamed for release. To know once again the power and ecstasy of spreading his wings and owning the heavens.

Aurora's face flooded his mind, her innocent blue eyes stoking the fire in his blood. *Get out of my head.* Why did he think of her?

It was intolerable.

Yet something about her had awakened his libido, and now it roared like a caged beast, demanding satisfaction. No way would he chase her like a lust blinded mortal. But if *she* came to *him*, he'd take her, and this infuriating fascination with her would end.

But right now, he had a far more urgent priority.

To find the missing child.

CHAPTER 6

AURORA

He strode out of the kitchen without a backward glance, and oxygen rushed into her deprived lungs, even though she didn't remember holding her breath.

I'm not losing my mind.

Clutching her phone like it was an anchor to reality, she risked glancing over her shoulder. The kitchen was all sleek gray stone and must have cost a fortune, but it was the view through the floor to ceiling windows that shook her mind.

Beyond a paved veranda, an impenetrable, lush forest spread across the horizon.

This is really happening.

He hadn't abducted her. She knew that was true, even when she'd accused him, but her panic had blinded her to logic.

He'd rescued her from that streak of violet light. The same light that had flashed through her mind in the second after she'd fallen from the astral planes.

A shudder inched along her arms. Was it sheer coincidence? Or was it her fault that the strange fissure had seemed to follow her?

He'd said it was nothing to do with her, and although she

couldn't see how he could possibly know something like that, for some reason she believed him.

It's because you want to believe him. Because then she didn't need to feel guilty for having inadvertently done something terrible while attempting to reach her mother's elusive world.

Either way, she was now stranded on an island with a guy who possessed far more extraordinary powers than telepathy. A guy who was determined to protect her from—what had he called them, the Guardians?—even if the prospect of her staying with him clearly pissed him off.

She sucked in a deep breath. She'd only caught a fleeting image of shadows in that eerie light, but menace leaked from them, chilling her heart.

But no matter how dangerous they were, there had to be a way she could go home. She couldn't just disappear off the face of the Earth. Her dad would be frantic and her mum …

She didn't want to think how it might affect her mum.

She needed to find him and get some more answers.

The hall, which like the kitchen reeked of understated wealth, was empty. And massive. More like a lobby to a grand hotel, except there was no artwork on the walls, statues on pedestals, or sofas and coffee tables scattered around for intimate gatherings.

Then again, who needed manmade art when you had a view of tropical paradise through the endless windows?

An imposing staircase beckoned, and although she'd much rather investigate the rest of the ground floor, she'd heard him go upstairs. She shoved her phone back in her pocket and made her way over. There were no banisters, and the stone steps were worn, as though a million feet had trod them over the centuries.

As she reached the top floor, it was eerily quiet. Three single timber doors were on her right, but directly ahead were a pair of enormous double doors that took up the entire wall. They were partially open and must have been twelve feet high and eight across, and if she didn't know better, she'd think he was trying to compensate for something.

Stop right there. She wasn't going to think about how his body had felt sprawled on top of her. Or remember the breath stealing pressure from his impressive erection.

Even if she just had. She ignored the needy flutters between her thighs and resisted the urge to wipe her suddenly sweaty hands on her jeans.

Slowly, she walked toward the doors, half expecting him to emerge from the room at any second. She cleared her throat. "Hello?" No answer. She pushed one of the doors open a little more. "I wanted to thank you."

She stepped inside and the view of the forest from his open balcony doors stopped her dead.

There was no balustrade enclosing the sweeping balcony. Who would build such a thing without any safety barriers?

She forced her feet to move, until she stood by the open doors. The forest stretched in every direction, and she caught a flash of sapphire ocean in the distance. The sky was a flawless azure, and the haunting call of exotic songbirds drifted in the air.

She could leave. But she had no idea where she was, and in that forest, and without her phone's GPS, she'd be hopelessly lost within a couple of minutes.

An arch led to what she guessed was his dressing room and bathroom, and she swept a glance around his bedroom. An immense bed dominated the space. Who needed a bed that big? It could easily sleep six.

And it probably did. Although she doubted much *sleeping* happened.

Just. Stop. It was none of her business what he did, and she certainly didn't care. It didn't stop her from stroking the silvergray bedspread that draped to the floor. From what she'd seen so far, he was a minimalist, whereas she loved having personal photos and all her stuff around, but she couldn't fault his taste.

The linen was soft and luxurious against her palm. She had the insane urge to climb on his bed and wrap his immaculate sheets around her naked body.

He'd never know.

She snatched back her hand and curled her fingers, her face burning with mortification.

Obviously, his irresistible pheromones infused everything in his villa. That was her story, and she was going to stick with it. The sooner she got out of his bedroom, the better.

And then he emerged through the arch. He must have just had a shower, as his hair was damp, and her throat dried at the sight of his sculpted, bronzed pecs and taut abdomen. Dark gold hair dusted his chest, arrowing toward his unzipped jeans, and it took *all* of her willpower to force her gaze back to his face.

His scorching gaze raked over her, but his expression was impassive. "Do you want something?"

Her legs were pressed against his bed and her cheeks were still hot from imagining how his sheets would feel against her naked skin. She couldn't blame him if he thought she had an ulterior motive for following him into his bedroom. Especially after the way her glance had inexcusably slid south.

At least he hadn't caught her caressing his bed linen.

She cleared her throat. She just had to ignore his half-naked body and stick to the plan.

"I wanted to thank you for rescuing me."

He prowled toward her like a panther stalking its prey, and all the questions she had fled her mesmerized mind.

"Do you?" He towered over her, golden and beautiful, like a god from ancient myths. His cologne was subtle and addictive and swirled through her senses like an elusive aphrodisiac.

It was hard to remain upright and not simply sink down onto his bed.

Focus. She blinked a couple of times in the hope that might break the mesmeric spell.

"Yes." Her voice was unforgivably husky, but she couldn't help it. "I really do appreciate it, and I wanted you to know."

His mouth quirked, as though he found her thanks amusing despite himself. Not quite the reaction she'd been hoping for. And did he really need to stand so close to her? She pushed her hands into her jeans pockets, so she wasn't tempted to glide her fingertips over his ripped chest.

"You're welcome." His voice was low and sexy, a velvet caress that promised to fulfil every fantasy she'd ever had.

What was she thinking? That was *not* the reason she'd come upstairs. She needed answers, and she might as well start with the most basic question.

"I don't even know your name?"

"Gabe."

"Gabe." She liked saying his name. It took longer than it should have to recall she was here for a reason, and secretly drooling over his name wasn't it. "I'm sorry I was weird in the kitchen. I was messed up with the teleportation shock."

His smile was like glimpsing the sun after a storm, breathtaking.

"You handled it well. Better than most humans do their first time."

What a strange way of putting it.

"I'd love to learn more about your teleportation system."

His eyes smoldered. She'd never believed such a phenomenon was possible. *What are we even talking about?*

"It's all in the DNA. Not something I can teach you."

His enigmatic answer fired a dozen more questions in her brain, but *DNA* was the reason she'd tried to breach dimensions in the first place, and it slapped her back to the present.

Back to why she needed to speak to him again.

"I don't want to sound ungrateful, but I really need more information on the Guardians. And I have to contact my parents, so they don't worry about not hearing from me."

Incredulity flashed across his face before his impassive mask shuttered his expression once again. She hitched in a shallow breath. What had just happened?

"I don't have a hidden repository of information on the Guardians. I've told you what I know."

All he'd told her were they were vicious aliens who had attempted to abduct her. He *had* to know more.

"But—"

"I'll set up a way for you to communicate with your parents later. Right now, I need to work."

Well, that was abrupt. But if he had to work, she could hardly expect him to drop everything to help her, even if she was desperate for answers.

"Okay, we'll talk about this later, then?"

"I've no doubt." He didn't sound as though he was looking forward to it.

He swung around and horror slammed through her. Two deep gashes ran from his shoulder blades down the length of his back, as if an acid-drenched ax had hacked through to the bone, eating the flesh, distorting the muscle.

The wounds were healed and looked ancient, but the passage of time hadn't disguised how agonizing the injuries must have been.

What in the name of god happened to him?

He rolled his powerful shoulders, and the condemning glance he flung her way was more than enough to confirm her shocked gasp hadn't remained inside her head. For endless seconds their gazes meshed, but there was no glimmer of understanding in his eyes. Anything she said wouldn't be welcome.

When he finally stalked away, she let out a shaky breath and made good her escape. But his injuries kept spinning in her mind.

Had he been tortured? She couldn't imagine any kind of accident would leave such horrific scarring.

It was none of her business. And it wasn't something she

could ask him. He'd made that very clear without even needing to utter a word. In any case, she had enough on her mind to worry about.

Once she was back in the kitchen, she picked the photo frame up from the floor and placed it on the worktop before running the tip of her finger over the glass.

When she was a child, she'd loved listening to her mum's stories of her own world, where telepathy was as natural as breathing. Distance didn't matter between those you loved. You could be on the other side of the planet and still be in contact. But although her telepathic link with her mum had always been strong, about ten years ago it had vanished.

There hadn't been any warning, but it had been the first sign of her mum's decline.

She sighed and turned away from the pressed flower. Although Gabe had said he'd help her later, she couldn't just sit around and wait for him to finish work.

Whenever she needed answers, she'd visit the astral planes. They'd never failed her. In fact, it was while she was there six years ago that she'd first had the idea to find her mother's parallel world.

Well, that hadn't turned out the way she'd dreamed, but the point was it always calmed her mind and allowed possibilities she'd never thought of to filter through.

It had to be worth a shot.

She sat cross-legged on the floor and took a few deep breaths. She'd cobbled together her own form of transcendental meditation around the same time she'd learned to read and had out-of-body experiences as a child long before she discovered the mystical astral planes. When her parents found out what she was doing, they'd given her basic safety rules to follow, along with advice not to tell anyone at school.

It was just another family secret she'd learned to keep, so the other kids wouldn't label her a freak.

She closed her eyes, and her mind calmed.

The astral planes glimmered and unfolded before her. Except something wasn't right, as though they were enclosed within a shimmering sphere of water, just out of her reach.

Unease fluttered through her, and she pushed harder, something she'd never needed to do before. But like two negative forms of magnetism, she couldn't get closer, couldn't connect.

She couldn't enter the astral planes.

Panic crawled up her chest, making it hard to breathe, hard to even think. It wasn't the astral planes that were surrounded by a protective force, preventing her entry.

It was *this island* keeping her entrapped.

Where on Earth am I?

Her throat tightened. This shouldn't be possible. It didn't *matter* where you were. Access to the astral planes was universal and had nothing to do with the laws of known physics. Technology wasn't advanced enough to do anything like this—whatever the bloody hell *this* was.

But all the facts in the world didn't mean shit. Because this was her reality.

And I can't break through it.

CHAPTER 7

GABE

Hours later, Gabe left his office and made his way downstairs and into his kitchen. Aurora wasn't there, but the silver frame she'd brought with her was propped up on his worktop. He stared at it for a couple of seconds, not sure why it held his attention. It was just a flower. But a reluctant compulsion made him pick the frame up and examine it.

Spectral fingers glided along his spine. He'd never seen anything like this before, and not just on Earth.

Anywhere.

It was fragile and beautiful, but something was … wrong. He didn't know what.

Get your fucking shit together. He replaced the frame and turned his back. There was nothing uncanny about it.

Where was she?

When she'd followed him upstairs earlier, he'd been convinced it was because she wanted him. The heat in her eyes, the warmth of her smile, and the sultry note in her voice hadn't been a figment of his imagination.

But once again she hadn't fallen under his archangelic spell. All she had wanted from him were more answers.

To questions *he* didn't have the damn answers for.

He dragged his fingers through his hair and cursed under his breath. His vow not to seduce her unless she begged, mocked him, since it was becoming increasingly obvious that was never going to happen.

Grimly, he made his way to the living room at the end of the villa. As he reached the half-open door, the sharp tang of fear spiced the air.

Aurora.

He slammed open the door, and although the room was in shadows, he saw her easily enough, curled up on a sofa and clutching a cushion.

"What's the matter?" His voice was harsher than he intended. What the hell had happened? She'd been fine the last time they'd spoken.

She clutched the pillow tighter. "Where *am* I?"

That was the reason she was so terrified? It seemed an extreme reaction. Although considering how well she'd taken everything so far, he guessed this delayed response was inevitable.

He shouldn't have left her alone for so long.

I was only upstairs, for fuck's sake.

He took her hand. His knuckles pressed against the cushion, and she gripped his fingers as though her life depended on it. It was oddly touching.

I did not just think that.

There was no reason for her not to know where they were. It wasn't as though she'd ever be able to find her way back here, once she left.

No mortal could.

"You'd never find my island on any map, but it's in the region you call the Bermuda Triangle."

"Okay," she whispered, and the fear that had drenched the air moments ago faded. Her thumb caressed his knuckles, a featherlight touch that shouldn't feel half as good as it did.

He cradled her face. Her uneven breath dusted his jaw and need glowed in her eyes. When had he moved so close to her?

Why did that even matter?

Temptation and lust thudded an erratic tattoo in his blood. Reason splintered, and only the need to possess this exasperating, enchanting, woman made any sense. He could almost taste her surrender, inhale her desire, and a tortured groan vibrated along his throat.

Her lips parted, a seductive invitation. It was all he needed.

She hitched in a ragged breath. "Are you some kind of crazy scientist?"

"*What?*" The word shot from him, unbidden, as frustrated need mangled his brain. "Do I look like a crazy scientist?"

Why was she speaking? *How* could she speak? They were about to kiss. She should be incapable of any coherent thought at all.

Like I am.

Their lips were almost touching. Her elusive scent of strawberry shampoo, with tantalizing hints of aroused woman, bewitched his bemused senses. She should be falling into his arms, not questioning his existence.

"What *are* you?"

She still had no idea. A warped part of him liked the fact she was so oblivious. Maybe that was the reason he found her so irresistible. Whatever, the moment to tell her his true identity had passed. It wasn't like it would make any difference to her situation.

Not that he was going to lie to her.

He forked his fingers into her hair, and her curls tumbled over his wrist. "I'm a mercenary."

"What have you done to your security system here?"

He was in danger of combusting and she wanted to know about his *security system?*

She wouldn't understand the extent of the security around his island even if he explained it to her. Humans' conception of physics was limited in the extreme. And nothing in the universe would ever compel him to admit that even *he* couldn't fully comprehend the reverse science involved.

But he had to tell her something.

"The island is protected by an energy field."

"I've never encountered anything like it. It's *unnatural.*"

She had no idea how close to the truth she was, with it being alien to all known laws of the universe.

"It's the only thing keeping the Guardians out. They can't see this island."

Her eyes were dark pools of desire and need pulsed from her with every heightened heartbeat. All he needed was one taste of her tempting lips, and all her questions would incinerate.

He barely managed to swallow his groan at the visceral image. His chest was constricted, his skin on fire, and his cock was hard as iron. *I've never craved a kiss so badly.*

"You said they're aliens? " Her voice was hushed, and he squeezed his eyes shut and pressed his forehead against hers. His breath rasped against her face, and he couldn't control it. Couldn't mask how much he wanted her, or how fucking hard it was to not just kiss her senseless until she couldn't even recall her own name.

He could hardly remember his own.

"Yeah." He ground out the word. "About as alien as you can get."

She shuddered, but he didn't trust himself to toss away the cushion and pull her fully into his arms. That cushion was his last line of defense.

This is crazy. He was an archangel. She was a human. *This shouldn't be happening.*

"Gabe." She breathed his name in a seductive sigh. It was the sexiest damn thing he'd heard in years. Her breath caressed his jaw, and he couldn't ignore it, no matter how hard he tried. "I need to contact my parents. To let them know I'm okay."

"I know." He had promised her, and he would keep his promise. But it wasn't that straightforward. First, he had to get her a laptop and then configure it so it could penetrate the energy field. The way his did.

She could use mine.

Not happening. No one touched his laptop but him.

He released her and shoved himself to his feet. She gazed up at him, looking so sweet and vulnerable he nearly lost it. It took more willpower than he'd ever admit, but he backed up a couple of steps and dragged in a lungful of oxygen.

She wanted him, but she never lost sight of her primary goal. Her ability to resist him fascinated and frustrated in equal measure. If he didn't get away from her, he was going to beg.

And that was unthinkable.

GABE LEANED back in his chair and stared at the ceiling of his office. The newly acquired laptop was on his desk, and once Aurora had finished in the shower, he could activate it for her use. Before leaving the island, he'd directed her to his bathroom, since it was the only one in the villa, and left one of his shirts out for her.

Don't imagine her under the spray.

Too late.

He stifled a groan and forced his mind back to business.

After shifting through the intel on the disc Jaylar had given him, he'd sent a telepathic message informing him he would take the case.

Like there had ever been any doubt of that.

The holographic images of the dark-haired young girl imprinted on his brain, but no matter how hard he tried, it churned up memories of another small girl. A child who had once cradled his heart in her tiny hands.

His hands fisted and he bowed his head, forcing the ancient memory back into the shadowy corners of his shredded soul. *My precious Helena.* He would never forget, and he would never forgive. But vengeance had corroded him long ago, and now there was nothing left but an echo of guilt and loss, and an elusive whisper of the love that had once embraced his life.

Slowly he flexed his fingers and forced open his eyes. The interminability of his existence stretched out before him, a bleak desert of fleeting interactions. Without his missions to give him focus, he would have sunk into madness long ago.

Long ago, I once did. He'd crawled out of the pit. Eventually.

The silence wrapped around him, a soothing cocoon. Brooding, he stared through the window as the moonlight turned the forest into a silvery mirage. He'd spent nights without number doing just this.

But tonight, the solitude only served to remind him that he wasn't alone.

He'd never had a problem ignoring a minor irritation before. And that's all she was. He could only hope the Guardians lost interest in her sooner rather than later, so he could return her home and forget she even existed.

In the window's reflection he saw Aurora appear at the door to his office. She didn't say anything and didn't attempt to enter the room. She was obviously waiting for him to acknowledge her.

Let her wait.

The seconds stretched into eternity. Anticipation sizzled through his blood, and in the end, it was he who could wait no longer.

He swung around in his chair and self-derision burned his

chest. Had he done it deliberately? The shirt he'd left out for her was blue, a perfect match for her eyes. She'd rolled up the sleeves to her elbows, and the shirt almost reached her knees. Her damp hair curled into enticing tendrils over her shoulders, and there was no hellish way she should look so utterly bewitching.

Cut the bullshit. He'd known exactly how she would look, dressed in his shirt.

His throat was dry, mouth parched. It was contemptible that merely the sight of her could affect him so profoundly.

There was only one thing for it. He'd have to keep away from her.

Banished from my own island. For helping a human.

"Is there anything to eat?" Her soft question punched through his grim thoughts, and he frowned.

"There's plenty of food in the kitchen." Not fresh stuff, admittedly, but only because he'd been away for weeks. The walk-in pantry was stocked to overflowing. "Help yourself to whatever you want."

"Thank you." Her smile was oddly touching. "And tomorrow we'll work out a plan on how we can beat the Guardians?" There was a hopeful note in her voice, and he couldn't bring himself to tell her there was no way for mortals to beat the Guardians. They just had to evade their radar.

He was too tired to have that conversation tonight. And damn it, he didn't want to shatter that thread of hope she was still clinging onto.

Which was crazy, because that was exactly what he had to do.

Tomorrow.

"Sure. Whatever." Side-stepping her question wasn't as easy as it should have been. *Move on.* "You can sleep in my bed." *Since I won't be here.*

More to the point, it was the only upstairs room, besides his office, he'd bothered to furnish.

A delicate blush heated her cheeks, and he couldn't drag his spellbound gaze away.

"I'm not going to share your bed."

The spell shattered. Did she seriously assume he wanted sex as payment for rescuing her?

He'd been accused of countless things in the past. Most of them justified. But he'd never demanded sex in payment for anything, and the fact Aurora so easily jumped to that conclusion burned like acid.

He shoved back his chair and prowled toward her. To her credit, she didn't run screaming from the room. Then again, she never behaved the way other mortals would in her position.

"Let's get one thing straight." Why was he standing so close to her? It was hard holding onto his justified disdain when all he wanted to do was scoop her into his arms and march into his bedroom. And damn it, before he'd ripped one button from that shirt, she'd be begging him not to leave her alone in his bed. Frustration roared through him. *Get out of here now.* "You're not as irresistible as you think you are."

CHAPTER 8

AURORA

Gabe towered over her, leashed power vibrating in the air. It should have been terrifying, but instead it was like she'd drunk a bottle of the finest champagne. Heady. Intoxicating.

Infuriated.

The alarming urge to grab his shirt and kiss his arrogant mouth slammed through her. *That would show him.*

Yeah, it would show him she was so desperate for his touch she didn't care what derisive comments he slung her way. He might be breath-takingly gorgeous and used to women falling at his feet. But just because he clearly had a problem with the fact he wanted *her,* was no reason for him to be so *rude.* "Don't blame me for your—"

The rest of her retort lodged in her throat as he gave her a satanic grin *and vanished.*

Into thin air.

She stumbled back against the doorframe and took a few calming breaths. It didn't do much for her racing heart.

Gingerly, she waved her hand in the space where he'd been just seconds ago. Yep. Definitely gone.

How does he do it?

That was a question for another day. Right now, she had a more important issue. Because if he thought she was going to just sit around and wait for him before trying to contact her parents, he was seriously deluded. She'd already wasted half the day doing just that.

His desk, on the other side of the spacious office by the window, was cleared of everything except a laptop.

It stood to reason that was the communication method he'd mentioned earlier. She'd have a quick look, to see if she could access her email account.

Guilt chewed through her as she trailed her fingertips over his desk, even though she tried to ignore it.

You can go anywhere. Except my office.

If he hadn't teleported in the middle of their conversation, she wouldn't have had to.

The laptop had an unrecognizable symbol on its top, like two moons circling a three ringed planet. She frowned and peered closer at the holographic image before opening it.

The air whooshed from her lungs as she gazed at the keyboard with its incomprehensible hieroglyphics.

So much for trying to contact her parents without Gabe's help.

She sat on his large leather chair. It was worn and warm, and the faintest hint of his intoxicating cologne caressed her senses.

And she could stop that right now. He wasn't *that* irresistible.

Yes, he is.

She still wasn't going to think about him.

The top drawer of his desk was slightly open. Like an invitation. She eyed it for a few seconds, while her stomach churned with a combination of hunger and nerves.

This could be my Pandora's Box.

Before she could change her mind, she opened the drawer.

A small pile of seashells was heaped in one corner. They were perfectly ordinary, and yet chills skittered along her arms. Whatever she'd expected to find, it certainly hadn't been something so personal.

So precious.

Close the drawer and walk away.

The only other item in the drawer was an A5 size canvas, face down. A faint glow emanated from it and unformed foreboding snaked through her chest. *Is it a force field?*

Her fingers clenched.

There was nothing here that could help her. She was *not* going to pick it up.

Her hand didn't get the memo. The material was cool and smooth, as though it was enclosed in wafer-thin glass—except it was very slightly pliant beneath her fingertips.

Not glasslike at all.

She pulled it from the drawer and turned it over. Vibrant colors and an overwhelming impression of love and happiness flooded her mind, momentarily stunning her reflexes.

Gabe. She clung onto that one irrefutable fact. It was Gabe in the uncannily realistic three-dimensional portrait. His dark blond hair created almost a halo-like effect and his fantastical eyes were so real she had the scary certainty they could see right into her soul.

Her stupefied brain took it all in. Focusing on the details. Refusing to believe the truth of her eyes.

He had one arm around a black-haired woman who was laughing up at him, and in his other arm he carried a small child, whose tiny hand was entangled in his hair.

But this Gabe had wings. Wings the color of clotted cream, with delicate streaks of pale gold glinting through them. Heavenly highlights brushed each individual feather with devoted precision.

Wings. *The man had wings.*

They were folded behind his back but were clear enough. And he was laughing, as though he hadn't a care in the world.

The photo was obviously enhanced. Except it wasn't a photo. It wasn't a painting or a holographic image. She had no idea what it was, but it really didn't matter.

The wings were fake. Because if they were real, that made him …

Non-human.

An alien.

An angel?

Squeezing her eyes shut, all she could see were the horrific scars on his back. *Exactly where wings would be.*

The painting wasn't magical, and the characters didn't move, but she had the uncanny notion that, if only she knew how, she could step into this scene, like Alice through the looking glass.

Stop. She inhaled a deep breath to center herself. *It'll take more than meditation to process this.* A bottle of whiskey might help.

Don't look at his wings. Of course they weren't real. Maybe he'd been celebrating Halloween or something.

With his family.

She bit her lip and focused on the woman, with her elaborate earrings, jewel-threaded hair, and delicate bangles. She had a regal bearing and was almost as tall as Gabe, and she sure had the face of a mythical fallen angel.

But she didn't have wings. Neither did the child.

The little girl's windswept, blonde hair fell in messy ringlets to her waist, and if she needed any more proof that this exquisite child was Gabe's, her eyes were a bewitching silver-and-blue-streaked green.

A strange pain squeezed her chest. It shouldn't come as a huge shock to discover he had a family. Just because he'd flirted with her—and saved her from the Guardians—didn't mean he was single. It didn't mean *anything*.

But it had never even occurred to her.

That's what happened when a gorgeous man paid her some attention. Her brain devolved into mush.

Or I'm losing my mind.

The fear she'd lived with for years, that one day she, like her mum, would forget the reality of her life.

That wasn't going to happen. *This. Is. Real.*

Somehow, she had to deal with it. Falling apart over a picture wouldn't get her anywhere. And although she didn't want to touch it again, she couldn't leave it out on his desk, proclaiming her guilt at having gone through his most personal items.

She picked it up, and her gaze snagged on a gold chain that glinted around the little girl's throat.

What ...? No way. It couldn't be. But, suspended from the delicate chain, was a familiar butterfly, and gold dust and minuscule rainbows glittered in the tiny, flawless wings.

It was identical to the necklace she had worn for the last six years, and instinctively she curled her fingers around it in a protective gesture.

Throughout her childhood she'd had recurring dreams of rainbows and gold dust and magnificent jewel-like butterfly wings and had been thrilled when her parents had offered to get a piece of jewelry specially commissioned for her eighteenth birthday. She had known exactly what she'd wanted.

It was an original, and she'd never seen anything quite like it.

Until now.

It's a coincidence. How could it be anything else?

But between each panicked beat of her heart, a relentless question echoed.

Are you sure about that?

Gabe

Eta Hyperium was a shithole. And that was an understatement. But since it was the hub of the slave trade, and every other illicit transaction imaginable, for the technologically advanced mortals of the Sextans Galaxy, it was never going to be anything else. Even the weather had given up millennia ago, and now the surface was a bleak landscape of withered trees and stunted wildlife that scavenged beneath the dying red sun.

And the sooner that sun got its shit together and swallowed the whole damn solar system, the better.

Gabe materialized in a dark corner just outside the main entrance of the biggest establishment. The place looked decrepit, but that façade concealed phenomenal security. Luckily, his DNA allowed him to circumvent it.

Although the owner knew damn well who and what he was, his cover as a megalomaniac half-blood demon always worked. None of the slime ball clientele would guess he was an under-cover archangel. Not in this savage sector of the universe.

He shouldered his way inside. Thick, noxious smoke filled the air, but worse than that was the scent of greed, depravity, and prohibitively expensive alcohol.

He swept his glance around the crowded tables. Where the hell was Eblis?

A hand slammed onto his shoulder. "Hey, Gabe. Been a while."

Gabe turned. "Got a minute?"

Eblis rippled his pearlescent wings, and patrons scattered hastily out of the way. No one wanted to draw Eblis' attention. He was one of the most feared traders in the Sector and one of the most powerful demons in existence.

He was also the sole owner of this complex, but that was something very few were aware of.

They approached a table, and the muscled occupants fled before the demon uttered a word.

"What's the deal?" Eblis undulated his wings as they sat, and with a flick of his finger to a half-naked waiter, indicated to bring them drinks. "Found a way to get back at her Celestial bitch-fuck?"

"I wish." Gabe relaxed against the circular sofa and hooked his arm over its back. If there was one species in Creation who loathed his goddess even more than the archangels, it was the demons. And while he and Eblis stood on opposite sides of the chasm that divided their races, they'd forged a bridge long ago.

"You here for business or pleasure?" Eblis' question refocused his mind. He despised the demon's lucrative trade, but Eblis made a great partner when it came to finding the best places to enjoy mindless debauchery.

No way was he returning to his villa until he'd been well and truly laid. He might be able to look at Aurora, then, without wanting to shove her against the nearest wall and fuck her senseless.

He'd left his own damn island to get away from her, intending to spend a couple of hours with fellow archangel, Zadkiel. But somehow, he'd ended up telling Zad about the encounter with the Guardians.

Not that Zad had been interested in that. But he'd been *way* too interested in the fact Gabe had saved a human female.

So he'd brought forward his plan to go visit Eblis. At least with the demon he wouldn't have the suicidal urge to tell him about Aurora.

"Both."

"Spill."

"Heard of any minors from the Andromeda Galaxy being traded recently?"

Their drinks arrived, the sizzling alcohol so potent one sniff of its fumes was enough to send weak-minded mortals comatose. Still not as strong as the brain rot Mephisto had produced earlier, though.

Eblis drained half his tankard before smashing it onto the table.

"None of these Sextans bastards can reach Andromeda, Gabe. They can't get anywhere without their crazy little spaceships. You know that. They couldn't even get to the Milky Way and that's their closest neighbor."

"You get occasional traders who can cross galaxies." He paused for effect. "Foreign captives always ratchet up the price."

Eblis didn't argue. They both knew that mortals who originated outside the Sextans Galaxy were smuggled in by the unscrupulous who weren't restricted to spaceship travel. They were descendants of immortals, who had inherited their ancestors' ability of interstellar teleportation.

"Details?"

Gabe showed him an image of Evalyne.

"She's a native of Medana." He placed a small star map globe on the table and opened the holographic image of the Beta Spiral of Andromeda. Medana was an insignificant little planet hidden within an obscure solar system. He didn't expect the demon to know the place offhand.

Eblis shifted, his feathers ruffling in a nonexistent breeze, and Gabe zoomed in further, suns and moons shooting by until the six-planet solar system of Evalyne's birth hovered above the table.

"I recognize this system." Eblis raised an eyebrow and glanced through the planet at Gabe. "Saw some pirates from Namtar in the Fornax Galaxy plotting the chart about three months ago."

The Fornax Galaxy, where demons had fled to millennia ago, seethed with a dark underbelly of pirates. If they'd expanded their operations into Andromeda, it was more than a single child at risk.

It could lead to intergalactic war.

CHAPTER 9

MEPHISTO

*M*ephisto teleported directly outside Gabe's villa. Aside from Gabe, he was one of only three archangels who could cross the island's fucked-up energy field, which was a big advantage right now, when he wanted to see for himself what the hell was going on.

Half an hour ago, Zad had contacted him to let him know that Gabe had rescued a human from the Guardians' clutches. Meph was under no illusion how furious Gabe would be if he ever discovered Zad had done such a thing, but that was tough.

When it came to the Guardians and Gabe, there were no secrets between Zad and Mephisto.

It was ironic that the reason Mephisto had missed Gabe's reckless gesture, and therefore been unable to stop him, was because he'd had to attend the centennial meeting with the Guardian elite. It was mind-numbing in the extreme but essential in order to ratify the terms of peace between all sentient beings in the universe—and the Guardians.

It was also off the record. Not even his fellow archangels knew of his diplomatic ties with the Guardians, and that was how he wanted it to stay. The treaty had been hammered out

69

eons before he'd been created, and a lot of the clauses were morally repugnant. But at least they served to muzzle the Guardians' otherwise insatiable urge to annihilate all forms of existence that didn't conform to their own.

A small price to pay in the scheme of things.

And Gabe had fucking risked everything.

He peered through the window into the living room. Dawn had broken, and he could easily see Aurora huddled on one of the chairs. She was asleep.

And what the fuck was she wearing? One of Gabe's *shirts*?

When he'd taunted Gabe about getting laid by a human from Earth, this was *not* what he'd had in mind.

He rapped on the window, and for good measure he also unfurled his wings. Nothing wrong in causing her to gibber with fright, considering she was the reason he had yet another mess to clear up.

He should have wiped her mind of her obsession two years ago. Mess averted. That knowledge didn't improve his mood.

Her eyes flew open, and she gripped the arms of the chair as she caught sight of him. For endless seconds their gazes meshed. *Why isn't she writhing on the floor in terror?*

He undulated his wings, well aware of the effect the rising sun would have on his magnificent feathers. Aurora didn't even twitch.

Reluctant fascination raked through him. She'd always interested him, but only because of her intriguing ideas. This was different. He'd never met a mortal who hadn't fallen to their knees, even if merely metaphorically, at the first sight of him.

He could almost understand why Gabe had brought her here.

Irrelevant. To maintain peace in the universe, she couldn't stay here, hidden from the Guardians' view.

Since it appeared she had no intention of opening the door for him, he did it himself with a telekinetic flourish, before strolling into the room.

"Hello, Aurora," he said and gave her a smile guaranteed to send most primitives into traumatic shock. It didn't appear to affect her in the slightest. *Why not?* It was a shame he hadn't discovered this fascinating aspect about her two years ago. "Driven your lord and master away already, have you?"

She didn't rise to his bait. Maybe he'd overestimated her, and his appearance had liquified her mind. That wouldn't go down well with Gabe. Even though he couldn't keep his pet, there were ways and means of obtaining that outcome that wouldn't piss Gabe off.

There was only one way to discover if he'd irreversibly damaged her, and he grazed the edge of her mind.

White hot acid speared into his brain, and he mentally reeled. What in the name of the holy fucking goddess was *that?*

"Get the fuck out of my *head*." She accompanied her tirade by practically leaping from the chair and taking a step toward him. He couldn't figure out whether he was enraged or entranced by her performance. "Who are you? One of Gabe's minions?"

Her entertainment value nosedived. He relished seeing her reaction when Gabe learned the truth about her.

Zad had told him Gabe was on his way to visit Eblis on Eta Hyperium. There were only two reasons why anyone would willingly go to that shitty little planet, and since Gabe abhorred Eblis' trade, that left the other option that the demon was an expert in procuring.

Very dirty sex.

Despite breaking one of the fundamental protocols that held the universe together, obviously the sex with Aurora hadn't been worth it. The thought amused him, and he offered her a soul scorching grin.

"Gabe wants to see you."

Aurora

Don't panic.

Aurora didn't drop her gaze from the winged stranger, even though his black eyes sent shivers racing along her spine. It was just as well she'd discovered that picture of Gabe. Otherwise those feathers would've totally freaked her out.

Concentrate. No way was she going to fall apart. *Pretend the wings aren't there.* "You haven't told me your name."

"You may address me as Lord Mephisto."

Wait. *Mephisto?* Gabe had mentioned that name. At least that meant they knew each other.

It didn't help settle her nerves.

"And Gabe sent you here to take me to him? Why didn't he come back himself?" It wasn't like he had to handle rush hour on the M25, was it?

"I can take you to him," Mephisto said. "But I'm not discussing it. Yes or no?"

Gabe had told her nothing could breach his island without his permission. Which meant Mephisto must be acting under Gabe's authority. And although she was still mad he'd vanished mid-conversation, she knew he'd never do anything to put her in danger.

She didn't trust Mephisto, but she trusted Gabe. "All right, then."

Mephisto didn't look impressed by her response, but if he imagined she was going to call him *Lord,* well. He was going to have a very long wait.

He bared his teeth in a mockery of a smile. "You need to change. You'll stand out like a virgin sacrifice where we're going." And with that, an outfit materialized at her feet.

AURORA EYED her reflection in Gabe's bathroom mirrors. *I'm not wearing this.* Mephisto was obviously depraved. She wasn't even sure why she'd put the outfit on, except she'd had the faint hope it wouldn't be as terrible as it looked.

It was.

She didn't have a problem with the six-inch stilettos or fishnet tights. The crotchless knickers might have been exciting under other circumstances, but at least the lurid red leather micro-mini skirt covered her assets. Just.

It was the scrap of leather that was supposed to pass as a bra, but had strategic slashes that showed off her nipples, that was the deal breaker. There was no way she was leaving the villa in this.

She pulled it off and found her underwear from the previous day. And then put Gabe's shirt back on.

He was standing in Gabe's bedroom as she left the bathroom, and the glint in his eyes suggested he knew exactly what she'd done. She resisted the overwhelming urge to cross her arms. She wouldn't give him the satisfaction of knowing he unnerved her.

"Come here." He spread open one wing, and it took every shred of courage to walk toward him instead of running back to the bathroom. He wrapped his wing around her, engulfing her in darkness, and she stiffened in shock as softness and strength and unimaginable power thrummed through every feather. *Archangel's wings ...*

His arm snaked around her in a crushing grip, and then she couldn't think anymore as her atoms exploded.

Instantaneously, her feet landed on solid ground. It took a second for her stomach to catch up. She kept her eyes screwed shut. *I just teleported.*

It wasn't the first time she'd done this. The only difference being, she hadn't *known* when she'd teleported with Gabe.

She forced open her eyes and tried to pull back from Mephisto. He didn't get the hint. His arm was an iron band around her waist and his wing encased her. She couldn't see anything but his moonlight-streaked, midnight feathers.

Slowly his wing slid down her body, sending shudders over

her skin. A horrible realization hit her, and she flattened her hand against her chest, just to confirm her worst fears. "What did you do with the shirt?"

And my necklace. She dug her fingernails into the palm of her hand and took a couple of long, shuddering breaths.

His hand splayed across her naked stomach. Like he owned her. "Be grateful I allowed you to keep the leather on for daring to disobey me."

"Where's my necklace?" She hoped he couldn't hear the rising panic in her voice. It was bad enough he'd made the shirt vanish and the disgusting bra appear, but even that faded beside the possibility he'd lost her beloved necklace.

"Didn't go with the look, babe." He sounded both bored and amused, and his wing glided lower, still concealing her breasts but curling around her thighs in blatant possession.

Part of her wanted to shove him away, maybe knee him in the nuts for good measure. Except he was built like a mountain, and she was under no illusion that anything she might do to him would have any effect. And while she hated the way he was holding her, at least he was concealing her nearly naked body from view.

She gritted her teeth and chanced a quick glance at their surroundings. It was dark, and strange incenses prickled her nose. Could be a club.

As Mephisto strolled forward, the crowd parted before him. Nerves spiked low in her stomach as some of the patrons glanced her way.

A human with strange, reptilian eyes and iridescent amphibian skin embraced a luminous haired creature with glowing, red flesh.

Humans? *Really?* But what else would they be? Anyone who had the kind of wealth that allowed them to go to the same clubs as winged beings, could obviously afford to pay for any kind of body modification they wanted.

She wasn't going to think it. *This club isn't full of aliens.*

And then Mephisto spoke. "Hey, Gabe."

Relief rushed through her in a torrent. She'd had a terrifying moment when she'd wondered if Mephisto had lied to her. That he hadn't brought her here to meet Gabe at all.

Thank god she was wrong. And then she saw him, sprawled on a sofa, completely ignoring her predicament as he focused on a couple of near-naked, snake-skinned women who were gyrating on a table in front of him.

Well, that was just great.

CHAPTER 10

GABE

What the hell was Mephisto doing here? He and Eblis loathed each other, and it had everything to do with the fact he was the first archangel their goddess had created after rejecting her flawed first children.

The demons.

He glanced at Eblis. Why wasn't he already shooting fire and brimstone in Meph's direction? But instead, he appeared enthralled by the archangel's appearance.

Yeah, right. Like that would ever happen. The brain-rot he'd been drinking must have been stronger than he thought.

Since Mephisto and Eblis appeared to be having a visual stand-off, he returned his attention to the dancers. Eblis had informed him with a smirk that they were both freelancers with their own spacecraft, but even the knowledge they were in control of their own fate did nothing for his disinterested libido.

What was so fucking special about Aurora?

"Mephie," Eblis said, and even after millennia, the derogatory nickname that no one else would dare utter still made Gabe grin. "Is that female morsel a gift for me?"

Presentiment scraped across his nerves, like rusty nails across a chalkboard. *It's not her.* Why couldn't he get her out of his head? She wasn't the only damn female in the universe. But the dread refused to diminish, and he turned to the other archangel.

And saw Aurora.

His heart thudded in his head, blocking out every other sound. What the hell was she doing with Mephisto?

He had his wing around her in a blatant gesture of possession. How dare he fucking touch her?

Rage thundered through him. And consuming everything was raw, acidic envy that Meph, the bastard, retained the ability to wrap her in his wings at all.

He shoved the table back with his boot, sending the entertainment sprawling across the floor. Mephisto shot him a demonic grin and slid his cursed wing down Aurora's body, and his heart jackknifed.

What in the cursed gods' names was she wearing?

Mesmerized, he stared at her exposed nipples peeking through the slashes in the scarlet leather. They were erect and enticing, and blood surged, arrowing directly to his damn cock.

"Not bad," Mephisto said. "For a mortal indigenous to Earth."

"Earth?" Eblis sounded enraptured. "You brought me a human from *Earth?*"

Ancient muscles flexed and contracted as phantom wings attempted to unfurl with outrage. He'd possessed his wings for only a fraction of his long existence, yet they were a part of him still.

A part of him forever.

And right now, he would give almost anything to possess them once again, to match Mephisto wingspan to wingspan and prove to creation that he was *once again whole.*

"Take your fucking hands off her."

The words thundered in his brain and directly into Mephisto's. For a fleeting second shock flared in Meph's eyes, as if Gabe's response had exceeded his expectations.

Then Mephisto drew back his wing with a flourish, exposing Aurora to half the depraved clientele of the club, and pushed her forward. She tottered on the spindly black stilettos, and he grabbed her wrist before she ended up on the floor.

Black fishnet stockings gave her legs an erotic silhouette, and lacy scarlet suspenders decorated her thighs. Primitive lust surged through him, and he forcibly sat her down on the sofa before taking one step toward Mephisto.

He'd pay for bringing her here.

"Jealous, Gabe?" Mephisto's voice was mocking, and it was all the invitation he needed. He grabbed Meph's throat and shoved him up against the wall, barely aware when the other archangel slammed a heavy fist into his ribs.

No one made a fool of him. Least of all another archangel.

Aurora

HER BACK RIGID, arms folded across her exposed breasts, Aurora stared as Gabe and Mephisto knocked lumps of stone from the walls, and no one attempted to stop them. It was obvious Gabe hadn't expected her. So why had the other one brought her here? Surely not just to start a fight?

Why am I stressing about that? If they wanted to beat the shit out of each other, it was nothing to do with her. Because seven terrifying words kept spinning around her brain.

You brought me a human from Earth.

She was no longer on Earth. She was on an alien planet, and the strange, exotic, and downright weird people in the club weren't into extreme forms of body modifications.

They're all real-life aliens.

After discovering teleportation was possible, the existence of other worlds teeming with intelligent life wasn't that much of a leap.

I'm not losing my grip on reality. Just because she'd left her own world, didn't make it any less real. And it didn't mean she'd never find her way back to it, either.

"Relax, babe," said the stranger sitting beside her, and she shot him a glance. Dear god. He had wings too. Was he another archangel? His dark golden eyes had flecks of amber, and his shoulder length hair was a couple of shades lighter than Gabe's. "Is this your first time off that primitive shithole of a planet? Don't worry. I'll look after you." His lascivious grin sent icy fingernails along her spine, and she leaped to her feet before she even knew what she was doing.

There was only one person here she'd trust to *look after her* or help her get back home. She sure as hell wasn't going to sit quietly in the corner while Gabe and Mephisto attempted to kill each other.

"Stop that *right now*." Her voice rang out, far louder than she'd intended, and she couldn't believe she'd even said it. They both swung around simultaneously to stare at her, as though she was an insect who'd suddenly discovered the power of speech. Shock speared through her. *That's probably all they think I am.*

"Sit down," Gabe growled as he raked his eyes over her as though he'd like nothing more than to sling her over his shoulder like a Viking conqueror. Wait. *What?* She was having dirty little fantasies about him right *now?* "Every fucking pervert in the place is looking at you."

That might be true, but he didn't need to sound like it was *her* fault. She fought the urge to tug on the hem of the skirt. It would only draw more attention to her half-exposed bottom.

"This outfit wasn't my idea." She tried to inject as much dignity in her words as she could and gave Mephisto a dark glare. He appeared to be enjoying himself.

"Park your asses, archangels," said the winged stranger. "The human may remain standing. I like the view."

Gabe grabbed her arm and shoved her onto the sofa before

sitting between her and Mephisto. He slammed his booted foot onto the table as waiters placed steaming tankards in front of the three guys.

Males.

Archangels.

Beings from mythology.

Clearly, she wasn't important enough to be served. And while she didn't much like the look of the drink, she was in desperate need of alcohol and she doubted this place served whiskey.

Keeping her arm wrapped across her exposed boobs, which was more awkward than it seemed, she reached for Gabe's tankard. His fingers wrapped around her wrist before she even came close.

"Drink that and die." He dropped her hand onto her lap, as though her flesh burned him. And not in a good way.

She flexed her fingers and a dozen retorts flashed through her mind. But she kept her mouth shut, because no way would she let him know his cavalier attitude wasn't annoying her, which was the right response. She was *hurt*.

"Have mine." Mephisto leered at her and pushed his tankard across the table. She'd rather drink weed killer than anything he offered her. Before she could do a grand refusal, Gabe bared his teeth at her.

"Don't, Aurora." Warning throbbed through each word. "That stuff will kill you."

"Shit, Gabe. You're no fun." Mephisto picked up his tankard and drained half the contents, never taking his gaze from her. Had he *really* just attempted to poison her?

"I think it's time I took a trip to Earth," the winged stranger said. "Been a while since I had a human. I don't remember them being so ..." He paused, clearly for effect, and she eyed him as nerves tumbled in her stomach. "Irreverent," he added with relish.

Gabe ordered a glass of water from a hovering waiter, and it appeared with dizzying speed.

"Humans haven't changed, Eblis." It was obvious he didn't mean that as a compliment.

The stranger—Eblis—slung his arm over the back of the sofa and scrutinized her. Prickles of alarm raced over her exposed flesh. Much as she wanted to stalk off, it was pointless. Where would she go?

Why didn't Gabe get her out of here?

"I'm opening a new fetish club," Eblis said. "Catering to the seriously depraved. Creatures who would literally rip each other apart for the chance to touch a human. Are you up for a trade? I'll ensure she remains undamaged, if you want her back."

Paralyzing terror slammed into her.

She was no longer on Earth. She had no idea of the laws, if any, that governed these so-called archangels. They were more like gangsters than anything with a heavenly connection, and their power appeared absolute.

Her hands were clammy, and insanity whispered through the outer edges of her mind. The cloudy atmosphere closed in on her, oppressive and alien, and a terrifying, yet oddly comforting, certainty flooded her.

She was going to faint. And then she was going to die.

CHAPTER 11

"She's not for sale." Gabe picked up his tankard and took a long swallow of the burning liquid. It was either that, or leap over the sofa and smash Eblis' head into the wall for daring to suggest such a thing.

He'd fought over Aurora enough for one night.

It was almost amusing.

Yeah, right.

"You've taken this female under your wing?"

Even after all this time, he didn't appreciate any allusion to his deficiency. Not even the most powerful of immortals broached the subject with him. Eblis was the only one who could say such a thing to him and get away with it.

It was ironic that if Gabe still possessed his wings, he and Eblis would still be blood enemies. Yet the loss of the one thing that defined both archangels and demons had been the catalyst for this unlikely bond between them.

"She's mine." The words were archaic, tantamount to ownership, but it was the only thing he could think of to ensure Eblis—and Mephisto—would no longer consider Aurora fair game.

"You should've said." Eblis snapped his fingers for more drinks. "I've no desire to trespass on your property."

Beside him, Aurora shuddered, and he waited for her caustic retort. Although the imperious way she'd addressed him and Meph just now had staggered him, he admired her nerve. There were few who would dare intervene between pissed-off archangels.

Even fewer who would live to breathe another day.

But she didn't say a word.

Frowning, he grasped her jaw and forced her to look at him. Her skin was ashen and oddly clammy, and her eyes were unfocused. After everything that had happened, she was going into shock *now*?

He picked up the glass of water and managed to get a few drops between her lips. He needed to get her back to his villa before she completely lost it.

"She's yours?" There was a hint of mockery in Mephisto's voice that he chose to ignore. "That won't stop the Guardians when she's not on your island."

How did he know about the Guardians? Unless Zad had told him. Gabe should've kept his mouth shut, but he'd been so fucking riled up earlier.

All he had to do to keep her safe was take her back to his sanctuary. The Guardians couldn't touch her there. But if he gave her his official protection, the Guardians wouldn't be able to touch her at all.

And neither would any immortal who wanted her. Not when they checked her aura and saw she belonged to him.

Why didn't I think of that before?

It would solve the problem of having her stay on his island. She could leave, go about her life. He'd never need to see her again, because she'd be safe, and the insidious guilt that he was somehow responsible for drawing the Guardians' attention to her in the first place, would die.

He'd never given his protection to a mortal before. And not just because the ritual involved a complex cleansing ceremony, where the mortal had to give an oath of allegiance and obedience to their immortal protector. On sacred ground on the night of a full moon.

It was because he'd never wanted to. Because it felt like a betrayal of his long-lost love.

But the alternative was to keep her in his sanctuary for who knew how long.

He didn't want to keep Aurora for a second longer than he had to. She would never need to understand the significance of what he was doing for her. All she had to know was the Guardians would never come near her again.

And fuck the ritual. Only one thing sealed the deal.

He held out his hand, palm up, to Mephisto.

Shock flashed across the other archangel's face. "You can't be serious."

"I am." Otherwise, how could he ever be sure of her safety? The Guardians might forget about her for decades, and then decide to take her. Without his protection, she would never be free of their shadow.

With obvious reluctance, Mephisto handed over his ceremonial athame.

Gabe turned to Aurora, who appeared frozen by the sight of the blade. He smothered a sigh, and before she got the chance to ask what he was doing, he cut open his palm, grasped her fingers, and made an identical incision on hers.

"What?" she wheezed, looking at him in horror. He pressed his hand over hers, mingling their blood, and her expression slid into something strange and ethereal, almost as though a part of her understood there was more to this ritual than its surface significance.

What the fuck does that even mean? He banished the lingering tendrils of guilt from his mind and said the words that would bind her to him.

"This human from Earth, Aurora, is under my protection."

That was it. All it took was the immortal pledge and a drop of immortal blood and Aurora was his.

Mephisto narrowed his eyes, obviously checking her aura for the unmistakable evidence that she was untouchable. He didn't bother checking it himself. The deed was done.

"Satisfied?" He wiped the tip of the blade on his forearm before handing it back. Surprisingly, Meph didn't make a mocking comeback. Instead, he frowned, as though something had distracted him.

Aurora took a shuddering breath, her gaze fixed on her palm. The wound was already healing, due to the immortal properties of his blood. "The Guardians can't get to me anymore?"

Her voice was barely above a whisper, but at least she was no longer mute with shock. He'd take that as a win.

"No. They can't touch you without incurring the wrath of the Immortals." More specifically, him.

"Okay." She glanced around the club and swallowed. *Get her out of here now.* He'd got the information he needed. Before he could tell her they were leaving, she added, "I really need the bathroom."

He shrugged at Eblis, who jerked his head at a nearby seven-foot, muscular bodyguard from one of the less civilized planets in the Sextans.

"Take this human to the restroom. She's valuable, you understand?"

"I don't need an *escort.*" She sounded outraged. Relief smashed through him that her near descent into shock hadn't done any permanent damage to her sassy tongue.

Anyone would think I enjoy her smart mouth.

And what if he did? It was no one else's business.

"It's for your own safety." Not everyone here could read auras and therefore understand an archangel had claimed her. Especially when Mephisto, the fucked-up pervert, had made her wear something so provocative. If Gabe's telekinetic power wasn't restricted to whichever planet he happened to be on at the time, he'd give her another of his own shirts to wear. Anything was better than what she had on right now.

But only because of where they were. It would be different if they were in his villa. She could wear that outfit all the time and he wouldn't complain.

He barely suppressed a groan at the prospect.

"Okay." Reluctance dripped from the word, but at least she didn't argue the point. She stood up and edged past Eblis, who, to his credit, avoided looking at her cute ass.

The crowd parted before the bodyguard, and Aurora sashayed across the floor on those astronomical heels, her arms crossed over her breasts and her head held high. She exuded a mesmeric air of confidence and could easily be mistaken, at first glance, for a minor demigoddess. After everything that had happened, any other human would be drooling in a corner as their brains leaked out of their ears. But except for that one shaky moment, she'd kept her shit together.

It was impressive.

Mephisto hooked one booted foot across his knee. "Isn't she just *adorable*."

The sarcasm sizzled in the air, but Gabe ignored it. He was more interested in the glimpses of Aurora's rounded ass that she displayed with every exaggerated step she took. His cock throbbed with frustrated need.

"Cut the crap." Eblis gave Mephisto a filthy glare that could reduce lesser beings to puddles of slime. "Since you didn't come bearing gifts, what the fuck are you doing here?"

"Just delivering Gabe's pet." Mephisto ruffled his feathers and glanced at Gabe. "You're welcome."

Aurora finally disappeared from his view, and he turned to

Mephisto. He had no idea why Meph thought it a good idea to bring her here, but that was a secondary detail. There was something they needed to get clear.

"Whatever interest you had in Aurora stops right now."

"My only interest in the human was her obsession with inter-dimensional travel. Do you know what she was doing on the astral planes the moment before you arrived?"

How the fuck did Meph know about that? He hadn't mentioned the astral planes when he'd seen Zad earlier.

But that wasn't even his main concern. Because an unwelcome memory stirred and thudded through his head. When he'd taken her to his island, the first thing she'd asked was if he'd pulled her through to another dimension.

Why did she ask that? It wasn't the most obvious thing a mortal would say after their first experience of teleportation. He'd thought it odd at the time but hadn't attached any significance to it.

There is no significance. Meph lied as easily as he breathed. Except he had the sick certainty that this time Meph was telling the truth.

That was crazy. Aurora wasn't from an advanced race of mortals who even understood the reality of alternate dimensions, let alone the complexities involved in breaching those dimensions.

But she has a telepathic shield like nothing I've encountered before.

"How the hell do you know where she was?"

"I tagged her phone."

So that was why he'd felt Meph's presence when he'd picked up the device. Because the bastard had been spying on her.

It was preferable to the alternative. At least Aurora hadn't been involved with Mephisto.

"She was in trance. So what?" Even he could hear the belligerence in his voice. But he didn't like the direction Meph was heading.

"She deliberately breached dimensions. I saw her."

The hell she did.

"That's why the Guardians are after her." Eblis exhaled a long breath. "Nothing random about *that.*"

Denial thudded like a tribal drum inside his head. Aside from anything else, why would anyone try to cross dimensions while on the astral planes? "The Guardians got it wrong."

"I was there, Gabe." For once, Mephisto was serious. "There's no mistake. It's all the excuse they need to hunt her across the universe. She'll never escape them."

He clenched his fists, fighting the fury that pounded through his blood. He'd given Aurora his pledge of protection *and it meant nothing.*

If she had breached dimensions, she had given the Guardians, the self-appointed keepers of laws so ancient their reasoning was lost in the fog of time, carte blanche to exact retribution—and his protection was void. She would only be safe within the energy field that surrounded his island.

Only the beloveds of Immortals were immune from the Guardians' grasping claws, whatever the provocation. Unlike bestowing protection, a beloved was their Immortal's equal. There was no need for the blood exchange. It was love that granted the same, and greater, immunity.

Aurora wasn't, and could never be, his beloved.

The Guardians wouldn't move onto another victim when they got tired of looking for her. They would hunt her down until they found her because they were vindictive, tenacious fuckers.

Was it something I did? The terrified question she'd asked after he'd taken her to his island hammered through his mind. He'd been so sure of her innocence. He'd even been plagued by guilt that it was *his* fault she'd been targeted.

But she had known the truth all along. What else had she kept hidden from him?

"Tell me one thing." It was fucking eating him alive. "Why did you drag me into this shitstorm?"

Confusion glinted in Mephisto's eyes for a fleeting microsecond, but it was enough. He had nothing to do with Gabe's involuntary teleportation. Gabe had been so sure Meph was responsible he hadn't even considered any other possibility.

What other possibility could there be?

"I'm working on how that happened." Mephisto sounded unusually grim.

"You do that." Something dark and savage surged through him, scorching his blood. He needed answers that even Meph couldn't give him, and by all the gods, he wouldn't be distracted by Aurora's blue eyes and deceptive innocence again.

He marched through the club, focused on only one thing. She'd tell him what he demanded, if it was the last damn thing she did.

The bodyguard was standing outside the bathroom door but instantly stepped aside at Gabe's approach. He smashed open the door, dislodging the spindly chair Aurora had obviously used as a makeshift barricade, and she was sitting cross-legged on the floor of the mirrored powder room.

Her eyes were closed and her breathing shallow. She didn't stir at his entrance and appeared oblivious when he kicked the door shut.

And then it hit him. She was ascending into the astral planes.

Why the fuck is she doing that now?

It didn't matter. And he'd be damned if he'd wait for her to return in her own sweet time.

He crouched, gripped her shoulders, and glared into her calm face. The fact she was so serene while fire consumed his reason *because of her* pushed him over the edge.

"Get the hell back here, Aurora, or I swear I'll follow and flay your soul until you scream for mercy."

CHAPTER 12

GABE

Gabe didn't wait for her response. There was no point, since she'd never obey him anyway, and within a nanosecond, he followed her.

Jagged discordance scraped through him, and echoes of unnatural chaos vibrated. It had been millennia since he'd last been here, but this was nothing like the tranquil realm he recalled.

Any other time he might have investigated. But Aurora was right ahead, glowing with pure energy. Reluctant awe rippled through him.

Breathtaking ...

Concentrate. She was a fucking menace. And before she could do any more damage, he needed to pull her back into her physical body.

The second he grasped her, they fell from the incorporeal realm and collided on the cold, tiled, floor of the bathroom.

Panting, Aurora faced him on her hands and knees, her hair tumbling over her shoulders. She looked feral and furious and infinitely fuckable.

"You could've killed me doing that."

"Unlikely." What the fuck was her deal with the astral planes? Involuntarily, he drew in a deep breath, savoring the scent of his soap and shampoo on her, mingled with supple leather and aroused woman.

He would *not* be distracted. He'd discover her truth. But damn, it was hard to focus.

"What are you doing in here, anyway?"

She had the gall to speak to *him* in that accusing tone?

"Tell me what you were doing in the astral planes before I arrived in Cornwall."

Confusion clouded her face. How could Meph be right about her? There had been a mistake. Had to be.

"I told you. I was in trance. I've always loved the spiritual realm."

He glared into her eyes. She was holding something back, but unlike when he'd first met her, this time he wouldn't dismiss his suspicion.

"Were you attempting to breach dimensions?"

The words thudded in the space between them, sounding even more unthinkable now he faced her. There was no way this fragile human could do such a thing. *But what isn't she telling me?*

There was no hint of fear on her face. *Let me be wrong.*

She took a shuddering breath, and his treacherous gaze slid to her enticing breasts. Lust scorched his blood and he was so fucking hard it hurt. Godsdamnit, why did his brains scramble every time he was near her?

"Yes."

It was a soft, breathy confession, and for an eternal second, he couldn't even comprehend what she had just admitted.

"*Yes?*" The word scraped his throat. "You deliberately opened a rift?" She was mistaken. It had been accidental. *Why can't I accept her guilt?*

It hit him that he was on all fours, facing her, and he reared up, fury pumping through his arteries. He kneeled before no one, but he was incapable of standing.

She followed him, a mirror image, and even though she was kneeling before him, in a sacrificial outfit— a despised human, no less—there was no hint of reverence in her manner. She faced him as though they were equals.

I should destroy her, right here, right now.

"But you don't understand. I'm not—"

He wrapped his hand around her throat. Her pulse fluttered against his fingers, so delicate, so easily extinguished. Her lips parted and her shallow breath fanned his face in an illicit caress. She didn't struggle or try and push him away, and he couldn't tear his gaze from her beautiful blue eyes.

It would take no effort to end her existence. An act of mercy compared to the Guardians' brand of justice.

"You've no idea what you've done." And the gods alone knew how she'd managed it. "You could have unraveled the strands of the universe."

Her eyes darkened, but it wasn't terror tainting the charged atmosphere. Awareness sizzled along his flesh, and he plunged his fingers through her hair, his grip merciless. She reached for him then, but not to push him away.

She grasped his shirt and held on tight.

An agonized groan flayed him. Instead of squeezing the life from her, his thumb caressed the silken skin of her vulnerable throat. A shiver rippled through her, and a delicate blush suffused her cheeks as one hand slid up and cradled his jaw.

"What are you?" she whispered as the tips of her fingers stroked his face. Her touch was as light as a feather, oddly tender, and a strange burning sensation filled his chest, the way it had when she'd pushed him from the face of danger.

A danger she'd brought on herself.

Her touch should mean nothing. She was no longer merely a despised human.

She was a human who had flouted a fundamental law of the universe.

A mortal whose fate was to die for her sin.

Yet he couldn't untangle his fingers from her hair, or release her tempting throat, and he sure as hell didn't want to stop her gentle caress.

Why did she ask him, when Eblis had already told her the answer?

"You know what I am." His voice was raw with need. Why could he barely recall his own name whenever she was near?

"An archangel." Awe threaded the words. And then mystified comprehension filled her eyes. "The Archangel *Gabriel?*"

He bared his teeth. It was the closest he could get to a grin. "Don't faint on me now, human."

Her hand glided from his face to his shoulder, and even through his shirt, her touch was like fire.

Curse the fates. He'd wanted to kiss her from the second they'd met. Human or not, hunted or not, made no difference. Her lips tempted him, her body invited him, and he could drown in the innocent depths of her eyes.

She's not innocent. She had deliberately opened a rift between dimensions.

He didn't care. Nothing mattered but slaking this unholy desire between them.

"What happened to your wings?"

Involuntarily his grip tightened around her throat. How dare she question him on such a thing? How dare she question him *at all?*

She was disrespectful, disobedient, and he couldn't dislodge her from his mind. But some lines could never be crossed.

"Don't you ever ask me that again."

Her nails dug into his shoulders, her eyes widening, and he relaxed his death grip. She swallowed, an erotic caress against his palm, and even now, when she'd asked the one thing that could guarantee instant death, he couldn't let her go.

She panted, sucking air into her lungs, and fury glinted in her eyes. "Why not?"

And still she questioned him.

It was unprecedented. There was no reason why her insolence stoked the fire in his blood or incinerated his defenses, but every word she uttered was a sultry enticement.

He didn't owe her an explanation. Yet he couldn't ignore her. "Because you don't need to know."

"Bastard," she breathed, but the curse sounded like an endearment on her tongue and his grin was feral. Finally, she'd got something right.

"To the bone," he growled before finally claiming her lips.

She tasted wild and sweet, and he released her throat so he could wrap his arm around her. Her tongue teased him, and her fingers plunged through his hair, taking and giving with every frenzied beat of their hearts.

This shouldn't feel so good. *It's only a kiss.*

It was everything.

He ripped his mouth from hers. Her eyes were dark, her breathing ragged, and a fierce wave of possessiveness surged through him. *She's under my protection.* He'd never allow anything to harm her.

Stop. He was losing his godsdamned mind. There was only one way to reclaim his sanity and conquer this lust for all time.

"Tell me you want me." It was a harsh command, but she didn't instantly obey. He hadn't expected her to.

It's why she's so irresistible.

He cupped her ass. Was she naked beneath that minuscule skirt?

"Yes," she breathed, her fingers tangling in his hair, her eyes glazed with passion.

"Yes, what?" He needed to hear her say it. Wanted her to admit she was as ensnared as he within the web of this blistering desire.

She pressed closer, her lips teasing his ear, and her exposed nipples tortured him through the fabric of his shirt. Why the hell were they still wearing clothes?

"I want you." Her confession splintered the last threads of his control, and he kissed her again, but there was nothing soft or teasing about this one. He plundered her mouth, demanding her surrender, and she didn't yield.

Her refusal to succumb was electrifying, even if part of him had expected it. Relished it.

Craved it.

His hand slid down her body, exploring her waist, hip, and naked silken thigh. The lace on her decadent scarlet garters burned his fingers, and her sigh stirred erogenous zones he hadn't even known existed.

He didn't want her to submit, but a crazy part of him wanted to hear her beg. To know she wanted him more than her next breath.

And not because he was an archangel.

"You want me to stop?" He growled the words against her bruised lips as his hand cupped her sex. *Gods.* The strip of leather was crotchless. She was hot and wet, and bucked helplessly as he stroked his fingers over her swollen clit.

"No," she gasped frantically, clutching his shoulders as though he was her lifeline. "Don't you dare stop."

"Not a chance." He slid a finger inside her and she clenched her muscles, entrapping him in a silken cocoon. *Slow down.* He gritted his teeth and breathed in her evocative scent. He didn't know why he wanted to prolong this torture. *Just do it and get her out of your system.*

"Gabe," she moaned, arching her back. Her cheeks were flushed, her lips full and inviting, and her hair tumbled down her back.

She was bewitching, magnificent. The need to see her beautiful eyes as she convulsed around his cock consumed him.

A sliver of reason whispered in the back of his mind. *It's only a fuck.* A fundamental need. It had been so long since he'd wanted a woman. That was the only reason he was so damned obsessed with her.

Why her? Why now?

She's a human. But even that reminder didn't make any difference.

He screwed his eyes shut but could still see her face, anyway.

"It doesn't mean anything." Had he said that aloud? He didn't know, didn't care. Nothing else mattered but the need to make her his. "It's just one godsdamn fuck."

Don't look in her eyes.

He twisted her around, and the seductive curves of her ass cradled the rigid length of his erection. Her shocked intake of breath fueled the blaze in his blood, and when she rocked her hips, increasing the friction, his unraveling control gave up the fight.

He cupped her breasts, teasing her nipples with his thumbs. She groaned, and the sound of her frustration wound him tighter than ever. With a guttural curse, he released her breasts and swept her hair back from her face, exposing her naked shoulder.

There was no reason why the delectable column of her neck should be so provocative, but logic had perished the moment they'd kissed. If he didn't have her now, he was going to fucking die.

With degrading lack of finesse, he ripped open his pants and then gripped her hips. The perfection of her ass, framed in the tattered red leather of her skirt, was a visual feast and her pussy mesmerized.

His mouth watered.

Later.

His cock nudged her wet slit and her seductive tremor vibrated throughout his entire body. He wanted to savor and cherish the first time he possessed her, but a ferocious primal imperative to claim and conquer scorched whatever remained of his reason.

He thrust into her and an agonized groan tore from his throat as her tight sheath expanded around him. She fell forward, ass in the air, her head cradled on her arms, and her staggered gasps of shock were all he could hear.

She was hot and wet and so fucking tight around him he could hardly breathe. He pulled out, an excruciating drag of flesh against flesh, and stared, entranced, by the sight of his cock invading her irresistible heat.

She quivered, and it was too much. He pushed into her again and her embrace was silken fire, licking over and into his cock, igniting his blood and infecting his sanity. He palmed her butt cheek and his other hand glided around her waist and between her thighs.

So hot and wet. His cock stretched her delicate folds, and he teased her clit as her choked moans filled his head. She writhed beneath him, and he pushed in deeper, to the hilt, his heavy balls slamming against her tender flesh.

Her thrusts matched his, a frenzied maelstrom of mindless lust and ragged breaths. She shuddered, squeezed him tighter than should have been possible, and convulsed in waves of raw, uninhibited pleasure.

It was too much. He followed her over the edge, gripping her thigh as he pumped into her. It felt so fucking good, felt so fucking right, to fill her with his seed. To hear her erratic gasps and feel her body tremble at his onslaught.

He collapsed, bracing his weight on his hands as he covered her body, entrapping her. The evocative scent of sex and satisfaction drenched the air, and he couldn't resist dropping a kiss on her bare shoulder.

Buried deep inside her, his cock stirred, as hard as ever. He'd come, and it had blown his fucking mind, but damn if he didn't want her again. Right now. Why the fuck not?

An unformed warning vibrated in the dark corners of his mind. *Danger ...*

She suddenly severed their connection by sprawling onto the floor. Shock staggered through him. *We're still in Eblis' club.* How had he forgotten that?

When was the last time he'd been so captivated by a woman that he'd literally forgotten where he was?

He shoved the unsettling notion aside and brushed the tangled hair from her face. Her eyes were closed, her mouth open, and she was sucking in oxygen as though she'd almost drowned. An unaccustomed thread of tenderness flickered through him. "Hey, are you okay?"

Her eyes opened, but she didn't look at him.

"I'm fine." Her voice was hoarse and didn't help with the whole wanting her again thing. She pushed herself upright and he rolled back onto his knees. Something wasn't right, but he couldn't imagine what. Hadn't he just given her the best fucking orgasm of her life?

She pushed back her hair from her flushed face and shot him an oddly hostile glance. What the hell was *that* for?

"Can you take me home, now?"

They had just had mind-blowing sex, and she wanted to go *home?* By rights, she should be worshipping at his feet, begging him to never leave her. But when had Aurora ever been bedazzled by his archangelic radiance?

That wasn't even why he was almost speechless. It was because *he* still wanted *her.* Back when he fucked around, he'd rarely wanted to go a second round with the same woman. At least, not without an alcohol break.

Why hasn't my brain cleared?

"No." He practically snarled the word at her as he shoved his cock back into his pants. "You're not going anywhere." Except back to his island, where she'd have to stay for the rest of her damn life.

"Why not?" she shot back with another venomous glare. "You got what you wanted. It didn't *mean* anything. It was only a goddamn fuck."

She had the nerve to throw his own words back in his face?

But it didn't mean anything to her? *Really?*

He couldn't even figure out why her comment pissed him off so much. She was right. Except for one thing.

"Don't give me that. You wanted this as much as I did." And now he was defending himself? Against a *human?*

She exhaled a long breath and gripped her fingers together on her lap. He was reluctantly fascinated that she was clearly trying to stay calm and rational, when there was nothing remotely rational about this entire situation.

Even now, after her insult, *after they'd had sex,* he was as ensnared with her as ever.

It was a demeaning admission.

Danger ... He crushed the thought. He was in no fucking danger from her.

"All right." She inclined her head as though she was bestowing a great favor. "Let's forget about that, then. It's safe, now. You can return me home."

If only. "It's not safe and you can never return home."

She licked her lips, and fear flared in her eyes. Instead of victory that he'd finally got through to her, he felt like a total bastard.

"But you gave me your protection." She swallowed, clearly having problems with that word, but it didn't stop her continuing. "The Guardians can't touch me now."

"Yeah, about that." He leaned into her space, daring her to

retreat, knowing that she wouldn't. She didn't even blink, and still her blue eyes threatened to deceive him with their innocence. "My protection means nothing since you breached dimensions."

CHAPTER 13

AURORA

He's lying. The panicked denial tumbled around Aurora's head, but deep inside she knew the truth.

She really had opened a doorway to her mum's world. That scary violet lightning *had* been her fault.

And her experiment was the reason why the Guardians were after her.

Her stomach heaved, and she had the mortifying certainty she was about to vomit. She dug her nails into her palms and focused on the pain. Counted to ten in her head. Ignored the insidious whisper that invited her to sink into sweet oblivion where she wouldn't need to think anymore.

Finally, she risked glancing at Gabe again. His hair was tangled, but apart from that, he didn't look as though he'd just had earth-shattering sex.

Then again, he probably hadn't. *Just a goddamn fuck.* Brilliant. Really put her in her place in the great scheme of things.

It didn't change the reality, though.

I just had sex with an archangel. The unnerving urge to laugh bubbled in her chest. And once she started, she didn't think she'd be able to stop.

"I'm stuck here, then?" Her voice sounded weird and squeaky, like she'd just sucked on helium. Maybe she had. Maybe everything that had happened since she'd met Gabe was a hallucination.

Maybe she was losing her identity.

This. Is. Real. She wasn't going to fall apart. She had to think logically. Figure out a solution. It was hovering right there, on the edge of her mind.

And then it unfolded, like a magical answer to all her prayers. "That energy source that protects your island. Haven't you discovered a way to utilize it to protect individuals, no matter where they are?"

Please say yes. She held her breath, even though a cynical fragment of her brain mocked her hopes. If he had that technology, he would have shared it with her already.

His features darkened, like she'd just questioned his integrity, and he rose to his feet in a magnificent flourish. "No."

That was it? Just an unadorned *no*?

There was no way she could spend the rest of her life isolated on a deserted island.

With or without Gabe's electrifying presence.

She could stop thinking about that right now. No way were they having sex again. It took a couple of lust-clouded seconds to remember what they'd been talking about.

She stood, with far less grace than Gabe had, wobbled on her stilettos, and took a deep breath for courage. She'd never been religious, but if archangels were real … "Could you please ask God to intercede on my behalf?"

"Which god did you have in mind?"

His question echoed in her ears, and the implication wasn't encouraging. "I'm sorry?"

His grin was anything but friendly. "You want a consultation with a god. I wouldn't advise it, but out of interest, which one do you think would lower themselves to assist *you*?"

There was only the slightest emphasis on his final word, but it was enough to let her know just how insignificant she was in his terrifying world.

Not that she'd let him see her wavering courage.

"Your god." What other one was she supposed to appeal to? Zeus?

Wait, maybe there really *was* a Zeus, after all? How would that be more unbelievable than the fact she'd just shagged an archangel?

"My goddess barely acknowledges your right to exist."

A strange, rushing noise, like she was standing by Niagara Falls, filled her head.

Goddess.

She locked down the rising panic. "But this isn't fair. Don't I even get a trial?"

"There's nothing fair about it." He sounded feral. "What gave you that idea?"

A phantom fist tightened around her heart. "But you're an archangel. You must have some influence. I mean, your goddess is the highest power, isn't she?"

His lip curled, and not in a good way. "She's always liked to think so."

In other words, no.

How had the legends got it all so wrong? Mythology was real, but so different to the fairy stories it was frightening. Before she could think better of it, she grabbed his biceps, and despite her predicament, his rock-hard muscles sent quivers of need through her.

Seriously? Fuck off, hormones.

Gabe had saved her once. She knew, if she could just get through to him, he could save her again.

Somehow.

"Could you plead my case with her? If she knows my reasons, surely she'll—"

"Throw you to the Guardians herself." He gripped her shoulders, and it shouldn't have felt so good, not when her entire future hung in the balance. "I haven't spoken to that bitch in millennia, Aurora. And if I ever see her again, pleading to her nonexistent compassion will be the last thing on my mind."

Millennia. Gabe hadn't seen her in millennia.

He was thousands of years old. He was an *immortal.* Superficially, she'd accepted that the moment she'd accepted he was an archangel.

But she'd never really thought about what it meant. Because he didn't look ancient. He looked as though he hadn't yet hit thirty.

And he clearly didn't worship his goddess.

Her eyes stung, and violet streaks flashed in front of her eyes. She blinked rapidly, but it didn't help readjust the warped laws of the universe or clear her vision.

The violet lightning splintered behind Gabe and then coalesced into a single entity. Long silvery fingers pushed through the fracture, and terror clawed through her heart.

The Guardians had found her.

Time froze as the violet shard expanded as if it were a door that had been violently flung open. Horror skated along her arms, and she clutched onto Gabe as a willowy gray alien with a huge dome head and reflective almond eyes stepped through the chasm.

An alien. The Guardians were gray aliens.

Gabe swung around and cursed viciously in that strangely familiar language he'd used before. She didn't even have time to suck in a petrified breath before he wrapped his arms around her and teleported them out of there.

Aurora reeled as his bedroom came into focus. Relief flooded her. She was safe. He hadn't left her behind to be taken.

I never thought he would.

And then her relief shattered as a single thought scorched her reason.

Gray aliens were real, and they were more than anyone had ever imagined.

He relaxed his vice-like grip around her but still held her in his arms. She didn't have the strength to push him away. She didn't *want* to push him away. Garbled fragments of a newly discovered, terrifying reality stabbed through her brain.

"The Guardians." The words tangled on her tongue, because they conjured up something magnificent and warrior-like—even if they were the bad guys. "Why didn't you tell me what they really were?" Renewed panic slammed against her chest. Or was that her heart? "They're not even human."

"I told you they weren't human." His voice was harsh, but his fingers were tender as he caressed her back. "*I'm* not human."

Logically, she knew that. But he looked like a man, not a monster, and she had no problem talking with him. Arguing, even. She'd even had sex with him! And he could be reasoned with. There was no way she could imagine doing any of those things with the Guardians.

Wasn't that what he'd been trying to tell her all along?

"You look human." It was a terrible response and she knew it, but her grasp on what she'd always believed logical and scientific was crumbling around her. Even the knowledge of her own unique heritage faded when compared to the mind-boggling reality that truly existed in this universe.

"Only superficially."

She had no intention of releasing her grip on that illusion of superficiality, either. Gabe she could accept. But deep in a primitive chasm of her psyche, she rejected the existence of the Guardians.

"Do they have spacecrafts?" *Shut up.* But the need to understand was stronger than the instinct to run. Even metaphorically.

"No." Gabe's kaleidoscopic gaze bore into her, oddly calming.

"They've never used that technology to my knowledge. We assume the energy they harvest from the Dark Matter they inhabit provides them with their version of teleportation."

Dark Matter was more a case of what science concluded it *wasn't*, rather than reliable data of what it *was*. And it seemed even archangels didn't know all its secrets.

"So that violet light is—what, their teleportation device?"

"Something like that. More like an interstellar elevator. Except when you enter the fracture, you arrive at your destination instantaneously."

A shudder inched along her spine. Within the space of a couple of days she'd breached dimensions, hooked up with an archangel, and traveled by teleportation. But the discovery that gray aliens existed was just one thing too much.

"All the claims of alien abductions—they're *real?*"

He shrugged. "Probably."

She was breathing way too fast but couldn't control it, not even when waves of dizziness collided inside her head. "But they don't keep the people they abduct. They gave them back."

He cradled her face with one hand, and his thumb stroked her heated skin. "They release some of their victims. They don't just take humans from Earth."

Of course they didn't. They had an interstellar elevator. They could go anywhere they wanted to.

"There's no way they could be persuaded to—" Her mouth was dry, and the words were hard to form. Ignorance might not be a defense in the eyes of the law, but there must be a loophole, somehow. "Give me a full pardon?"

"For your crime?" His gaze roved over her face, and incredibly her terror ebbed, like the tide receding from the shore. "If they ever get their hands on you, they'd never let you go."

His words were terrifying, but the crippling fear became fainter with every beat of her heart. She pressed her hand against his chest, and even through his shirt, the solid heat of his pectorals sent flickers of need over her exposed flesh. Yes, she wanted him. But it was more than raw sexual desire that drained the horror that was so close to drowning her sense of self.

With Gabe, she was safe. In this unfamiliar world, he was the only one she could trust. It was a primitive imperative, a fundamental survival tactic, but it was so much more than that.

Her touch was only light, but his pupils expanded, obliterating the mesmerizing magic of his irises. But he was no less compelling for that.

She wanted to kiss him, hold him tight, never let him go. Wanted his arms around her and feel the brutal strength of his body claiming her once again. But finally, he was answering her questions. And there was so much she craved to learn about this staggering new existence she now inhabited.

Even if the truth couldn't set her free. Ignorance was far worse.

"Are they immortal?" Her whisper drifted between them, the underlying currents of heat far more potent than the words she spoke.

"I don't know." His admission was shocking, and not just because the Archangel Gabriel didn't know the answer. It was *because* he'd told her. And it was unaccountably arousing.

"Are you?"

He smiled, but it didn't reach his eyes, and for an eternal second, unimaginable grief brushed her quivering soul.

"Define immortal." He forked his fingers through her hair and cupped the back of her head. "Compared to a human's lifespan, maybe I am. Compared to those in the Alpha Pantheon, I don't even come close."

Awe shivered through her, but even knowing all this, when she looked at him, she didn't see a powerful immortal who could teleport at will.

All she saw was a man who was prepared to disrupt his existence in order to keep her safe.

Her hand glided from his pecs and curled around his throat. The way he'd held her in anger so recently, yet even then, when murder had glinted in his eyes, she hadn't been afraid that he'd hurt her.

His grip had been bruising, but it had been blatantly sexual, and his sharp intake of breath now was all she needed to know that her touch affected him just as profoundly.

"Can you die?" It didn't seem possible, but it was all a matter of perspective. After all, to a butterfly a human would appear immortal.

"I haven't yet."

What a strange response. Didn't he know if he could die or not?

With one arm wrapped around her waist and his other hand cradling the back of her head, he walked her backwards to the bed.

"Really?" she gasped, as with a lightning-fast reaction, he had her flat on her back on the bed. Before she could even follow up her accusation, he straddled her thighs and his wicked grin of triumph at her easy defeat was breathtaking.

I wasn't resisting.

"Really," he confirmed, and leisurely unbuttoned his shirt.

Her mouth dried as his spectacular, bronzed chest came into view. All her fleeting fantasies of how he would look naked were pitiful compared to the real thing. How easy it would be to simply worship his masculine magnificence. It was what she wanted, after all.

She let out a ragged huff of breath. She might liquefy every time he touched her, but that didn't mean she was a total walkover.

"What happened to just one—" The word stuck in her throat. How ridiculous was that? *Fuck* was the perfect description for what they'd shared in that bathroom. She still couldn't say it.

"Time?" she substituted and attempted to glare at him, but he didn't laugh at her absurd prudery.

"It wasn't set in stone." He threw another evil grin her way before tossing his shirt onto the floor. "This time I want to watch your face as you come."

If she had any defenses left, they would have melted like ice before a furnace. Even though being taken from behind had been shocking and exciting, and all but turned her brain to pulp, a tiny sliver of hurt throbbed through her.

It was as though he hadn't wanted to see her face. As though it didn't matter who she was, just so long as she was willing.

He was an archangel. This wasn't the start of a new relationship. He didn't want her to be abducted by the Guardians, but that didn't mean he felt anything more than lust for her.

That's all I feel for him.

She still couldn't keep her mouth shut, though. "Is that all you ever think about? Sex?"

"When I'm with you?" He unclipped the suspenders and rolled the top of her stocking along her thigh, without breaking eye-contact. "Yes."

She propped herself up on her elbows and watched, fascinated, as he discarded her stilettos before continuing to roll one stocking, and then the other, down her legs before he dropped them beside him on the bed.

"I'm going to burn every last piece of that outfit," he said as he stood over her on the bed and tugged his pants down his legs. "But we might as well enjoy it in the meantime."

She was enjoying herself already. His body was a sculpted work of art, all rippling muscles, sleek flesh, and a dusting of dark blond hair that arrowed into his black boxer briefs. Her gaze snagged on his massive bulge, and she had the terrible certainty she was going to drool.

With expert ease, he toed off his boots and discarded his pants. All without losing his balance and crashing on top of her.

"I suppose you've had plenty of practice." *Please don't let me have said that out loud.* The quizzical look on his face crushed that hope. No way was she going to tell him what she really meant. He might be her savior, but his ego was big enough. She scrabbled for coherent words that would make sense of her random comment and came up blank. "Secluded island. No interruptions." *Shut. Up.* Her mouth just kept on going. "I can't even imagine how many women you've tied up in this bed."

Did I just say tied up? Where had that come from? Even her Viking fantasies didn't go that far.

Just because he hadn't wobbled while contorting his body was no need for her to devolve into a gibbering wreck. Gymnasts also possessed perfect balance. Why couldn't she just bite her tongue when nerves got the better of her?

Instead of bestowing one of his toe-curling, evil grins her way, a fleeting shadow darkened his face.

"No." Reluctance dripped from the word, as though he answered her against his will. "I've never brought a woman here before."

His confession curled like warm honey through her veins. It shouldn't matter whether she was the only one he'd brought to his island, and yet it did.

Don't fall for an archangel's silver tongue. Except he wasn't trying to flatter her. It was the stark truth.

Deep in her heart she knew it, even if she had no idea how she could be so sure.

"Gabe," she whispered, although she had no idea what she was going to say.

He fell to his knees, one of the stockings in his hand, and this time his smile was all sin. "You talk too much."

Once again, he straddled her hips, his subtle, exotic cologne making her head spin, and his expanse of naked chest was close enough to lick.

Before she got the chance to follow that delicious thought

through, he eased her onto her back. Without taking his mesmeric gaze from her, he tied the stocking around her wrist.

Wait. *What?*

She tugged ineffectually against the knot as he fixed the other end to his bedpost.

"*Excuse* me?" Her accusation was all breathy, more like an enticement to continue.

"Why, what else have you done?" Without waiting for her answer, he restrained her other wrist before rolling back on his knees and admiring his handiwork with a satisfied gleam in his eyes. "This leather shit has to go."

She was all for that. Not that she'd mind wearing it if Gabe had given it to her, but right now, naked was all she wanted to be.

He held out his hand, and a million glittering atoms appeared, dancing in the air above his fingers. She couldn't blink, couldn't breathe, as within nanoseconds they coalesced, and a wicked looking dagger glinted in his hand.

CHAPTER 14

AURORA

"*D*on't wriggle," he warned, and she didn't even feel the chill of the blade touch her skin as it sliced through the leather as though it was silk.

He peeled the severed leather over her breasts, exposing her fully to his gaze. But still he looked into her eyes, and although she was tethered to his bed, and was pinned beneath his powerful body, it was the beauty of his irises that truly held her captive.

"Your silence suggests you're impressed by the skill of my magnificent dagger." His teasing voice was smoky, but it was his smile that was the true aphrodisiac.

"Your dagger is a pretty impressive trick."

"That's harsh." He spun the thing around on the tip of his finger, its deadly blade gleaming. "I don't do tricks."

She laughed, couldn't help it. "All right. It's *magnificent*."

He tossed the dagger into the air before catching it by its worn hilt and shifted his weight so his erection brushed against the tender folds of her sex. She moaned, bit her lip, but couldn't stop moving restlessly against his rigid length.

The tip of his nose brushed hers. It was a featherlight touch, unexpectedly tender, and the pit of her stomach knotted with an absurd pleasure that bordered on pain.

"How gratifying to know my weapon meets with your approval."

His breath against her mouth was an erotic caress. She wanted to spear her fingers through his hair, wind her arms around his shoulders, and drag him onto her needy body. But, inexplicably, he maintained a whisper of distance between his chest and her aching breasts. And there was nothing she could do about it, because he had *tied her up*.

She tugged on the restraints, but they didn't unravel. She hadn't expected them to. It was beyond thrilling to be so utterly at his mercy. Without any control over what happened next.

"And leaves you speechless," he growled, which was the hottest damn thing she'd ever heard.

She clenched her fists and arched her back in a futile effort to feel his gorgeous body crush hers. He grinned, clearly loving the way she couldn't stop writhing beneath him, and she let out a frustrated groan. "I'm *so* going to pay you back for this."

"Promises," he mocked before brushing an electrifying kiss across her erect nipple. A mortifying squeak escaped her throat, but he didn't seem to notice. His full attention was focused on worshipping her breasts. Licking and sucking, and spirals of agonizing pleasure ignited her sensitized clit.

"Killing me," she gasped as she clung onto the fishnets as if they were an anchor to sanity.

Gabe raised his head, his jaw still grazing her tender flesh. "Don't die yet. I haven't finished."

She choked on another laugh. Who knew archangels had such a crazy sense of humor? "I'm not promising anything."

His fingers stroked and caressed, and his mouth and tongue were instruments of sweet torture as he inched farther down her body. It was an effort, but she managed to raise her head so she could watch his leisurely progress. Why was he taking so long? She gave a frantic wiggle, and he glanced up, masculine satisfaction radiating from him like an immortal halo.

"I'm *serious*," she panted. His archangelic radiance *wouldn't* distract her, and she didn't even care that he knew how desperate she was.

"Hold that thought," he responded before flourishing his dagger again. "I like it when you beg me."

"I'm—I'm *not* begging you," she spluttered, but they both knew she was.

His magnificent weapon sliced through the skirt before he tossed the ruined garment across the floor. "I'll make it worth your while."

She didn't doubt that. She just didn't want to *wait*.

With a final glint of his blade, the G-string slithered from her body. The dagger vanished, and he teased her damp heat with his finger. The breath caught in her throat and she couldn't tear her gaze from his face.

It was only sex. But despite his taunt of yesterday, the Archangel Gabriel found her *irresistible*.

The knowledge was as potent as the fire from his touch. She collapsed back onto the bed and the world tipped out of focus as his tongue swirled over her aroused clit.

It was forever and no time at all before he raised his head, his ragged breath sending shivers of pleasure across her damp flesh. His fingers played with her hips and waist, and delirium hovered on a hazy horizon.

Words fluttered in her mind, somehow making a connection to her tongue. "I *am* going to die if you don't hurry up."

"I don't do hurry up." And they both knew *that* was a lie. Did he really want her to beg?

"Please." It came out as an undignified sob as she writhed helplessly.

He rose over her, his face so close to hers she could taste her scent on his warm breath. "Is that the best you can do?"

She redoubled her efforts to escape her bonds, but that wasn't saying much. Every molecule screamed for release, and she wasn't talking about her restraints.

"Yes," she gasped, infuriated and aroused that he insisted on a reply when she could barely even think.

"You need to work on that." As he taunted her, he roughly kneed her thighs apart and the savage gleam in his eyes told her he was as close to the edge as she.

Primal power surged through her and she wrapped her legs around him, his rigid cock pressing against her wet sex. *When did he take off his briefs?* Not that it mattered. He was an archangel. He could do almost anything.

She squirmed, frantic with need, but still he didn't take her. His hands smashed down on either side of her head, bracing his weight. His tangled hair framed his face, his tautly muscled shoulders filled her world, and the head of his erection nudged her swollen clit.

"Archangel." Barely aware she'd spoken aloud, the evocative image spilled through her mind. "Gabriel." She dragged out each syllable, savoring the taste of his name on her tongue.

He cursed in his own language, which sent another frisson of desire sizzling through her blood, and slid the head of his cock over her wet slit. The exquisite pressure teased and probed, and another dry sob of frustration escaped her parched throat.

"You want something, Aurora?" He panted into her face, looking more like a hedonistic demon of pleasure than an archangel.

"Yes." Her fingers clawed uselessly, but he wouldn't come close enough so she could kiss him. "*Yes.*"

"Tell me." His thick erection continued to torment her, and she quivered with agonizing anticipation. "Do you want my cock inside you? Is that what you want?"

No way was she saying that. She dug her heels into his butt, her muscles straining with effort, but he was as hard as iron and as immovable as a mountain.

"Just *do* it." Had she *screamed*?

"Say it." His mouth all but touched hers, their erratic breaths mingling as one. "Say the words."

His growled command was intoxicating, incinerating her reservations to ash. "I want your cock inside me."

His eyes glittered with lust, and raw power sizzled through her veins. A surreal conviction drifted through her mind. She was the one in bonds, but it wasn't Gabe who held ultimate power in this game.

"And?" His harsh word cut through her daze, and she blinked up at him, uncomprehending. "What else do you want me to do? *Tell me.*"

She licked her dry lips. He watched the movement like a hawk.

"I want you to …" The word lodged in her throat. The crazy inhibition had no place in a world inhabited by archangels and aliens and cold-hearted goddesses. "Fuck me. Hard and fast. And I want it *now*."

He rammed into her, so *hard* and *fast*, her breath stalled in her lungs. His possession was absolute, enslaving her body and shattering her mind. All she could do was ride the wave with him, or risk drowning in the sensual torrent.

"You're a great fuck, Aurora." His words scorched through her, filthy and erotic. "You're so tight and hot. It's fucking insane."

She'd forgotten how to speak, how to think. Nothing else mattered but this man, *this archangel*, who looked at her with such ferocious intensity and who fucked her as if the world was about to end.

And then it did end, in a cascade of sparkling rainbows that filled her universe and transported her body. Unthinking, unaware, she wrapped her arms around his shoulders and clung on tight as he came, hot and brutal, and in that moment, nirvana shimmered in her soul.

CHAPTER 15

GABE

Eyes closed, his harsh breath searing his chest, Gabe's muscles slowly relaxed. Aurora was soft and warm beneath him, her arms still clasped around his shoulders.

Her heart hammered against his chest, her uneven gasps of breath teased his throat, and every few seconds delicate tremors consumed her. Satisfaction unfurled deep inside a buried chasm of his ruined soul, and he savored the scent of woman, of sex, and the unique flavor that was Aurora.

It had been an age since he'd taken a woman. But he hadn't forgotten the inevitable aftermath. The overpowering need to untangle limbs and sever contact. To find his own space, without having to deal with any messy fallout from a temporarily enraptured mortal.

No such sense of self-preservation washed through him now. And his cock, still buried inside her tight cleft, stirred.

Again.

He should have known once—*twice*—would never be enough to sate the madness in his blood when it came to Aurora. She was too fascinating, too aggravating, to be cleansed from his system so easily.

She's the only one I've wanted in countless years.

All true. But it still didn't explain why he continued to lie here, content to wind her hair around his finger and enjoy how she clung to him as her erratic breathing gradually calmed.

"You untied me." She sounded drowsy, sated, and slightly surprised.

That made two of them. He'd had no intention of releasing her until they were finished, but instinct had taken over.

He'd wanted to feel her arms around him. Why not? It didn't mean anything deeper beyond the physical contact.

Even if he'd avoided that kind of intimate, physical contact in his distant past when he'd fucked around.

"Are you complaining?" He brushed his lips against her temple.

Her faint hum of amusement washed through him like a soothing balm. It made no sense, but he wasn't about to fight it. He'd take any elusive façade of peace and embrace it while he could.

If he was sure of anything, it was this. His fascination with her wouldn't last long.

"No." She drifted her fingers across his shoulders, perilously close to his scars. Unlike previous lovers, she wouldn't pretend they didn't exist. She had no clue that mortals simply did not question an archangel. And even if she did, he doubted it would make any difference to her.

He didn't want to deflect her questions yet again and shatter the mood. But he didn't have to, as her fingers slid to his nape and her gentle massage was unexpected, soothing … extraordinary.

How easy it would be to roll onto his side, tug her close, and fall into blissful oblivion. But a dark, alien, serpent twisted deep in his gut, and he lifted his head so he could see her face.

Her eyes were half-closed, her cheeks flushed, and a small smile tilted her lips. She looked satisfied and happy. Why shouldn't she? This had been his plan from the moment he'd seen the bottomless insanity glitter in her eyes when she'd discovered the truth of the Guardians.

Yeah, he was all heart when it came to Aurora. He'd wanted to banish the terror that threatened to eat her alive, but the sex had been all about mutual lust. Nothing wrong with that.

Yet the unease grew, like a malignant tumor, extinguishing the lingering tendrils of peace in his soul.

She had no option but to stay on his island for the rest of her life. Would it make her incarceration more palatable if she fell for him? If she loved him, she wouldn't miss her former life. Millennia ago, he'd witnessed the blinding devotion a mortal could have for an archangel, at the expense of everything and everyone else.

Not that he'd ever craved that for himself. It was a one-sided obsession and he had no use for that. Whenever a mortal had professed undying devotion, he'd got out of there fast and never saw them again.

It was easier that way. Kinder, even.

But Aurora. He didn't want her to fall. Didn't want to witness her inevitable slide into bitterness when she finally accepted that he'd never return her feelings.

He just wanted this strange encounter to continue, without complicated emotions getting in the way and destroying what they'd found.

Was that too much to ask? If he laid down the ground rules now, before she lost her heart?

Slowly, she opened her eyes. They were so damn beautiful that he almost forgot why he had to warn her at all.

"Gabe," she whispered. Why did he enjoy the sound of his name on her lips? "We need to talk."

Her words were arrows through his chest. *Too late.* She gazed at him in adoration, and there was no mistaking the tenderness in her tone. He heaved himself up and braced his weight on his hands, his wrists grazing her shoulders, but couldn't find the strength to leave the bed.

"Not now." His voice was harsh. *Not ever.* With damning reluctance, he withdrew from her warm embrace and rolled onto his back beside her. "Go to sleep."

He should have known she wouldn't obey. She curled onto her side and stroked his chest. He closed his eyes, so he didn't have to see her, but her gentle touch was as potent as ever.

"Later," she said, ignoring his attempts at protecting the fragile construct of her heart. "This can't wait."

"It can." To underline his point, he flung his arm across his eyes. He was in no mood for an argument. And it didn't matter how logically he presented his case, she wouldn't agree with him. There was plenty of time for them to talk about it tomorrow.

Or next week.

"It's important." She leaned against him, her soft curves not helping his resolve at all.

This strategy wasn't working. He rolled on top of her once again, pinning her to the bed. He'd saved her sanity earlier. It would be no problem seducing her so thoroughly that she forgot about her declarations of love and devotion.

Until the next time. He wasn't going to think about the next time.

"Be quiet." His mouth grazed hers and his cock hardened as she gave a submissive sigh. This was the answer. Fucking her into compliance until she was too damn exhausted to think, never mind speak.

"We can't risk a third time."

Her breathy comment managed to penetrate his rising lust and he stared down at her in bemusement. Of anything he'd been hoping to avoid her saying, this sure as hell hadn't been it.

As declarations of love and devotion went, it was bizarre. And he'd been on the receiving end of some eccentric proclamations in centuries past.

His best strategy was to ignore it. Except he couldn't. "We can't risk what a third time?"

"You know." She gave him a pained look, as though she thought he was being deliberately obtuse. "Unprotected sex."

Unprotected sex? She was thinking about that, when he was concerned she'd been falling for him?

It was almost funny. Shame he didn't feel like laughing. "And your point is?"

There was an edge in his voice. He couldn't help it. He still couldn't quite believe he'd so misjudged her mood.

And why did the fact she *wasn't* on the brink of declaring undying love for him, irk him?

Sex with Aurora was interfering with the higher functions of his brain.

"My point?" She gazed at him, confusion clouding her eyes. "Well, I don't want to get pregnant, do I?"

Ancient pain compressed his chest, and buried memories flooded his mind.

Helena. The child of his heart. The child of his love.

His miracle.

"No." His voice was flat, while savage regret wrenched through his psyche, all but paralyzing him. "You won't get pregnant."

"But it's *possible*," she insisted, oblivious to the truth. "I'm not on any birth control, and even though it's the wrong time of the month, I don't want to take any chances." There was a thread of panic in her tone, as though the possibility of conceiving the offspring of an archangel horrified her.

And she was right to be horrified. Except Aurora would —*could*—never conceive his child.

He pushed himself off her and collapsed onto his back. He'd never had a conversation like this before. Among those who possessed immortal blood, it wasn't an issue, and for others they either knew the chances of conception were zero, or else they harbored a deluded desire to bear his child against all the odds.

Usually, mortals were too damn enthralled by the experience to even think of something so ... *normal.*

When had Aurora ever reacted like a regular human?

He was under no obligation to explain. If she chose not to believe his word, that was her problem. Yet he couldn't dismiss her questions as easily as he wished.

"Archangels don't procreate." They hadn't for millennia. "You don't have to worry about that."

She stirred, and he knew this wasn't finished yet. *Just leave the fucking room.* It was his modus operandi, after all. Instead, he screwed his eyes shut, and Helena's sweet smile greeted him, her unruly curls framing her face, and her enchanting laughter echoed through the dusty void that had once been his heart.

"Why don't I? You've got all the right equipment. And you can't tell me archangels don't procreate, because I know they do."

His eyes snapped open, and she was propped on her elbow, gazing down at him. Denial burned through him, but it didn't disguise the truth. Because she was right.

But she had no *right* to throw that in his face. How dare she contradict him and suggest he lied?

Because she's Aurora. And that was the only reason she was in his bed. It was her disregard for all protocols that so ensnared him.

It didn't mean he had to indulge her.

Her eyes widened in alarm, although he had no idea why. And then she brushed the tips of her fingers over his shoulder in an oddly conciliatory gesture.

"I'm sorry." She sounded contrite, and he exhaled a measured breath, relieved they could put this behind them without any need for further discussion. "It's just as the myths of archangels are true, I'm guessing so are the stories of the—" She hesitated, clearly searching for the right word, and disbelief shimmered in his mind. She wasn't going there. She wouldn't dare. "Nephilim?"

She went there. This was killing him from the inside out. And she didn't have a clue.

"Yes." His voice was harsh, and he sat up, dislodging her gentle caress. *Never explain.* But he couldn't stop the bitter words that demanded to be heard. "But like everything else from antiquity, humankind corrupted the truth."

He knew the stories that polluted the histories of Earth when it came to the beloved Nephilim. It was one of the reasons why he had little time for those born on this planet.

"We might have the right equipment," he tossed her words back at her with the scorn they deserved, "but archangels were never intended to procreate. Yet some did. But only with those you might quaintly refer to as their soul mate."

Soul mate. The words tasted sour on his tongue, but the appalled expression on her face was enough for him to know she had instantly understood the implications associated with that hated term.

"I'm so sorry." Her whisper brushed against his shoulder, and her obvious distress pierced through the memories that threatened to suck him into the abyss.

"It's all right." It wasn't. It would never be *all right*. But she looked so devastated that he had to reassure her.

None of this made any fucking sense. Why did he feel the need to alleviate her discomfort when it was self-inflicted by her insistence to continually question him?

"I didn't mean to pry." Her voice was soft, and he had the strangest feeling she confessed to a great sin. He sighed heavily. Projecting, much?

He was the one who had sinned. And his loved ones had paid a horrific price.

Aurora would never discover the depths of his guilt.

"Go to sleep, Aurora." It wasn't a request. He was done with talking, but he couldn't stop himself from glancing at her once again. She was only a mortal, a human from Earth, and yet in the last few moments he'd shared more with her than he had with anyone in millennia.

Why?

There was no answer. Only the irresistible allure of taking her into his arms and losing himself once again in her welcoming body.

He wasn't enslaved to her charms. He refused to succumb to the demands of his lust. Grimly, he grabbed his shirt and dragged it on before leaving the bed.

She didn't say anything. At the door he battled the urge to glance at her.

No.

Jaw set, he went into his office, his haven, and pulled open the top drawer in his desk.

Helena laughed up at him from the only picture that remained of her. His gaze slid to her mother, and even now, after all these endless centuries, the familiar agony of futile fury and hopeless devotion ripped through his decayed heart.

He'd been unable to save either of them. They were gone. And they could never return.

Eleni. His first love. His only love.

She had captivated him with her smart mouth and refusal to acknowledge his archangelic superiority. But then, Eleni hadn't been a mere human. She'd possessed immortal blood herself, and her pride in her Nephilim heritage shone through everything she said, everything she did. She bowed to no one and, despite fighting her charms for more than three years, his surrender was inevitable.

He'd irrevocably fallen the moment he looked into her fearless dark eyes. Had fallen more surely every time they spoke, every time she refused his advances, and every time she laughed at his attempts of flattery.

Because she'd known. Right from the start, she'd known this was more than a fleeting liaison. They belonged together, and theirs was a partnership of equals.

Eleni was his beloved. The only one he'd ever loved. She was the reason he could never love again.

She was his heart.

And she was gone.

Forty years. That's all the time they'd had together.

And the miracle of creating their precious Helena.

He shoved the memories back into the haunted corners of his mind. Nothing good came of sinking into the labyrinth of his past. He didn't have time for it, anyway.

A child needed his help.

Last night, before Meph had arrived with Aurora, he'd secured a piece of intel. Eblis, who had no compunction listening into the thoughts and telepathic communication of those who frequented his club, recalled a group of pirates had been discussing the home solar system of the missing child, Evalyne.

With a thought command, Gabe's sleek data device emerged from the surface of his desk. Superficially, it could be mistaken for an Earth-based laptop, but that's where the similarity ended.

He logged onto the intergalactic network. Namtar was a mineral rich planet in the small galaxy of Fornax, where Eblis said the pirates had originated from. It wasn't a sector of the universe he frequented, and before he contacted a certain high ranking demon in that galaxy, he wanted to access all the information he could about the various pirate tribes.

It wasn't much to go on, but at least it was a start.

CHAPTER 16

AURORA

*A*urora sighed as she gazed at the double rainbows that crowned the aquamarine sky before vanishing beyond the ocean's distant horizon. Gold particles shimmered in the warm air, and then a strange undulation rippled across the peaceful vista.

Spellbound, she held her breath as the rainbows and gold dust transformed from a picturesque paradise into a pair of dazzling wings.

The dream fragmented and floated away, and an eerie sense of discordance whispered across her soul.

Wings. *Butterfly* wings?

She stirred, for once not comforted by her childhood dream, and a familiar fear swept over her.

What am I?

Am I real?

Her nails dug into her palms, chasing away the remnants of nighttime fantasy. A pleasurable ache warmed her muscles, and she smiled before she curled on her side and snuggled beneath the bed sheets.

The silence soaked into her and awareness weaved through her mind.

She gasped and her eyes flew open. She was facing the wide glass doors, and sunlight streamed in, bathing the room in a golden glow. Broken images of archangels and gray aliens tumbled through her mind, and she sat up, clutching the sheet to her breasts.

I'm safe, here.

Her galloping heart slowed, and she took a few calming breaths. Where was Gabe? What did archangels even *do* when they weren't rescuing humans from alien abduction?

Had he left her alone, again? After the night they'd shared?

It was only sex. How many times did she have to remind herself? But even so, a part of her had hoped things would be ... different, now.

Idiot.

She had plans, and they didn't involve staying in bed all day, waiting for him to reappear. Although if she was honest, she had no idea what time of day it was. Things like time got confusing when you planet hopped.

Two days. That's how long she had known Gabe.

I think ...

She twisted around and spied the shirt of his she'd worn yesterday before Mephisto's visit in a heap by the door to his bathroom. She inched her way off the bed and padded across the room, the sheet trailing on the floor behind her like an impressive train.

She pulled on the shirt and hugged her waist before slowly making her way to the bedroom door. Last night—this morning? —in Eblis' club when she thought she was safe from the Guardians, she'd entered the astral planes. She'd just wanted to check that she *could*. That she hadn't somehow lost the ability.

There hadn't been any psychic barrier, and for a brief, glorious moment, relief had whispered through her.

And then vanished as terrifying waves of disaster smashed into her. But before she'd been able to make sense of it, Gabe had dragged her back to her body.

And they'd had brain exploding sex.

Twice.

The door to his office was open. She walked along the landing, her heart thundering in her chest. Was he in there?

She reached the door, and the breath caught in her throat. He was slumped over his desk, his head cushioned on his folded arms. He didn't look like an archangel. He looked like a man exhausted by grief and ancient heartache.

Empathy at his loss crushed her chest, even though she barely knew him. Even though he hadn't admitted to any such loss. Yet when he'd told her archangels *could* procreate, the raw suffering in his voice had told her everything.

Thank goodness she hadn't confessed about finding the picture of his family. He might have saved her from the Guardians, but she didn't think he'd forgive her for that transgression.

Not when that beautiful, regal woman had been his *soul mate*.

It didn't matter how long ago his woman and child had died. He still loved them. Would always love them. So fiercely that he still couldn't speak about them.

How must it feel, to be loved by an archangel?

Don't go there.

It would never happen. And she sure as hell wasn't about to fall in love with *him*.

That would be a disaster. Her heart would wither, and she'd never be able to get her life back on track. Because one thing was for sure. She had no intention of staying on his island for the rest of her life.

She needed to find a loophole in the Guardians' draconian laws, otherwise she'd never see her family again. Just as her mother had never seen her family again after she had left her own world. And while her mum loved her dad and was happy to stay with him, eventually her mind had shut down under the strain.

Her mum clung to the edges of sanity by insisting there was only one world. *This* world. By denying her heritage, she had scrubbed her mind of all telepathic links. The precious link Aurora had shared with her since she had been a child.

But even that hadn't been enough to halt the fog that insidiously crept through her mind.

A sliver of fear sent a shiver along Aurora's arms. She hadn't traveled to another dimension like her mother had. But if she could never return home, she might just as well have.

Would she wake up one day and believe this was *all there was?* That her life up until meeting Gabe was nothing but a strange, barely recalled dream?

But while her dad loved her mum with all his heart and would do anything for her, all Gabe felt for her was lust and a sense of responsibility.

That was no way to live. And there was no way she was *going* to, either.

Gabe raised his head and their gazes locked. Heat flared in his eyes, and it was obvious he found her tangled hair, and the crumpled shirt she wore, irresistible.

Stop thinking that word. Yet she couldn't help it when his focus on her was so compelling.

His shirt was unbuttoned, showing off his perfectly toned chest, and stubble darkened his jaw. It should be illegal for a man to look so mouth-wateringly fuckable.

From force of habit, her fingers went to her throat, but her necklace hadn't miraculously reappeared while she'd been asleep. What was she thinking? Mephisto had most likely destroyed it without a second's hesitation.

"Morning." Her voice was husky. She sounded like she was begging for it, and that wasn't far wrong.

"Afternoon." His scorching gaze slid over her body, and she resisted the urge to curl her toes, and possibly melt over his floor while she was at it. "Come here."

She'd taken a couple of steps toward him before she even realized. How did that even happen? They needed to talk, and they wouldn't if she got close enough for them to kiss.

She came to an abrupt halt. *It's just chemistry.* And she couldn't afford to be distracted *all* the time when in Gabe's company.

"Gabe."

"Aurora," he countered, his smoky voice a caress for her senses. It was obvious what he had in mind, and if she didn't get her imagination out of the gutter, another day would slide by and she'd be no closer to her goal of freedom.

Focus. "I need to contact my parents. I've been staying with them since I finished Uni. I can't just disappear for a few days without letting them know I'm still alive." They weren't due home until today—*I think it's today*—and she didn't want them registering her as a missing person with every police force in the country.

He frowned, and she thought he was going to take issue with her *few days* comment, but he appeared to think better of it.

"That's for you." He glanced at the laptop she'd tried to access yesterday. "I can hook you up to your Internet so you can send them an email."

Excitement flared through her. The way he'd said *your Internet* suggested there was another network out there, something far more powerful. Exactly what she'd been hoping for.

"Thanks." She took another couple of unintentional steps toward him. He was like a star and she an adrift moon, impossibly captured within his orbit. All she had to do was make sure she didn't fall under his radiance and burn. "Is there a cosmic net or something that you use? I mean, I don't suppose you have much use for the net on Earth."

His eyes narrowed. Clearly, she had to work on her subtlety skills. "Why?"

"I want to research the Guardians."

"I've told you about them."

Maybe this wasn't going to be as easy as she hoped. "I know. But I want to see if I can find a loophole."

"There's no loophole." There was a grim edge to his voice. "Do you think I wouldn't have told you if I knew something like that?"

He had a point. After all, he'd had eternity to discover everything about the Guardians. But that didn't mean he *had*.

Another few steps and she was standing by his desk. So close to him, she could breathe in his wild, exotic scent, and the heat from his body lured her like a bewitched moth to his immortal flame. She wanted to crawl onto his lap and lose herself in his embrace. Who was she trying to fool? If he said nothing could be done to beat the Guardians, did she really think she'd uncover something revolutionary?

Her drugged gaze slid down his naked chest before snagging on his thighs. After leaving the bed, he'd dragged on a pair of shorts. The incongruity of an archangel wearing shorts caused a strange twisting sensation in the pit of her stomach.

It was so *normal*. It was hard to reconcile that this gorgeous man before her wasn't even human. She had firsthand evidence that he could teleport, and he hung out with winged creatures, but it didn't change the way she saw him.

"I'd like to try." Her voice was soft.

He exhaled a long-suffering sigh. "Okay. But don't get your hopes up. Those bastards' clauses are ironclad."

AFTER A QUICK TRIP to the bathroom, she made her way to his kitchen. Although she'd eaten yesterday, it hadn't been a lot, and she was starving. Unlike yesterday, there was now an enormous basket of exotic fruits on the table, as well as freshly baked bread. There was even a selection of teas in an adorable wooden tea chest. Had he bought all of this while she'd been in the bathroom? Or had he just thought it into existence?

Either way, everything tasted amazing, even if she didn't recognize any of the fruit, and she'd just finished eating when he strolled into the kitchen. He'd obviously had a shower, and his damp hair was unbelievably sexy.

She cleared her throat and tried to refocus her brain. "This is all lovely. Thank you."

He shrugged and looked faintly taken aback by her remark. Did he really think her so ungrateful? "Didn't want you passing out on me."

"Are the fruits from your island?"

He glanced out of the window, almost as though he had no idea what she was talking about.

"No. I leave the rest of the island to the wildlife. I bought this from a trusted local." Then he gave her a wicked grin. "Local being relative. The fruit is from a planet in the Andromeda Galaxy."

"You're *joking*." Sure, the fruit had been a little on the fantastical side, but *alien*?

"The tea, on the other hand, I bought from a specialist store in London. You can thank me later." This time his lascivious grin sent her hormones into freefall.

"That's …" She struggled to find the words. Because there were no words. She sniffed, ridiculously touched that he had even remembered she drank tea, especially since it had only been a passing comment when they first met. "You're a big softie on the quiet."

Did I just call the Archangel Gabriel a big softie? She smiled up at him, even though a faint warning hummed through her mind, but she brushed it aside.

Just because she appreciated him, didn't mean she was in danger of falling.

He coughed, although he might possibly have been choking. "If you ever say that about me to anyone, I'll have to shoot you down in flames. Okay?"

"Fair enough." *Do I sound besotted?* She had the awful feeling she did. And she couldn't help herself. "If anyone asks, I'll tell them you're the most arrogant man I've ever met."

"And the insults just keep on coming."

She laughed. "Sorry. You just don't seem like an immortal to me."

"Please," he said. "Quit while you're ahead."

"Well, that's no fun."

His big body shook with silent laughter as he placed the alien laptop on the table and opened it. She hadn't even noticed he'd been holding anything. "I've reconfigured it. You shouldn't have any problems. Just give a thumbprint of your DNA here"—he pointed to the bottom right corner of the screen— "so it accepts your commands."

She pressed her thumb on the corner, and instantly the screen blazed into rainbow-bright life. Unfortunately, the keyboard was as indecipherable as before. "How do I use it?"

"Already thought of that." He shot her a grin before tapping a key and a wafer-thin, QWERTY keyboard slid out from beneath the alien one. "One of a kind, made to order. Just highlight any text you want to read, and it'll translate into English."

"Wow. That's impressive."

"This might help with your search." He placed a small crystal globe in front of her.

She touched the globe with the tip of her finger and tiny streaks of lightning flashed through it. "Does it work like a mouse?"

"Only superficially. You can use it that way without a problem. I access the network psychically and the globe works as a focal point, analyzing data on an organic level." He gave her an assessing look. "I don't know if it will work for you, but it might, with your unique brain structure."

How did he manage to make that sound so seductive?

"Okay, then." She kept her gaze fixed on the screen. The last thing she needed was him seeing how easily she was charmed by his words. She forcibly pushed it to the back of her mind as she examined the laptop, which didn't have any visible power sockets.

"How is everything powered here?" She doubted he was connected to any national grid, but he had light, air conditioning, and everything she'd used in the kitchen had worked—even though there hadn't been any plugs.

"Solar, hydro, and wind." This time his smile didn't reach his eyes. "I'm completely off the grid here."

"That's amazing." Probably not *that* amazing, considering who he was, but she was still impressed. "We've got solar panels—the only ones in the village, would you believe it? It's always been my parents' dream to be entirely self-sufficient, but it's hard in a cottage with a pocket-sized garden. Mum and Dad have been working for years to set up a wind farm for the village, but you wouldn't believe some of the opposition to it."

"Wouldn't I? These are humans you're talking about."

"Ouch. That's harsh. Not *all* humans are arseholes."

"I'll take your word for it."

She wasn't sure if he was joking or not. Although his voice was grim, there was the hint of a smile on his lips.

"In any case," she added, "I bet your methods of harnessing the elements are far more advanced than ours. Environmentalists would love the chance to share your technology."

His jaw tensed, as though she'd just struck a nerve. "It's not my technology. It was ancient knowledge here before I ever discovered Earth. And it's a damn sight better than the so-called advances made in your Age."

Ancient knowledge? *Before he had discovered Earth?*

Questions ricocheted through her mind. He was referring to lost civilizations. Great, unknowable cultures that had existed *before his time.*

It was like she'd discovered the key to a hidden treasure trove to the past. Was it possible, back then, that people from Earth were also telepathic? That losing the ability was a late deviation in evolution, and not something that had happened a million years ago?

"What—?"

"I'm not discussing it." The flirty manner of moments ago had vanished. He sounded as autocratic as the day they'd met.

Mentally, she kicked herself for pushing too far, too soon. She craved answers that he might be able to give, but her fascination had blinded her to one important thing.

If a great culture she knew nothing about had once existed, wasn't it also likely that was when Gabe's beautiful partner and child had lived?

She didn't want to remind him of that painful time. And her reasons weren't entirely altruistic, either.

It was nothing to do with her that he still missed them. Before she tumbled down that particular rabbit hole, she forced a smile to her face. "How do I log on?"

He came to her side, and his arm brushed hers as he placed a finger on the globe. It was hard to remain perfectly still when she wanted to rest her head against his powerful biceps. But if she did, it would be too easy to forget everything but the need to kiss him again, and it wouldn't stop with a kiss.

She couldn't let herself be distracted. She had to contact her parents.

Within seconds, the screen displayed a familiar search engine image. He stood up, breaking their tenuous contact, and she tried to ignore the chill that raced over her arm.

"I've accessed Earth's net. You won't have any problem

sending your parents an email." His gaze bored into her. "Don't promise them the impossible, Aurora."

He left the kitchen, and with a heavy sigh, she logged onto her account. There was so much she wanted to tell them. But how could she explain what she'd done, when by trying to help she had only made everything a million times worse?

Gabe was so sure she could never leave his island, and she was hellbent on finding a way. She couldn't tell her parents about that, either.

All she could do was reassure them she was okay and pretend she was staying with friends for a couple of weeks. She wasn't going to think beyond that just now. If she hadn't discovered an answer by then—well, she'd cross that bridge when she came to it.

When she finished, she left the kitchen. She wanted to freshen up before starting her search on the Guardians. Hopefully, Gabe hadn't left the villa yet, since she needed to ask him something.

He was sitting on the second step of the stairs, his forearms resting on his thighs, and a strange pain drilled through her chest. It wasn't just because he was so gorgeous it should be illegal. The kind of gorgeous who walked the red carpets and hung out with the beautiful people. It was because, despite everything she knew about him, she still saw him as a man.

But he was an archangel, an *alien*, and she had to remember that.

"Is it okay if I use your shower?"

"You don't have to ask." There was a rough note in his tone, almost as though her question had wounded him. "This is your home now, Aurora."

This would never be her home, and they both knew it. But he was trying to make her feel welcome, and that meant more to her than he would ever know.

"Thanks." There was a constriction blocking her throat, and

she avoided looking at him as she passed him on the stairs. Just in case he saw something in her eyes that he shouldn't.

Something she didn't want to face, couldn't risk, because if she allowed herself to fall for him it would be the biggest mistake she ever made.

CHAPTER 17

GABE

Gabe exhaled a tortured breath. In all the years he'd lived here, it had been his sanctuary, his island, but he'd never thought of it as his home.

Why had he said that to *her*?

There was no answer to that, so he followed her upstairs and into his bedroom. She was by the bathroom door and turned to give him an oddly shy smile.

"Do you mind if I borrow another one of your shirts? I'll wash this one today."

Curse the gods. The issue of her clothes hadn't even crossed his mind. "Help yourself." He folded his arms, so he wouldn't be tempted to wrap them around her.

She nodded, gave him another smile, and entered the bathroom.

He swallowed a groan. He'd lose his mind if all she wore was a succession of his shirts. When he finished this mission, they'd go on a virtual shopping spree. She could order whatever she wanted, and he'd throw in a few exotic pieces.

Damn. That was the wrong thing to think when he needed to

get to work. He didn't have time to find anything for her right now, which left only one option.

He grabbed a rucksack and teleported to where he'd met Aurora the other day. It was early evening, but still light, and he threw up a glamour before striding toward the village to find her house.

We've got solar panels—the only ones in the village.

Should be easy enough to find.

It took longer than he anticipated, but finally he found the cottage tucked down a lane on the other side of the village. A car was parked outside, and a man and woman were just walking up the path.

Great timing. He stifled a sigh and followed them up the path. As her father unlocked the door, her mother glanced over her shoulder. Whoa. She was the image of Aurora, twenty years from now. Except for her eyes, which were dark brown, and narrowed directly at him.

There was no way she could see him, but he rolled his shoulders, oddly uncomfortable by her apparent scrutiny. Now he knew where Aurora lived, there was nothing stopping him from teleporting directly into the house, but he didn't.

They went inside the cottage, and he marched toward the stairs.

"Where's Aurora?" her mum said. Despite himself, he glanced at her, and a shudder inched along his spine when she met his gaze. What the *fuck*?

"She's probably meeting up with friends," her dad said. "I'll send her a message and see if she's coming back tonight."

Gabe took the stairs two at a time as Aurora's mum gave her dad a vague answer. It didn't take long to find her room, seeing as there were only two bedrooms. How was it possible to cram so much stuff into such a tiny space?

He'd have to commission another piece of furniture, just so she had somewhere for all her possessions.

Although he'd done far worse things in the past, he felt like a thief as he filled the rucksack with her personal items. Did he really need to take it all? But if he didn't, he might leave behind the one thing that meant the most to her.

The rucksack was full, and he hadn't even found her clothes yet. He dumped it on her bed, which slotted beneath the eaves. It would be so much easier just to transport the wardrobe and chest of drawers in their entirety, but that would raise too many questions. And while he didn't usually care about questions that he had no intention of answering, if her bedroom furniture vanished, it would freak out her parents. Which would upset Aurora.

He really was fucking losing it.

There was a case under her bed, so he hauled that out and transferred the contents of her drawers into it. Belatedly it occurred to him that she might not appreciate him going through her underwear.

Too late now. What the fuck had possessed him to start this? He should've just let her wear his damn shirts.

He yanked the clothes from her wardrobe and draped them over his arm, hangers included. The sooner he got out of here the better.

Warning prickled along the back of his neck and he swung around, senses alert. Aurora's mother stood at the door, her gaze fixed on the bed.

Shit. He'd forgotten to fling a glamour over the rucksack and case. Not that it mattered. He'd enter her mind and wipe the last couple of seconds from her memory.

He didn't get the chance. She looked at him again and her voice filled his head.

I remember you.

Staggered, he couldn't even respond as she tilted her head, her eyes never leaving his.

No, she said in his mind. There was a questioning note in the word, but he still couldn't answer her. *It wasn't you …*

What the hell was happening? It shouldn't be possible for any mortal to initiate telepathic contact with him. He recalled what Aurora had told him the day they met.

The only other person in her family who was telepathic was her mum.

Aurora had inherited her beautiful, unique, brain from her mother. And her mother could see through his glamour as easily as any immortal.

He shifted focus and scanned her aura. An eerie shiver scudded along his spine. Her aura glowed, but it was shredded, as though a giant claw had ripped through the fabric of her existence.

But she possessed not a drop of immortal blood.

"What are you?" Her voice was hushed, but she didn't sound terrified by his presence.

An answer glimmered in his mind, and he responded without speaking. *What are* you?

Where have you taken my child?

It didn't surprise him that she ignored his question. She was Aurora's mother, after all.

"She's safe," he said.

A flicker of fear—of understanding?—glittered in her eyes.

"Keep her safe." There was an urgent note in her voice. "Promise me."

A section of his brain couldn't believe he was even having this conversation, but he didn't hesitate. "I promise she'll come to no harm under my protection."

"And bring her home again."

Regret burned his chest. "I can't promise that."

Her eyes glazed. "Tell him I didn't mean to forget," she whispered.

What was she talking about?

"Tell who?" he demanded, but she gazed at him as though she had no idea what he meant.

He didn't have time for this, but her words haunted him. Was she speaking of Mephisto? Except something didn't feel right. Meph had tracked Aurora for a specific reason, but that had nothing to do with her mother.

He'd figure it out later. Without another word, he swung the rucksack over his shoulder, picked up the case, and teleported.

Aurora was still in the bathroom when he returned. He placed everything on the bed, and then had the urge to disappear again before she emerged.

He had no idea how she'd react to what he'd done. Any other mortal would likely kiss his feet in gratitude at his benevolence. Aurora might just as easily hate that he'd collected her personal things without her permission and not hesitate to let him know.

Why didn't he just admit it? It was her unpredictability he found so addictive.

She strolled into the bedroom, wearing one of his black shirts and towel-drying her hair. He'd definitely done the right thing. The sooner she had her own clothes to wear, the less distracting he'd find her.

Yeah, keep hoping that.

Her welcoming smile froze as she caught sight of his haul on the bed. He couldn't tell whether that was a good or bad sign.

"What?" she managed at last, coming over to the bed and running her hand over her clothes. "These are *mine.*"

"It made sense." He hunched his shoulders and glared at the pile of clothes. It was disconcerting that he had no defense if she took exception to his action.

He was a fucking archangel. It didn't *matter* if she agreed or not with what he did.

"You went to my home and collected all of my things?"

"They were no good to you there."

"I know, but …" Her voice trailed away. She appeared to be having a problem telling him what she thought, which had to be a first. "Well, I didn't expect you to go to all this trouble."

"It was no trouble."

She bit her lip. "It's just if my parents see my room's been cleared out before they get my message, they'll think the worst."

"About your mother." He waited until her reluctant gaze met his. There was little point telling her that her mother had seen straight through his glamour, as he doubted that would mean much to Aurora. "She's one of the strongest telepaths I've ever encountered." And he wasn't just referring to telepathic mortals, either.

"You met my mother?" Horror etched her face. And was that a thread of fear in her voice?

Sure, he hadn't intended to speak to her parents, but why was she so upset that he had?

"Yes. Briefly." Clearly, his response didn't reassure her as he had hoped, since she hitched in a ragged breath as though she was having trouble processing what he was saying. "She was fine," he added, even though that in itself was odd, since humans were generally anything but fine when in the presence of an archangel. He decided to keep that to himself.

"Wait. How do you know she's a strong telepath?"

"She spoke to me telepathically." Well, fuck. Aurora had that ability. What was stopping them from communicating that way? It had never even occurred to him before, but the possibility intrigued him.

"She did *what*?"

Unease prickled. Aurora hugged her waist, her body tense, as though his answer was of paramount importance. He was missing something, and he didn't have a clue what it was.

"It was unexpected." To hell with it. He might as well tell her.

"She shouldn't have been able to even see me, much less initiate contact."

She stared at him, desperate hope pulsing in the charged air between them. "Are you sure you didn't just probe her mind by accident and read her thoughts that way?"

"No, I didn't." If he probed a mind it was never by accident, and the thoughts he harvested were read by design. While abilities varied between different species, the principles of not invading an unknowing mind remained the same throughout every telepathic race.

Then again, Aurora didn't come from a primarily telepathic race. She had no idea of the etiquette involved.

And it was all academic. Mortal rules didn't apply when it came to the gods and their descendants.

Or archangels and demons.

She let out a ragged breath, and his irritation at her accusation—especially since she had some justification for it—faded. She'd been thrust into a strange new world and throughout everything that had happened she'd been amazingly resilient, except for that one moment in Eblis' club. But this glimpse of vulnerability was different. Deeper, somehow.

It shouldn't matter. He had a missing child to find. And yet he couldn't walk away.

"What's the problem, Aurora? Why does it matter so much to you that she spoke to me?"

Her smile was strained and didn't reach her eyes. "Because she stopped speaking to me that way years ago."

"Why?"

"When we were on that other planet, you asked me if I'd deliberately breached dimensions."

"I don't see the connection."

She swallowed. "When I was a child, Mum used to tell me stories about her home all the time. We were linked telepathically from when I was born. Poor Dad, he must have felt left out at times. But about ten years ago she just cut off our link. No warning. And she wouldn't explain it. But it was as though she'd cut off, I don't know, half of my brain and one of my limbs. She just wasn't *there* anymore."

The raw pain in her voice clawed through him. He understood more than she would ever realize.

He and Eleni had been telepathically linked, and the void she'd left behind had been … immense. And although he was oddly touched that she had confided something so personal, he still wasn't sure how this was linked to her breaching dimensions. "Why are you telling me this now?"

"It was awful." There was a tremor in her voice. "It was as though she needed to close the door on her past life, just so she could survive in this one. But shutting me out didn't help, Gabe. She's still fading away from us. I thought if I could bring back some proof that her world really did exist, she'd remember everything again."

That her world really did exist?

"Theoretically, I should have arrived at the exact place where the flowers grew. If anything could help her remember it would be the flowers. I wanted to bring some back for her, that's all."

Where the flowers grew.

Ice skated along his arms as he recalled the silver frame with its strange, ethereal bloom that she'd dropped in his kitchen. The eerie certainty he'd experienced of something being not quite *right* with it.

No. He couldn't imagine what she was trying to tell him, but it wasn't that her mother came from *another dimension*.

"And yes, I admit I wanted to find out more about that side of my heritage. Who wouldn't? But I had no idea it would be so dangerous or that I was breaking cosmic laws."

"Are you trying to tell me …" The words lodged in his throat. There was no way this could be true. "What are you trying to tell me?"

Wariness flashed in her eyes. He had the oddest conviction that his reaction wasn't what she'd been expecting. So what the hell *had* she expected?

"My parents are from different dimensions." The words were reluctant, as though she'd never spoken them before. *Of course she hasn't.* It wasn't the kind of thing anyone would share. "They met in their dreams when they were still children and kind of grew up together. Later, they communicated on the astral planes. And then … they fell in love."

He guessed that theoretically it was possible to dream of those who existed in another dimension. Why not? And she had just revealed the astral planes weren't confined to one dimension or another. Which meant they were potentially accessible to all sentient beings.

Except for the Guardians.

Somehow, Aurora's parents had succeeded in a trans-dimensional physical union.

And then the truth slammed through him.

Aurora is the result of a trans-dimensional union.

Awe shivered through his soul. It had been so long since anything had so fundamentally shaken the core of his existence that he had no idea what to even say to her.

There was nothing that marked her as such an extraordinary being. Her damp hair curled around her face, the freckles that dusted her nose and cheeks were still ridiculously appealing, and her eyes were the prettiest blue he had ever seen.

"What happened?" His voice was hushed. Her parents had flouted the most elemental laws of the universe—and had lived, undetected by the Guardians.

But the Guardians were of this dimension. Aurora's mother came from another. Was that how she had avoided detection?

"When they were teenagers, they found they could communicate without needing the dreamworld or the astral planes. They were telepathically linked. But the thing is, that's the sum total of my dad's psychic ability. He can't even link to me."

Another eerie shiver scuttled over his flesh. It took this to another level entirely when her parents had been still able to connect outside of the spiritual realms.

At least he now knew the reason for Aurora's extraordinary mental barriers. She had inherited them from a species of human he'd had no idea even existed.

"One day when they were sharing thoughts she simply walked from her world into my dad's arms. The same place we met the other day."

"How did she evade the Guardians?"

"She never mentioned them. She just took one step. That's all. And then the gateway or whatever it was that had opened for her closed. Permanently. But because of my heritage I was sure I could access my mum's dimension. And … I was right."

"There has to be more to it than that. Something must have triggered a split between this world and your mother's."

She hesitated, and he took her hand. Just as Mephisto had asserted, Aurora had been fully aware of what she was doing. And now he knew her reasons, he couldn't even blame her.

The damage had been done, and even if he understood why she had done it, it didn't change the outcome. Nothing could change that, but in his eyes, at least, she didn't deserve to be condemned to a lifetime of confinement for simply trying to discover her maternal origins.

Her smile was infinitely sad, and something deep in his chest ached in response.

"Somehow when they were psychically connected to each other, they also simultaneously opened a physical breach between their worlds. If I could do that, using the flower as my anchor, then theoretically there was nothing to stop me from walking into her world."

CHAPTER 18

GABE

Before meeting Aurora, Gabe would never have considered such a theory had a hope of success. Even discounting the inherent danger of the Guardians, the likelihood of a mortal managing to breach dimensions was mind-boggling.

And that didn't even touch on the tricky question of finding the right parallel dimension in the first place.

Then again, nothing about her actions had been random. She knew exactly where she was going.

To the world where half of her DNA originated.

"You had it all worked out." He couldn't prevent the thread of admiration in his tone. It wasn't her fault she'd been ignorant of the ancient protocols.

"I thought so. It's a shame I didn't have a Plan B for when an avenging archangel swept me off my feet, though."

He still had no idea how that had happened. But one thing was for sure. "Lucky I did."

"Gabe." There was a cautious note in her voice he didn't like. She must know by now she could say anything to him, without judgment. "Please tell me you've come across this before. I can't be the only one whose parents are from different dimensions."

Ah, gods. He wanted to reassure her. Tell her of course she wasn't the only one. To ease the fear he could so easily guess was churning through her psyche.

The words hovered in his mind, loathed, yet so apt.

The fear that she was an anomaly of creation.

Yet he couldn't lie to her, because it wouldn't change the truth, and she deserved nothing less. But as he gazed into her eyes, a truly outrageous notion rocked his existence.

Just because he had never known this to happen before *didn't mean it hadn't.*

It wasn't possible. Something of that magnitude would be common knowledge among the elite immortals. Even if it was never spoken of. And whether the Alphas liked it or not, archangels were numbered among the elite.

But no one had known of Aurora.

"You're the first I've encountered." His voice was low. She flinched, as though he'd inflicted a blow, and he sucked in a deep breath. "But that doesn't necessarily mean that you *are* the only one."

"But you wouldn't bet on it?" She sighed and squeezed his fingers. "Thanks, anyway. Nothing like having it confirmed from the highest power that you're a total freak of nature."

"Highest power?" he mocked, but her smile was half-hearted. It was obvious he'd just crushed one of her most secretly held hopes. "Hey, cheer up. You're in great company. I've been called that and far worse in my time."

"I find *that* hard to believe."

"I know, right?" He smirked and flexed his muscles and was rewarded when she laughed. He didn't usually find anything amusing when he recalled the origins of his creation and the bitter fallout that followed. "I'm beyond perfection."

"And so modest, too."

He wound chestnut strands of her damp hair around his finger and gently tugged. He was so tempted to stay with her, but he needed to work. "Let me show you how to access the intergalactic web before I leave."

"You're going out?"

"Yeah." There was no point telling her where he was going. He doubted she'd even heard of the Fornax Galaxy.

From the corner of his eye, through his open balcony doors, he caught a distant flash of wings approaching his villa from the forest. Looked like Azrael, one of the few who could penetrate the island's defenses.

Shit. He didn't want Az meeting Aurora and asking questions. Within a blink, he teleported them to the kitchen, and while Aurora gripped the edge of the table, he logged on. She'd soon figure out how to navigate the interstellar net.

Hey, Gabe. Azrael's voice filled his head. *You home?*

Be right there.

"Catch you later," he said to Aurora. "I'll bring food back for us." He leaned forward to kiss her and then froze.

Just leave. He took a step back, unnerved. He wasn't into that kind of intimacy. Just because he wanted Aurora, didn't change that fact.

"Okay, then." She nodded and gingerly sat down, without even a glance in his direction.

If he didn't leave right now, Az was going to stroll in the door. He gave an unintelligible grunt, unsure why he was making such a big deal of it all, and teleported onto the front terrace.

Azrael's iridescent feathers shimmered in the sunlight as he landed next to Gabe. Folding his wings, he rolled his shoulders before casting a curious glance at the villa, as though he sensed Aurora's presence.

Either that, or Mephisto had spoken to him, and Az had come to have a look at her for himself.

Gabe folded his arms. Not fucking happening.

"Something's screwing with the astral planes," Az said.

It was so not what he'd expected the other archangel to say, the word blurted from him. "*What?*"

Unlike most of the archangels who had given up visiting the astral planes after they'd annihilated the celestial city of their creation, Az had become obsessed with that realm and maintaining its harmonious balance.

Discounting when he had followed Aurora there yesterday, he'd only been in that realm once since the fall of their city. And he hadn't gone willingly.

Once again, Az glanced at the villa. If he was wanting an invitation to go inside, he was going to have a very long wait.

"I've never encountered anything like it before," Az said. "It's pure chaos."

And Gabe had a good idea who had caused that chaos. He gave Az a death stare. No way would he admit to her guilt. Not to Az. Not to anyone.

"The levels are collapsing," Az continued, obviously not concerned by Gabe's lack of response, or his deadly glare. "It's like a physical entity was let loose and smashed its way through."

He couldn't stay silent any longer. "Except you can't physically enter that realm."

The astral planes, the ultimate haven of healing and renewal, would recover. But if Az or any immortal guessed Aurora might have something to do with the chaos, she would be held accountable.

They'd have to get through him, first.

"Guess who was there, attempting a cover up?" Az said, ignoring Gabe's last comment. "Mephisto."

What the hell was Mephisto doing there? "It could be a natural phenomenon. Mephisto likes to know what's going on."

Except Meph knew what Aurora had done. And if he'd discovered it was her actions that had caused the collapse, why would he try to cover it up?

Azrael's fingers curled around the hilt of his katana. "If that was a natural phenomenon, then the universe is fucked. It was an outside force. Meph knows more than he's telling me."

That was no revelation. Mephisto always knew more than he shared.

Az shot Gabe an assessing glance. "You don't know anything about it?"

His senses went on red alert. Az didn't need Mephisto to tell him anything. He'd found incriminating evidence against Aurora himself.

That didn't mean Gabe was going to admit to anything, and this island wasn't under any official jurisdiction. Aurora was safe from everything, so long as she remained here.

"Why would I know anything about it? The astral planes aren't my favorite place in the universe."

"That's why I couldn't understand it. There's a lingering echo of your presence scattered throughout the levels. But it's distorted almost beyond recognition."

"I visited the realm briefly yesterday." No need to go into details.

"No," Az said. "That wasn't it." Before Gabe could even wrap his brain around that bizarre comment, Az added, "Are the rumors true? You saved a human from the Guardians?"

Obviously, the events from Eblis' club had leaked. Hardly a surprise, considering how many witnesses there had been. He guessed his cover in that sector as a megalomaniac half-blood demon had been blown.

"I wasn't going to let those little fuckers take her."

"And you brought her here." That wasn't even a question. Az knew too much of Gabe's past. Knew that in all the universe, this island was the only place the Guardians could never access. "Any chance of meeting this irresistible female?"

"No."

Az was silent for a heartbeat. "Be careful, Gabe. The Guardians never forget."

With that stark reminder, Az teleported. Gabe glowered at the lush forest, torn between contacting Mephisto and risking raising suspicions Meph hadn't yet considered, or staying silent. But he needed answers.

Mephisto.

What? Meph sounded distracted, which wasn't like him at all.

Have you met Aurora's mother?

A sense of irritated disgust permeated Gabe's mind as Mephisto answered. *Why the fuck would I have done that?*

That confirmed it. She hadn't been referring to Mephisto. Based on what Aurora had told him, it was possible her mother hadn't meant anything by her comment.

Except he wasn't convinced.

What did you discover on the astral planes?

There was a long silence. So profound, an uneasy thought surfaced. Had Meph severed their connection without him realizing it?

Don't worry. Sarcasm reeked from each word. *I've cleaned up your crap. No one will trace anything back to you.*

With that, he cut their communication, and Gabe frowned.

He was more than willing to shoulder the blame if it saved Aurora's head. But why, when they both knew the truth, had Meph made it sound as if the collapse on the astral planes was down to *him?*

Something was going on and he had no idea what the hell it was.

Aurora

WHEN GABE TELEPORTED from the kitchen, Aurora let out a soft groan. She'd hoped that by sharing her secret with him he could give her some answers, or at least reassure her that she wasn't the only one with such a mixed heritage. Instead, he'd confirmed she was even more of a freak than she'd ever feared. Although it *had* been sweet of him to try and make her feel better by telling her he'd been called worse. Not that she believed him. Besides, she had more important things to worry about.

He spoke to Mum. She couldn't wrap her head around it. And she'd been so shocked, she hadn't even asked him what her mum had said to him.

She leaned back in the chair. Possible answers to the mysteries of the universe were literally at her fingertips, but Gabe's evocative scent enveloped her in soft cotton and wicked thoughts. Absently, she stroked his shirt sleeve, and her fingers tingled at the contact.

This was insane. She couldn't concentrate while she still wore his shirt. And there was no need to. All her clothes were upstairs. It wouldn't take five minutes to change, and then she could start work.

In his bedroom, she picked out a T-shirt and pair of shorts and quickly pulled them on. She had no idea where she was going to put all the stuff he'd taken from her wardrobe. But they couldn't stay on the bed.

She scooped up the clothes and glanced around the room. Near the doors that lead onto his balcony was a grand-looking sofa. It wasn't the perfect solution, but draping her clothes over the back of that was preferable to finding room in his wardrobe. Not that she thought he'd mind, but sharing his dressing space seemed a bit too personal. In any case, this was only a temporary arrangement.

It didn't take long to cover his sofa, and she had to admit, the aesthetics weren't great. With a sigh, she hauled her case over, but it was too big to slide underneath, so she set it to one side.

And a glint of gold on the polished stone floor caught her eye.

She gasped and picked up the delicate chain as relief streaked through her. It was her butterfly necklace. Mephisto hadn't destroyed it after all.

Sunlight streamed in through the open doors, and the tiny rainbows and flecks of gold shimmered and glittered like a minuscule fantasy world.

Why had this image haunted her for so many years? She'd never really questioned it before. It was just something she had always dreamed of and had wanted to craft into a piece of unique jewelry.

Her priority was to discover all she could about the Guardians and find a way home that wouldn't put herself, or her parents, in danger.

But first she was going to search for information on archangelic artifacts. Because it didn't matter how insane the idea was, she couldn't shift the conviction that the answers to her current problems were hidden in the origin of the necklace.

NIGHT HAD FALLEN, thick and black, outside the villa, when she finally admitted defeat in her search for archangelic answers.

Talk about contradictory. Aliens apparently were just as invested as humans when it came to relying on gossip and speculation. Every civilization—and she'd found a mind-blowing number of different civilizations—had their own theories.

She wasn't sure if it was comforting or not to discover that archangels, in some form or another, were known throughout the universe.

If any genuine information was out there, the ancient truth of the archangels had been buried long ago in the hazy stream of time.

She'd even tried searching specifically for information on the Archangel Gabriel but turned up the same ambiguous results. It didn't come close to describing the man she knew.

Hopeless. She propped her elbows on the kitchen table and

cradled her head. Maybe her searches needed refining, but so far nothing had come close to showing her a replica of her necklace.

And nothing ever would, because no one, apart from the archangels themselves, knew anything about those precious gifts.

What? Where had that thought come from?

She curled her fingers around the butterfly wings, but the certainty persisted.

The archangels crafted the necklace as a token of their devotion for their beloved. And the tradition had evolved, and perished, in antiquity.

Shivers scudded over her arms. Was someone—some*thing*—invading her mind?

She disconnected from the net, but the conviction that she was right about the necklace refused to leave her.

And that belief hadn't come from an outside force. It was as much a part of her as her unique DNA.

She shook her head.

Focus.

The truth was, discovering hidden secrets of the archangels wasn't going to set her free. It was the Guardians' secrets she needed to unearth.

CHAPTER 19

GABE

Since Eblis hadn't known which pirate tribe from Namtar had been discussing the Medana solar system in his club, Gabe visited the leader of the most disreputable. They were known for trading minors from the more primitive planets in the Fornax Galaxy, which was despicable enough. But abducting them from another Galaxy altogether wasn't something that could be allowed to go unpunished, even if he hadn't been investigating Evalyne's disappearance.

He could have teleported directly to the leader's HQ, but that didn't serve his purpose. He strode along the back streets, his archangelic radiance all but blinding anyone foolish enough to glance in his direction.

Not that anyone would guess who he was. As a rule, archangels didn't visit the Fornax Galaxy without invitation, and they sure as hell didn't trespass on pirate dominated turf.

But his cover as a pissed off, megalomaniac, half-blood demon ensured no one would question him—or report his appearance to those in power.

With a psychic blast, the door exploded, security measures frying. Pirates scattered, and within moments he discovered their leader and flung up a teleportation blockade around him so he couldn't escape.

"This is outrageous." The pirate backed up against the wall, terror leaking from him. "We pay our protection dues to the Council."

Gabe delivered a lethal smile, and the pirate's knees buckled. "Do I look like a member of the Council?"

"Then what—"

"Intergalactic abductions."

Fear flared in the pirate's eyes, and it was enough. Gabe tore through his mind, relentless, searching for information. The pirate collapsed onto the floor, his head jerking like a marionette, but his thoughts were garbled, incoherent.

Underground cults and the search for archangelic blood?

One thing was certain. He wasn't responsible for Evalyne's disappearance.

"Speak." Gabe's voice was deadly.

"Anzu," the pirate gasped. "It's where the cradle of belief thrives. Where the faith that the cursed bloodline survives. That's all I know."

Gabe released his psychic grip and stepped back. Anzu was the largest planet in the Seventh System of Fornax, named after the first demon who had claimed the planet for his own.

Looked like he needed to pay the Primus of the Seventh System a visit.

GABE TOOK a shower as soon as he returned to his villa and scrubbed the stench of the pirates from his body. It was good to be home where Aurora waited for him. She was clean, pure, and would help him forget about the scum he'd just been dealing with.

And then his smile slid into a frown. *Home?*

It was the second time in as many days that word had fallen so easily into his mind. Until he'd brought Aurora here, he couldn't even remember the last time he'd considered anywhere as being his home.

Lies. He knew.

Because the last time he'd had a home, far from here, Eleni lived there.

Aurora

AURORA KNEW the exact moment Gabe returned, even though he didn't walk in through the front door. His presence brushed through her, an impossibly tangible thing, and she glanced over her shoulder, although she knew he wouldn't be there.

It didn't make any difference. He was back.

She stood, stretching her cramped muscles. God, she was starving. She hoped he'd remembered to bring back something to eat. It had been hours since she'd had the fruit.

As she went upstairs, she tried not to dwell on what he'd been doing since she had last seen him. But when she entered his bedroom and heard the shower, her mind went there anyway.

The shower stopped. She straightened her spine and forcibly relaxed her tense muscles. He'd slept with her to clear his system. This was a great wake-up call before she did something completely stupid.

Such as fall for him.

He strolled into the bedroom, a damp, gorgeous god of creation, and the smile he bestowed her way tightened her stomach and sent illicit tingles racing over her skin.

With just a smile. Then again, his smile was a thing of heavenly magnificence.

"You're back." Inside, she groaned at her truly terrible remark, but he didn't appear to mind. Not if the state of his semi-aroused cock was any indication.

Stop looking. She wasn't looking, but she couldn't help noticing these things from the corner of her eye, could she?

She wouldn't fall into his arms the second he returned. That would just make her look sex-deprived and desperate for his attention.

"And I'm starving." His eyes darkened, and it was obvious he wasn't talking about food. She dug her nails into her palms to stop herself from wrapping herself around him.

"Good." Unfortunately, her voice was husky. *Focus.* "So am I. What did you bring back?"

He blinked glorious long eyelashes that she would die for, and she forgot what she had even asked him.

"Ah." There was an odd note in his voice, and if he'd been, say, a human, it would have sounded contrite. "Food. I forgot."

He came closer. Why did he have to smell so delicious? Like an exotic rainforest. Dangerous and forbidden. How long could she hold her breath before passing out?

"I haven't eaten all day." He gripped the bedpost, and she was sure he only did it in order to show off his perfectly proportioned biceps. She tore her fascinated gaze from his bronzed muscles. *Don't encourage him.* His ego was big enough.

That wasn't the only big thing about him, either.

"Okay, then. I'm sure we can find something in your kitchen." She had no idea what she was even saying, but if he came any closer, she was going to have to retreat before she fell at his feet. His big feet.

She swallowed a groan. Her primitive brain always took over when it came to Gabe.

"I'll go get something." His smoldering gaze drifted over her, from head to toe and back again, scorching her skin like a lick of flame, before he turned and strolled toward his dressing room.

Her mouth dried. He had a seriously sexy rear. A tiny moan

escaped, and she hastily turned it into a cough before Gabe noticed.

He pulled on a pair of black jeans.

He's going commando. It was insanely erotic.

"Did you discover a loophole?" He turned to face her and slowly tugged his jeans over his far from disinterested erection.

"Your net is as bad as ours. I'd find one thing, only to have it contradicted on the next site." And she wasn't just talking about the Guardians. But he didn't need to know that.

"I never said it was infallible." He appeared to find it amusing that she might have thought otherwise. "You need to dig deep, just like on Earth's net."

He shrugged on a black shirt. Who knew watching a man get dressed could be such an electrifying experience?

"I found one reference that suggested the Guardians hate immortals even more than they do mortals." She'd discovered that on a site dedicated to paranoid theories, and although there hadn't been any attempts to back up any of their wild claims, the comment about the Guardians had intrigued her. "Is it true they aren't allowed to abduct those with the blood of gods in their veins?"

His smile faded. Maybe he hadn't expected her to discover that? She almost wished she hadn't, if this was the result.

Stop. It was just a smile. And she needed information. She couldn't stop researching just in case Gabe didn't like the answers she found.

"It's true." He sounded reluctant, but at least he hadn't ignored her, or teleported mid-conversation. That was a massive improvement on a couple of days ago.

"And were they around for thousands of years before the ancient gods and goddesses?" It had driven her wild when she'd uncovered that, only to discover every lead she followed ended in a dead end. There were plenty of fanatical theories of who, or what, the Guardians might be, and why they might hate the rest of known life in the universe. But there was no consensus, and verified facts appeared to be nonexistent.

"Try millions of years." There was a grim note in his voice. "They should have become extinct long before the Alphas evolved."

"The Alphas?" He'd mentioned them to her once before, only then he'd called them the Alpha Pantheon. "Who are they?"

He shoved his bare feet into a pair of black trainers, and she knew this discussion was over. "Megalomaniacal pains in the ass. Grab some plates and glasses. I won't be long."

And with a smile that gave *sin* a whole new level of meaning, he teleported.

BACK IN THE KITCHEN, Aurora laid the table with fine porcelain and crystal ware she'd found in his cabinets. As though this was perfectly natural and she and Gabe were a regular couple, intending to share a takeaway together at home.

Only a seriously deluded woman would think there was anything in the least bit normal about any of this.

She knew all that. But it made no difference. Because a tiny, obstinate, core of her found nothing extraordinary in this fantastical new life.

Even when he reappeared without warning, she didn't drop the cutlery she was holding. She was getting used to his teleportation. It was almost as though she'd been aware of such things all her life and had just needed ... a reminder.

Deep inside, her heart quavered at how unquestionably her brain was accepting it all. If that wasn't a warning about how easy it was to lose her grip on reality, she didn't know what was.

Don't forget my real life.

"I didn't know what you'd like, so I bought the lot." He placed a dizzying array of dishes onto the table.

"American Express?" She was joking. Kind of. *Did* Gabe pay for stuff? Why would an archangel need to pay for things in any case?

Did this food even originate on planet Earth?

"MasterCard," he said, deadpan. "For the air miles."

She laughed and pulled off one of the lids. The mouthwatering aroma of exotic spices from the unrecognizable delicacies made her stomach growl.

Not from Earth, then.

"Seriously, though. Do you really have credit cards? *Money?*"

"Sure." He strolled to a door that earlier that day she had discovered led to a cellar. She hadn't investigated further. She'd watched too many slasher movies as a teen to fall for *that* one. "My investments have the potential to topple governments both here and on a couple of other worlds. It's not that hard to amass several fortunes when you're considered immortal." He disappeared through the door. "You could call it a hobby of mine."

"That and sex," she said under her breath. She sat at the table, tugged her chain from beneath her top, and curled her fingers around the familiar pendant.

"I heard that." His voice echoed from the depths of the cellar, and her face heated. He also, apparently, had supersonic hearing. "If you want a decadent appetizer before the meal, I'm up for that." He stepped back into the kitchen, holding a couple of dust-covered bottles of wine and wearing a lascivious grin. "We can always reheat the food later."

Without meaning to, she licked her lips. "Tempting. But I might pass out from lack of food."

Standing behind her chair, he pulled the cork from one of the bottles, leaned over her shoulder, and poured the wine into her glass.

"Tell me what you think of this."

The heat from his body enveloped her, and his tantalizing cologne fried any sane thoughts she might have had. She tried not to hyperventilate and hoped like hell he couldn't hear the way her heart hammered in her chest.

She kept her eyes fixed on her glass. His warm breath sent erotic tremors across her neck, and she struggled not to bury her last remaining sliver of pride and fling her arms around him.

Food was so overrated.

There was a dull thud as he dropped the bottle onto the table. And then he scooped up her pendant and the chain bit into her skin as he yanked it up to take a closer look.

"Ouch." She squinted up at him, but he was glaring at her necklace as if it personally offended him. "What are you doing?"

"Where did you get this?" The accusation thudded in the air between them, and she swallowed down the hurt that stabbed through her. Did he think she'd stolen it from him?

And then realization crashed through. Did that mean he still had his daughter's necklace in the villa?

"It was an eighteenth birthday gift from my parents." Should she tell him? What did she have to lose? "I had it specially commissioned."

He stared at her, and for an eternal moment she saw raw, bleak longing in his eyes, and the cold abyss of loss dragged icy fingers across her soul.

They're not butterfly wings.

Chills skated across her arms. Why had she never seen it before? They were archangel wings. The gift from an archangel to his beloved.

Deep in her heart, a small chasm cracked open. *How do I know this?*

Slowly the chain slid through his fingers. "You had this specially commissioned?"

His voice was even. No one would ever guess the agony behind those words. Not unless they *knew.*

She clenched her fists on her lap and tensed her muscles

against her overpowering instinct to wrap her arms around him. He wouldn't thank her for it.

"Yes." She couldn't help the choked note in her voice.

"Why?" The accusation this time was stark, and another shaft of pain arrowed through her heart. How many centuries had he mourned the loss of his loved ones? How would it feel, to be loved so absolutely by an archangel?

By Gabe?

She recoiled, terror stabbing through her chest. She didn't want to know. Didn't want to imagine. Because it forced her to face something she'd been trying to ignore from the day she had met him.

How would it feel to love Gabe?

"I ..." Her voice cracked and she cleared her throat, no longer able to look into those mesmeric eyes. Because now she'd glimpsed the suffering behind the beauty, and it ripped her apart. "Ever since I can remember I used to dream of rainbows and gold dust and"—*don't say archangel wings*—"wings. I don't know why. But the strangest thing of all, is once I started wearing this necklace, the dreams stopped."

Did they stop? Or do I just no longer remember them?

"You dreamed of this?" His voice was harsh, but she could hear the anguish in his words, and it was killing her. "How could you dream of *this*, Aurora? This exact design?"

"I don't know." How could there be a connection between her dreams and the necklace she'd seen in Gabe's picture? "Why? What does it mean to you?"

Please don't brush my question aside. And that's when she knew she was losing the fight.

I'm falling ...

"It's very similar to an ancient archangelic design." He sounded as if the words were being torn from his shattered soul, and again she had to smother the need to pull him into her arms. And never let him go. "We'd harness fragments of the rainbows that glinted over our city. Trap particles of the gold that glittered in the air. And bind them into our wings for all eternity."

It sounded beautiful. She had the absurd desire to weep.

"City?" Her voice was hushed. "You had a city, Gabe?"

Bleak resignation flashed over his face, gone in a second, but it made her heart ache.

"Yes." He pulled out the chair next to her. "It was the place of our creation, the hell of our incarceration. It no longer exists."

He picked up the bottle and poured himself a glass before tipping the dark amber liquid down his throat in one long swallow.

It didn't matter how desperately she wanted to know more about his fabulous city or the mystery of the archangel wings. She knew this precious moment of confidences had passed.

For as long as she could remember, up until her eighteenth birthday, she'd dreamed of magical rainbows, glittering gold dust, and ethereal wings.

It had been as much a part of her as her telepathic ability.

But she'd inherited that from her mother. Where had the dreams of an ancient archangelic necklace come from?

And why?

CHAPTER 20

GABE

*E*yes closed, Gabe sucked oxygen into his parched lungs. His forehead rested against Aurora's, and her orgasmic scream echoed in his mind.

His name.

She'd screamed his name as she had come.

She was soft and warm, and her legs still entrapped him in her silken embrace as they lay on his bed in the early hours of the following morning. A thread of unease drifted through his sated mind. How many times had he taken her? Why did he find her so irresistible, even now, seconds after climax?

He should be craving distance. Feel suffocated by her lingering touch. Hadn't he tried to convince himself that the only reason he was so obsessed with her was because it had been so long since he'd had a woman?

It was no longer a convincing argument. Had it ever been?

He enjoyed her company. Even before they'd had sex. In the short time they'd been together, he'd got used to having her here.

Used to the way she'd turned his life upside down.

Her eyelashes flickered. She looked enchanting and exhausted and guilt ate through him. But all she had to do was look at him and he wanted her. As though he was trying to create as many memories as possible.

Because their time together was so inevitably brief.

Silence settled around them, an elusive illusion of comfort, as she slipped into sleep. And only then did he realize their fingers were entwined.

Much as he wanted to remain here with her, he had to work. With a heavy sigh, he eased his fingers from hers.

She stirred, frowned, and momentarily tightened her grip on him. "My beloved archangel."

The words were soft, sleep-drugged, and a shudder crawled along his spine at her whispered endearment.

My beloved archangel. Only Eleni had ever called him that. Only she had ever dared.

Only Eleni had ever possessed the right.

Fascination and dread-filled hope thundered through him as he stared at Aurora's sleeping face.

It wasn't possible. He knew that. Eleni was dead, and dead forever. She could never return.

Aurora's words meant nothing.

They meant everything.

He raked his hand through his hair and gripped the back of his neck. It didn't shift the crazy thoughts pounding through his head.

Why did she possess a necklace so similar to the one he had once given to Eleni?

Stop. There was no connection between Eleni and Aurora. He couldn't risk traveling that path, clinging to a dream, when he knew, in his heart, it could never be.

But what if it was more than a dream?

There was only one other he could talk to about this. Only one other who could truly understand.

Zad.

~

IT DIDN'T TAKE LONG to track him down. He was knee deep in the latest devastating earthquake that had recently hit the Pacific.

Gabe stood on a bank of steaming rubble and watched the other archangel, second only to Mephisto in age, leave the medical team he'd been organizing and make his way across the broken landscape toward him.

"Is it worth it?" Gabe narrowed his eyes against the gritty atmosphere and surveyed the ruined city. Zad haunted natural disasters on Earth as if they were a drug.

"Got to be worth a try."

They'd had similar conversations a million times in the past. As far as Gabe was concerned, humans could just get the hell on with it. Somehow or another their species always survived, no matter what the Earth or cosmos threw at them.

They survived. Whether they deserved to or not.

Strange. He and Zad had both lost those who meant everything to them. Yet while Gabe had turned his back on humanity, Zad had embraced them.

Gabe would never again open his arms to the human race.

Aurora's face filled his vision, obliterating the ravaged land. She was a human, and he'd done far more than merely open his arms to her. He'd broken ancient covenants for her.

But then, she wasn't wholly indigenous to Earth. She was a unique, incredible hybrid who possessed the genetic material from two dimensions. He would never lay the blame of the past on *her* shoulders.

Yet he'd saved her before he'd known her true heritage.

Again, the futile hope that she was so much more than she could ever be echoed through his heart. It would be the answer for his insatiable desire, and the reason he craved her company.

"Is this about the woman you rescued from the Guardians?" Zad's voice dragged him back to the present.

"Yes."

"It's no longer an inconvenience having her on your island." It wasn't a question. "The sex must be spectacular."

"It's not the—" He clamped his jaw shut. Zad was the last one he'd discuss his sex life with. "She had a necklace. It's an exact replica of the ones we gave our beloveds. And do you know why she has it? Because she used to dream of archangel wings and rainbows as a child. She had it commissioned to her specific design."

Zad gazed into the distance, his hands shoved into the pockets of his dusty jeans. Was Zad even going to acknowledge his words?

Finally, the other archangel turned to him, his face an inscrutable mask.

"It doesn't mean anything. Children throughout the ages, throughout the universe, dream of rainbows and archangels for no other reason than both are"—he shrugged, and a mirthless smile tugged at his lips—"fantastical."

Gabe forcibly relaxed his clenched fists. A buried sliver of sanity in a dark corner of his mind urged him to shut up, to leave, to forget about this madness.

But he couldn't let it go. Not yet. Not while there was still the tiniest thread of hope in his heart.

"That's not all. When she was asleep, she said—" The words lodged in his throat, burning. How could he repeat them, after so long? To anyone, but most of all to Zad, who had also loved Eleni?

Zad's mahogany wings rippled in the breeze, and Gabe saw how his muscles tensed, and he understood. Because even after all this time, he, too, struggled against the instinct to soar to the mythical heavens.

"It doesn't matter what she said." Beneath his even tone, there was a harsh note of finality in Zad's voice. "She's not Eleni, Gabe. Neither first-generation Nephilim nor their descendants have souls to return to us. We've always known that."

The knowledge was seared into the fabric of his being. The offspring of an archangel and a human, and all their descendants, was eternally damned. But still the irrational hope had flared that somehow, against every possibility and despite her Nephilim heritage, his Eleni had been reborn.

It was a fool's dream. And while he was many things, he was no longer a fool. The necklace was a coincidence. There was no universal convergence, no karmic confluence.

Aurora hadn't said she dreamed of *archangel* wings, after all. Aurora was not Eleni.

He would never have the chance to love her again, hear her laughter or hold her in his arms. Or be given a second chance to save her life the way he'd been unable to save her so many years ago.

"How long must we serve penance?" The words tore from him, bloodied chunks of his soul that would never heal.

"It's not a sin to love again." There was weary acceptance in Zad's voice. "You're not betraying Eleni's memory."

Gabe's laugh was harsh, a mirthless sound in the arid air. Archangels rarely fell in love, and when they did, it was forever.

"You know we can have only one beloved." The words ate into his heart like acid. "Like you said, it's only spectacular sex."

Zad finally turned to look at him, and Gabe saw fleeting desolation reflected in the other archangel's dark eyes. "With the right one, sex heals the soul."

CHAPTER 21

AURORA

"*F*inished." The little girl leaned back in her chair, and Aurora could see what she had been doing. Painting seashells, in every color of the rainbow. "Can we give them to him now?"

I can't understand what you're saying. Yet the strange language made perfect sense.

"As soon as he gets home." She was thinking in English. And yet the words were exotic, foreign. Unknowable.

The child's laughter was pure and carefree, and Aurora smiled, vaguely bemused, although she wasn't quite sure why.

Who is this child?

She seemed oddly familiar, with her curly blonde hair and kaleidoscopic eyes.

An elusive question drifted through her mind. *Is this a dream?*

She glanced around the kitchen and unease trickled along her spine. Had she been here before?

A shadow blocked out the sun and then *he* was there, and the world was filled with light and love as he pulled her and the child into his arms.

Silken feathers teased and caressed, belying their inherent strength, and she gasped, disoriented, as his wings embraced and claimed.

His wings.

"Aurora." The way he breathed her name, so husky and seductive, sent tremors of an entirely different nature dancing over her skin. She wound her arms around his neck as he tugged his fingers through her hair, and the sun dimmed into a pre-dawn glow.

The dream fluttered through her mind, fading into mist-shrouded corners, and the intangible boundary between fantasy and memory merged, became one, as Gabe's mouth claimed hers.

SITTING in the shade on Gabe's terrace, elusive tendrils of Aurora's early-morning dream haunted the edges of her mind, but the harder she tried to remember the details, the fainter they became.

It was so frustrating. She wasn't sure why. It was only a dream. Yet she couldn't shake the certainty that if she could remember it, so many things would fall into place.

She let out a long breath. There was nothing to fall into place. What did that even mean? Right now, she was on Gabe's island, but her real life was back in Cornwall.

There was no way she would ever forget that.

And that's why she needed to stop obsessing over what Gabe was doing today and get back to researching the Guardians. It didn't matter that after they'd spent the night having amazing sex, he'd disappeared this morning without even saying goodbye.

Her number one priority was discovering a way she could safely return home. But whenever she was with Gabe, that urgency faded.

Just as she had feared.

It was too easy to forget how impossible this was between them. The knowledge that one day she would never see him again twisted her heart inside out.

It was so much more than sex. And now she had to deal with the consequences of being stupid enough to fall for an archangel.

She was a mortal. How could she hope to defeat the protocols of an alien species that was older than anything she could imagine?

It wouldn't be a hardship, staying on Gabe's island, where she was safe. With him.

Isolated from everyone and everything she had ever loved. Crippled with guilt over abandoning her parents.

Inevitably growing old, while Gabe stayed forever in his gorgeous, irresistible prime.

And I'll never have a family of my own.

She couldn't accept that future. Not when she knew how fragile a person's grasp on reality could be. Her parents shared an overwhelming love, but in the end even that hadn't been enough.

Her goal was clear. Find a loophole in the ancient laws governing the Guardians' rights and discover a chink in their armored protocols. Just because no one else ever had, didn't mean it couldn't be done.

Maybe no one had ever tried.

Grimly, she logged into her email account to check if there was a reply from her dad. She'd sent a message to both of her parents, but she doubted her mum would reply, since she'd given up checking her email over a year ago.

Except she had.

A reply from her mother was sitting in the inbox.

Wild hope flared. Maybe her telepathic interaction with Gabe yesterday had pulled her back from the shadows?

She opened the message.

He said we were never to speak of it, but how could we keep it a secret from our only child? I tried not to forget. Please forgive me, Aurora. And find your way home.

This was *so* not the response she'd been expecting. She didn't even know how to reply. A quick glance at her dad's message confirmed that whatever her mum was talking about, she hadn't discussed it with him.

Much as she wanted to find out who the mysterious *he* was, she couldn't risk her mum's fragile health by asking in an email. All she could do was reassure her that everything was fine.

There's nothing to forgive. Don't worry about me! I'll be home ASAP.

SINCE YESTERDAY HADN'T GIVEN her anything to go on, she'd approach her research from a different angle today.

Guardian abductions.

And tumbled into a vortex of increasingly paranoid conspiracy theories. It was kind of shocking to discover that trait wasn't confined to humans of Earth.

There were countless hypotheses as to why they abducted in the first place, and all of them were horrible. But the one that really snagged her attention was the idea they did it to feed their insatiable drug habit.

Feeding on the terror of mortals.

Sometimes those who had been taken turned up again, their memories hazy, their sanity compromised, and evidence of torture apparent. But at least they were still alive.

Hours later, she stumbled across the anomalies.

Hidden in obscure archives were brief reports of those suspected to have been abducted by them but who hadn't returned alive. Those whose bodies had been drained of all fluid.

She dug deeper, her stomach churning with horror at the images scrolling across the screen.

And almost missed it.

She zoomed in on the unfocused image. Around the woman's neck was a chain. And the pendant was in the shape of wings.

Not just any wings. Even the poor quality of the image couldn't disguise the shimmering rainbows or glittering gold dust that seemed to pulse with a life of its own.

Involuntarily, she curled her fingers around her necklace. She couldn't shift the conviction there was a reason why this victim had possessed an identical piece of jewelry to the one Gabe's daughter had worn. If only she could work it out. Where was Gabe when she needed to talk to him?

It was as though he heard her unspoken wish, as from the corner of her eye she saw him materialize.

"Gabe come here. You'll never—" The words lodged in her throat as Mephisto, arms folded, dominated the terrace.

"Aurora." His voice was low, but the menace in that one word sent a shudder along her spine.

She refused to wilt under his unblinking gaze. "Gabe's not here."

"It's not Gabe I want to speak with."

Well, shit.

Mephisto appeared far more intimidating when he wasn't flashing his evil smile around. She flattened her hands on her thighs to stop them from shaking. No way did she want this arrogant bastard to guess how much he unnerved her.

"What do you want to know?"

His lips thinned. It appeared he didn't like being questioned by a mere mortal.

"Tell me exactly what you did on the astral planes."

"You know what I was doing. And so does Gabe."

Mephisto unfolded his arms and his wings rippled in majestic affront. A merciless, immortal, predator stalking his prey.

She forced a panicked breath into her lungs. She wouldn't give him the satisfaction of falling into a terrified heap at his feet.

"Tell Gabe whatever fucking fairy story you like. It won't work with me. I'll ask you one last time. What did you do on the astral planes?"

She could tell him about her mother. But this was the archangel who, for his own twisted motives, had taken her to that club. He wouldn't care about her reasons, unlike Gabe. Somehow, recalling Gabe's support gave her a shot of courage, and she pushed herself to her feet.

"I made a mistake." It hurt, having to confess that to Mephisto, but it was only the truth. "And now I'm paying for it."

His arm shot out, and although he didn't touch anything, the laptop catapulted across the table and smashed onto the terrace.

"You're paying for it?" He didn't raise his voice, but his eyes burned crimson. She wanted to run and hide from the malice pulsing from him but couldn't move a muscle. "I don't see that. It's the Archangel Gabriel who's paying your debt, and I want to know what the fuck you did to him on the astral planes."

Iced fear stabbed through her. What did he mean that Gabe was paying her debt? Immortals were beyond the grasp of the Guardians. She'd discovered that, and Gabe had confirmed it.

But what if we're both wrong?

"Is Gabe in danger?" She'd never forgive herself. "I thought he was safe from them?"

Mephisto's lip curled in contempt. "Last chance. Tell me how you dragged Gabe through the astral planes without his knowledge. If I'd known that was your plan, I would have fried your miserable brain two years ago."

He thought *she* was responsible for Gabe's arrival in the village? Through the astral planes? How did that even make any sense?

"I don't have any idea how he—"

"Don't think I won't rip open your mind to find the truth if I have to, human."

She believed him. And he would leave nothing of her mind behind afterward.

"I'm telling you the truth. I didn't drag Gabe into anything."

A phantom hand grasped her fingers and she staggered at the brutal grip. Mephisto's fiery glare scorched her flesh, and it took every shred of willpower she possessed to remain standing upright.

"What are you?" Frustration throbbed with every word. It was obvious he wasn't used to asking that question.

He tightened his psychic grip on her fingers. Pain raced up her arm and speared through her chest, arrowing toward her heart.

He was going to kill her. For now, he was playing, like a cat with a mouse, but he'd soon tire of that game. He'd rip through her mind, clawing for answers. And find nothing.

How easy it would be to fall to her knees. To grovel at his feet and beg for mercy. *He'd spare my life, then.*

The certainty was absolute. Ancient knowledge. And with it came a cold fury that ignited her paralyzed brain and pumped blood through her deadened fingers. She straightened her spine and pushed back with her mind. *Fuck you, Meph.*

Mephisto recoiled, denial spiking from him like supercharged lightning. The air around them crackled with singed energy as the crimson in his eyes faded and his psychic grip vanished. Their gazes clashed, but the deadly disdain had given way to incredulity. *Awe.*

She no longer feared him as a terrifying creature who could crush her to dust with merely a look.

And he knew it.

A thud echoed behind her and then Gabe was there, grabbing Mephisto's biceps, and the uncanny connection severed.

"Back off." It was a deadly warning.

Mephisto wrenched himself free, his eyes never leaving Aurora.

"How can this be?" His voice was oddly hushed, and shivers skated over her arms.

Gabe appeared oblivious to Mephisto's strange behavior. "Don't come near Aurora again."

"She's just a human." Mephisto stared at Gabe as if he'd never seen him before. Was it her imagination or did he sound as though he was trying to convince himself as much as Gabe?

"Get out of here."

Mephisto gave her one last, inscrutable glance. And then he vanished.

Mephisto

MEPHISTO FOUND Zad at a Taoist retreat hidden deep in the sacred mountains of China. He leaned against a timber support of the hut Zad had acquired and glowered at the magnificent panorama.

I'm mistaken. No, he wasn't. But he'd been trying to convince himself for hours because the alternative shook the foundations of everything he had ever believed in.

To think it had taken a mortal to make him question a fundamental truth.

But then, Eleni had never been *just* a mortal.

No wonder he'd been intrigued by Aurora when he'd found her at that lecture. Something in him had recognized her for who she truly was.

It explained the uniqueness of her aura when he had checked it after Gabe had given her his protection at Eblis' club. It hadn't shown the usual glow of a mortal claimed by an archangel. Truth was, Mephisto had never seen anything quite like her aura before, and he sure as hell hadn't noticed the sign of unbreakable archangelic devotion.

But when she'd stood up to him earlier, when she'd thrust into his mind, the image of Eleni had burst through his brain. It was so visceral that for one terrifying moment he'd feared for his sanity.

It isn't possible. But it didn't change the fact.

Eleni had been reborn.

CHAPTER 22

MEPHISTO

Zad emerged from the hut and propped his shoulder against the other timber support. He was covered in dust from whatever disaster he'd recently returned from, and silence stretched between them, as it had so many times in the past.

But this time he found no solace, no comfort, as this silence hung like a thick blanket of fog, a suffocating mantle ravaging the fabric of his existence.

Finally, he could stand it no longer.

"Demon spawn are soulless. That was ancient knowledge by the time we discovered Earth."

It wasn't a question. They both knew the answer. By rights, he should keep his mouth shut, bury this secret the way he had buried so many others.

But this discovery was different. He needed to confide, or lose his mind, and who else could he speak to but Zad?

Zad didn't deign to answer. Mephisto hadn't expected him to. Not yet.

"By default, so were the Nephilim."

Zad folded his arms and unfurled the tips of his wings. An

unspoken warning. His expression might have been carved from granite.

Mephisto reined in the fury that thundered through his veins. Fury that something he had failed to question, something he had taken as an absolute truth *was a lie.* "Nephilim could never be reborn. That's an irrefutable fact."

"What's your point?" There was an uncharacteristic edge in Zad's voice and Mephisto almost backed off. There was still time. He didn't have to burden his oldest friend with such a soul-shattering revelation.

But the knowledge was eating him alive. And for once, his need took precedence over the compulsion to protect.

The name that had once been so familiar to him lodged in his throat, but he pushed it out, anyway. "Eleni is *back*, Zad."

"No, she isn't."

Mephisto gave a bitter laugh. "She is. The human from Cornwall, of all fucking places, is living proof of how we were deceived."

Slowly, Zad straightened and turned to look at him. Wild, desperate, hope flared in his eyes, but there was something else. A fleeting glimpse of astounded comprehension that made no sense.

"Have you discussed your hypothesis with Gabe?" Zad's voice was hoarse, and despite his words, Mephisto knew the other archangel believed.

"He doesn't have a clue." And neither, apparently, did Eleni. Frustration throbbed through him and he smashed his fist into the timber support. It splintered, and the hut sagged like a drunken goblin. "How many others have returned without our knowledge, Zad? Lived and died without knowing their true heritage?"

Zad shook his head, but it seemed in response to his thoughts, not Mephisto's question. "Eleni's death almost destroyed him once. He can't find out who she really is, Meph."

It was the question he'd wanted to discuss, but he hadn't expected this response.

"Why not? Even when she dies, it's not the end, like we always believed."

"Eleni may be here now. It doesn't mean she'll return again. Without that guarantee, we can't risk telling Gabe. I don't think we could bring him back from the abyss a second time."

Gabe

GABE BATTENED down the rabid need to follow Mephisto's trail and hammer the crap out of him. How *dare* he touch Aurora?

After his visit with Zad, he'd resolved to keep her at arm's length. To protect her, as he had vowed, but nothing more.

His determination had crumbled the second he'd seen Mephisto towering over her.

But as he took her hand and saw how she gritted her teeth against the pain, the truth uncoiled deep in his chest. It was more than fury that another archangel had disregarded the ancient bonds of ownership and touched a mortal under his protection.

Not going there.

Rage he could deal with. But not the fear he might have arrived too late to save her. That Mephisto might, despite everything, have pillaged Aurora's mind and left a vacant, broken creature in her place.

"This might hurt." He enveloped her injured hand between his. Mephisto, the sadistic bastard, had torn fragile tendons and muscles. Nothing he couldn't fix, but that wasn't the fucking point. "You'd better sit down."

"I'm all right." She glanced at his hands. "You can heal." It wasn't a question. "Can you bring back the dead as well?"

"No." He broke his concentration to look at her. Her teeth

were clenched, and her face was drained of color, but she offered him a grimace that she clearly believed resembled a reassuring smile. For some reason it caused an odd stabbing sensation through his chest. "Bringing back the dead is beyond our powers. Healing others is just a side benefit of our ability to naturally regenerate."

She let out a huff of laughter. "Good job Meph didn't go straight for the mind-suck, then."

His gaze sharpened. While he often referred to Mephisto as Meph, he was damn sure he hadn't in front of Aurora. And no one called the other archangel that to his face, apart from Zad. Gabe wasn't even convinced Mephisto liked Zad abbreviating his name.

Eleni had always called him that, though. She'd been able to get away with almost anything, even with Mephisto.

Stop. He wouldn't fall into that beguiling web again.

"He won't come near you again." Once more, that crippling fear scraped through him. What if he hadn't arrived in time to save her from the other archangel's wrath? "He had no right coming here."

"He was pretty shaken up." She flexed her fingers. "Wow. You're good."

The color was returning to her cheeks, her eyes were no longer shadowed with pain, and she wasn't shivering in terror that the most powerful archangel in existence had almost destroyed her.

He was pretty shaken up. Who ever said that about Mephisto, let alone a human who had been within seconds of having their brain pulverized by him?

"Should be as good as new. Let me know if you get any twinges."

She curled her healed hand against her breasts and flattened her other hand against his heart. Such a light touch, yet the imprint of her palm scorched his flesh through his shirt.

Gods, he wanted her. To hold her and touch her and know that she really was all right. To lose himself inside her again, to reach that elusive pinnacle where, for a few blissful moments, his guilt receded, and peace bathed his soul.

"Thanks, Gabe." Her voice was soft, and her blue eyes hypnotized him. "I might have held him off for a few more seconds, but I know how close he was to crushing my brain."

He almost told her Mephisto had intended no such thing. It was odd, this compunction he had to protect her from the harsh truths. It didn't even make any sense. She already knew the truth.

"He won't make that mistake twice." It was unlikely he and Mephisto would cross paths again until Aurora—

The knowledge seared his brain.

Until Aurora is dead.

And a human lived only a few score years at most. No time at all when compared to the lifespan of an archangel. He'd have his island back and Mephisto would put this day into the archives and they'd resume their previous relationship as if nothing had come between them.

A few score years. A fleeting lifespan.

An eternity alone.

But she was here with him now, and now was all they had. But instead of scooping her into his arms and fucking her until this unnatural knot of panic subsided, he sat on her chair and pulled her onto his lap.

Just let me hold you.

"I'm sorry about your laptop." Her hands were on his shoulders, her warm body all but touching him.

"It's fixable." And even if it wasn't, so what? It was only a piece of technology, manufactured by one of the most advanced civilizations in the Andromeda Galaxy. An irreparably damaged laptop could be replaced.

But there was only one Aurora.

He buried his face against her neck. She was a mortal, a

human. So fragile that if he held his breath, he could hear the beat of her heart and the rush of blood in her veins. He shouldn't still want her so desperately, yet he couldn't get enough.

When was the last time a woman had so ensnared him?

It was a rhetorical question. There had only ever been one.

"Gabe." There was an unmistakable note of concern in her voice, and his arms tightened around her. He didn't want her permanently worrying. "Is the fact you saved me from the Guardians causing you problems with—well, anyone?"

She was worrying about *him*?

"Wouldn't matter to me." He tugged her closer and breathed in deep, relishing her purity. It had been forever since someone had showed such simple concern for him. "The only ones who might have complained gave up all pretense at responsibility millennia ago."

Aurora

AURORA FRAMED his face with her hands, stroking her thumbs over his cheekbones. His overnight shadow grazed her skin with an erotic caress. How strange that it had never occurred to her before that archangels might shave.

But it was hard to remember he was an immortal when he held her like this. When, every time she looked at him, she didn't see a fantastical creature, but a man.

"You mean the Alphas?" He'd mentioned them a couple of times, but she hadn't found anything about them during her research.

His smile was grim. "They never come anywhere near this side of the universe anymore. Too primitive for them."

Which meant it was unlikely Mephisto was referring to them. Maybe the debt he'd been so furious about was nothing more than the fact Gabe was now responsible for her safety.

"Are they your ancestors?"

He sighed heavily but didn't brush off her question. A strange little pain weaved through her heart. He was slowly opening up to her. And maybe he didn't even know it.

"You could say that. At least, they're the forebears of all immortals alive today."

There was an odd echo of desolation in his voice that pierced her heart. Could she ever learn all there was to know about him?

She ignored the tiny warning in the back of her head. It was too late for that. She didn't just want him, she cared about him. And deep inside she knew he felt more than base lust for her.

It had been in his voice as he'd healed her hand. In his furtive glances every time she'd winced. It wasn't love and it couldn't lead anywhere permanent. But for now, it was enough.

It had to be. Because now was all they would ever have.

And then his mesmeric gaze caught hers, and she knew *now* would never be enough.

Don't ruin the little that we have. If he guessed she was falling, he'd back off and they would never share another intimate moment like this again.

"Are there many of them? The Alphas?"

"Countless." There was a husky note in his voice. But he didn't slip his hands beneath her T-shirt the way she wanted him to.

"Who's in charge?" She tenderly brushed the tips of her fingers along the contours of his face. She loved touching him. She was afraid she might never want to let him go.

He didn't take up her unspoken offer. Was he holding back on purpose? He never had before.

"Who's in charge of the universe?" He laughed, and the lingering trace of despair in his eyes dissolved. "No one. Everyone. You know how it is."

She had no idea how it was, and right now she didn't care, when he looked at her as though she was the only one in the universe he saw.

She had to stop reading more into every glance he bestowed her way, or she'd never be able to put her heart back together again.

"Fate? Destiny?" She'd never really believed in either, despite the extraordinary way her parents had met, but now she was willing to seriously consider almost anything.

"Why not? The universe is a random bitch and goes by any number of names."

"I can't even imagine all the things you must have seen."

"You don't want to. You'd have nightmares."

He wasn't joking. What terrible events had he witnessed? She had the crazy wish she could take all his pain away, even if it was for only a moment.

As if that was even possible.

"There must be some good in the universe."

"Yes." The tips of his fingers caressed her waist, and even through her T-shirt delicious tremors raced over her skin. "And it's never where you expect to find it."

She leaned in closer, and the tantalizing scent of hot, aroused male flooded her senses. Slowly she speared her fingers into his hair, cradling his temples. "There must be more good than evil out there?"

"All creation cares about is balance. Good and evil is a matter of perspective."

"That's not very reassuring."

"I know." His smile was infinitely sad. "The universe is fucked. What can I say?"

"Maybe it is," she conceded. "But it's the same universe I found you. That makes it pretty amazing."

His laugh was irresistible. How easy it would be to think he had no concept of suffering or loss.

But she'd seen beneath his arrogant façade to the mortal beneath. His loss, no matter how long ago it had occurred, was still raw.

Was this moment of carefree laughter another façade?

Pain, as deep and desolate as any she'd experienced while watching her mother's memories fade, bit into her heart. How she wanted to believe that, when he was with her, Gabe could forget his past.

The irony seared her soul. She wanted her mother to remember, and for Gabe to forget.

All she had was now. She wouldn't waste it with regrets of what could never be.

"Is that a backhanded way of saying you think I'm amazing?" His gently mocking voice broke into her thoughts, and she smiled at him.

He was the Archangel Gabriel. Of course he was amazing. But he was so much more than that. "You're the man I want. Do you have a problem with that?"

"Do I look like I have a problem with that?" His muscles braced, clearly intending to stand, with her in his arms.

She untangled her fingers from his hair and gripped his shoulders. "Sit still."

"Are you giving me an order?" His lips quirked in amusement, but he remained seated. "Not even demigods are that brave around me."

"Good job I'm not a demigod, isn't it?"

He grinned and began to pull off her T-shirt. She slipped from his lap, gripped his wrists, and pinned him to the arms of the chair.

"Don't touch. Or do I have to hurt you?"

Gabe choked on another laugh. "I'd like to see you try."

"Be careful what you wish for." Heart pounding, making it hard to drag air into her lungs, she concentrated on unbuttoning his shirt. "Because you never know your luck. You might just get it."

CHAPTER 23

GABE

Gabe stifled the primal urge to rip off their clothes, drag Aurora into his arms, and slake the molten lust that surged through his blood. He'd tried to hold back, give her time to recover, but she didn't need time.

She needed him.

He gripped the arms of the chair, his biceps straining with the effort, and lashed down the instinct to assert control and take what she offered, on his terms.

"What are you planning?" Fascinated, he watched how she slid each button free with maddening deliberation, an enchanting frown of concentration etched on her brow.

"Wait and see." She glanced up, and the blush on her cheeks gave her an intriguing air of innocent seductress. "Not used to the woman taking control, are you?"

He heard the hint of triumph in her voice, and it was clear that thought gave her a great deal of satisfaction. She wanted to be the first who had ever had him pliant beneath her searching fingers.

A feral grin split his lips at her obvious delight. Even if it wasn't the truth. Back in his distant past, countless women had stripped him and worshipped him, while he lay there basking in their adoration.

But with every other woman who had taken the initiative, except for Eleni, he'd been content to let them feed their curiosity. He'd not had to rein in his desire as he was for Aurora. Hadn't needed to remain agonizingly still while she grappled with a simple thing like removing a shirt.

And unlike the others, she was far from incoherent with awe at the honor of being in his company. She was with him because …

Despite himself, a pained grunt escaped as she tugged his shirt from his pants. But still his thought hovered.

Aurora was with him because he was *the man she wanted*.

Not because he was an immortal or an archangel. Or even because of his reputation as a ruthless mercenary. But just because he was *him*.

She grasped the ends of his shirt in her fists and appeared unsure what to do next. Gods, he hoped she opened his pants. His cock was fucking killing him.

"Take off your shirt."

It would be so much easier to do as she asked. To pull her onto his lap and surrender to the lust that scalded his vision and blurred reality.

"No." He didn't even recognize his voice. He sounded like an addict craving his next fix. "You want me naked, you strip me."

She dropped the ends of his shirt and slid her hands up his abdomen, her touch light but sure. He instantly regretted his benevolence. *Can't take much more of this.*

"Is your body naturally perfect or do you work out?"

"Both." If he gripped the damn chair any harder, it was going to splinter. "How about you?"

Her fingers halted a whisper from his nipples.

"Me?" She sounded disbelieving that he could have said such a thing. "My body's hardly perfect, even if I do go to the gym."

He released a pained breath. Why had he thought it a good idea to let her take over? She was talking way too much. She always talked way too much.

And he would have her no other way.

Somehow, he ground the words between his teeth. "It's perfect to me."

She stared at him as if he was her entire world, and a strange pain deep inside corkscrewed through his chest. Plenty of females had gazed at him with adoration, but not like this. He couldn't even place it, only knew it had nothing to do with the mindless worship of an immortal being.

And then she gave a breathless laugh and stroked her thumbs over his nipples. He damn near came in his pants.

"I bet you say that to all the girls."

"Yeah." The word was feral. "Right."

She eased his shirt off his shoulders before tugging it from his body and dropping it onto the ground.

"Do you think …" She trailed off, and he wanted to tell her the time for thinking was past. He didn't care what she intended, he just wanted her to *do* it. "Do you think you'll have any more unexpected visitors? Should we go inside?"

There was an unmistakable crack as he finally splintered the chair's arms.

"No. To both." He sounded rabid. If anyone did turn up, he'd fucking slaughter them.

Her smile was strangely sweet as she inched her T-shirt up from her waist, and he watched, riveted, as she pulled it over her head and dropped it on top of his shirt.

"Wasn't going to get naked yet." Her voice was smoky, and it was agony to stay still and not touch. She hooked her thumbs into the band of her shorts. "I was going to make you wait for it."

An agonized groan escaped. "You *are* making me wait for it."

She kicked off her shorts, then glided her hands over his rigid thighs, a slow, torturous caress before she finally tugged at his belt. He hitched in a pained breath in a futile attempt to give her some leverage. She was taking forever to release him from purgatory. Was she doing it deliberately?

She gave a frustrated groan and yanked on his zipper.

"Fuck!" Still clutching the chair, he reared up, white pain blazing through him. "You damn near castrated me."

She slapped her hand across her mouth. His vision was blurred, but he could swear she was on the verge of laughing. Did she think he was joking?

"I'm so sorry." The words were muffled. Then she cradled his jaw. "I've never manhandled such an impressive weapon before."

Godsdamn, she *was* laughing. He was so staggered even the volcanic throb of his abused cock faded. It had been forever since a simple fuck had been so mystifyingly complex.

Or so much fun.

How the hell does this classify as being fun?

Undignified, yes. And yet he had the crazy urge to laugh with her.

He unhooked his fingers from the chair, and it dropped to the ground, before releasing the zipper, and relief flooded through him.

"Despite being immortal, my *impressive weapon* is also made of flesh and blood. And it damn well hurts."

Her smile faded, and he wished he'd kept his mouth shut. He didn't want her second guessing her every action.

"I didn't mean to hurt you, Gabe. It was an accident."

"That's good to know. If it had been deliberate, I'd be in trouble."

"Do you want me to …?" She didn't finish her question, but she didn't need to. He gave her a wicked grin.

"Sure."

With infinite care, she dragged his pants down his legs before straightening and resting her hands on his shoulders. She nibbled kisses along his jaw, delicate and provocative, and her uneven breath whispered against his skin. He molded the rounded curve of her ass, and she answered his unspoken demand by sinking against him as her mouth fastened on his throat.

Erotic darts of pleasure thundered through his blood, and even through her bra her erect nipples grazed his chest. He was desperate for her to be completely naked, to feel her skin against his.

But he'd wait until she was done. Even if it destroyed his sanity.

She sank to her knees between his thighs and the sight damn near finished him. As though this was the first time a woman had done such a thing, instead of times without number.

But it was the first time with Aurora.

She looked up at him through her eyelashes, an intoxicating combination of innocence and wanton seductress. Her rich chestnut hair tumbled around her shoulders, and he fought the desperate urge to plunge his fingers through those silken curls, to hold her close.

To force her to his will.

He sat and gripped the shattered chair arms once again.

"Where did I hurt you?" Her sultry whisper fanned his erection as she took him in her hand, her touch so light as if afraid he might break. He gritted his teeth against the order burning his tongue for her to *grip harder*. If she wanted to treat him like spun glass, then he would suffer it.

"Was it here?" Her fingers dusted his length, and a tortured growl rumbled through his chest.

"Yes." Not that he could recall now. His entire body throbbed with ecstatic anticipation, which was something he'd not experienced in … eternity.

He watched, mesmerized, as she bent over him, her hair caressing the insides of his thighs. Her wet mouth brushed against his rigid length, teasing, tasting, but leaving him wanting so much more.

She pulled back, panting, her head resting on his thigh, her lips parted in blatant invitation, with her hand wrapped around his cock. And he damn near forgot how to breathe.

"I don't think my mouth is big enough for you."

Somehow, he located his voice. "Your mouth is plenty big enough."

Her lips twitched. If she laughed now, he was going to lose what little restraint he retained. Did she really want him to disgrace himself in front of her?

"A girl could take that the wrong way, you know."

He grunted, a primitive sound, but coherent words failed him. *She's going to make me beg.*

Slowly, she licked him, and his control unraveled like cosmic filaments trapped within an intergalactic storm.

"Aurora." Her name razed his throat, and he would beg, if that's what it would take. "For gods' sakes, let me in."

Her hand tightened around him, exquisite agony, and her other hand cradled his aching balls. She shuffled unsteadily between his thighs, and he faintly recalled she was kneeling on hard, unforgiving stone.

And then he forgot everything as her mouth enslaved him.

Silken heat enveloped the head of his cock and he reared upward, instinctively, the need to possess pounding through his senses. He plunged both hands through her hair, twisting her curls around his fingers, forcing her along his rigid length.

Gods, it was exquisite. Her head nestled between his thighs, her hot breath erratic against his shaft as her mouth claimed him. It was agony, but he eased his grip on her head and she slid up a couple of inches, the friction a new kind of sensual torture. And then her fingers tightened around him, and it took all his willpower not to shove himself down her tempting throat and empty into her.

He wound her hair around his fists and watched, transfixed, as she worshipped his cock with her mouth and tongue. And still she tortured him with her fingers, trailing them over his rock-hard balls before cradling him in the palm of her hand.

Fuck, it was too much. And while the image of her on her knees was exhilarating, he wanted to feel her come around him as he pumped into her tight sheath.

As he claimed her once again.

Aurora

AURORA COULD HARDLY BREATHE, and was beyond thinking, as Gabe filled her mouth and filled her hands. He tasted of sex and sin, of primal desire and forbidden delights. Her jaw ached already, and they had barely started. But instead of taking what she offered, he pulled out.

"I haven't finished." Her words were jagged, and her jaw didn't feel as if it quite belonged to her.

There was a savage glow in his eyes. "Neither have I."

God, he was beautiful. Unblemished bronze flesh molded his strong, perfectly defined musculature, and his golden hair brushed his shoulders. He lifted her roughly in his arms, and for one surreal moment, she imagined him unfurling his glorious wings, enveloping her in the magical cocoon of softness and strength, the scent of arousal and devotion intoxicating her senses.

It's just a fantasy.

But it felt so real. As if she was remembering another time...

Mephisto. Disappointment cascaded through her, even as Gabe hoisted her onto the table. She was only recalling the feel of Mephisto's wings and imagining how it would feel with Gabe.

Except it wasn't that at all. It had nothing to do with Mephisto. The sensation was fading like a distant dream, but the fleeting certainty had been so visceral. So real.

It's a memory.

Gabe palmed her bottom and balanced her on the edge of the table. His gaze scorched her, his touch inflamed, yet goosebumps prickled her skin.

"Are you cold?" His question sizzled the air, and she clamped her legs around his waist. She was so desperate to feel his wings her mind was playing tricks. But she didn't need his wings because right now she had *him*. And he was all that mattered.

"I'm burning." She wound her arms across his shoulders and buried her fingers in his glorious hair. "For my archangel."

He stilled, and for a heartbeat she saw raw need glowing in his eyes.

"Then you'd better hold on." His growl was wild and inhuman, and his cock nudged her, a teasing, tantalizing kiss, but still he kept her waiting.

"Gabe." She was begging. She didn't care. "I need you inside me."

His grin was pure evil, forged in heaven and honed in hell, as he pushed into her, inch by magnificent inch, when she desperately craved a brutal possession.

She gripped his waist in a vise, dug her heels into his taut butt, and lifted herself from the edge of the table. The exquisite stretching of delicate flesh to accommodate his size was breathtaking.

With an inarticulate curse, he pinned her to the table. Her fingers were still tangled in his hair, and his hands imprisoned her hips. She squirmed helplessly beneath him, but his hold was absolute as her fingernails raked over his head. His big body shuddered, and the knowledge that he was so close to the edge thrilled her soul.

Her legs hitched higher, clamping around his back, pulling him so close his heartbeat echoed in her ears. Her muscles tightened around his invading length, a mind-blowing caress of silk and flame, and spirals of fire licked through her blood. Reality blurred as he came hard and fast, the pleasure so fierce it bordered on agony. She gripped him tight and forgot how to breathe, how to think. He was inside her, above her, the missing piece of her soul.

Sensation consumed, enslaved, and only one thought filled her world.

Gabe.

CHAPTER 24

AURORA

When Aurora emerged from the bathroom later that afternoon, there was no sign of Gabe. She refused to acknowledge the disappointment that stabbed through her. He had a life outside of this island that didn't include her, and she wasn't going to drive herself crazy by second guessing everything.

She'd continue with her research that Mephisto had interrupted.

Except he'd smashed the laptop.

Great.

Back in the kitchen, a large chest on the terrace caught her eye. Frowning, she went outside and crouched beside it. Dimly, she recalled a thud before Gabe had launched himself at Mephisto. This was obviously what he'd dropped.

She traced her fingers along the top of the timber chest. They slid into a concealed groove, and before she realized what she'd done, the entire top folded upon itself and disappeared down the back of the chest.

Shit. Guilt ate through her and she glanced back at the villa, half expecting Gabe to materialize. There was no way she was going to look through his personal possessions. She still felt bad enough that she had discovered that picture.

Despite her best intentions, her gaze snagged on the contents and her breath caught in her throat. The chest was filled with a child's beloved toys and books, and items of clothing.

She sat back on her heels and squeezed her eyes shut. It was like she'd wrenched open Gabe's heart. Why had she even touched the chest in the first place?

It was too late to regret that, now. She needed to find out how the mechanism worked and get it shut before he returned.

Gingerly, she probed the edge of the chest while trying not to look inside. And then he materialized at the other end of the terrace, and she jerked back so fast she almost fell onto her butt.

He strode toward her, and gibbered excuses raced through her mind as to what she was doing looking through his precious daughter's possessions. Just because that wasn't what she'd been doing, didn't make a lot of difference. It looked bad and she wouldn't blame him for losing his shit.

He stepped over the opened chest and placed something on the table behind her before sitting on a chair.

Okay, then. He was obviously waiting for her defense. Her mind was scarily blank. How pathetic would it sound to tell him she'd opened the chest without meaning to?

"You have a new laptop." There was the faintest trace of a tired smile on his face. She had the unnerving certainty he was oblivious to the open chest beside her.

Bemused, she glanced at the slender package on the table. *What am I missing?*

"Uh, good?" Her voice was unnaturally high, and she hitched in a shallow breath, but it had trouble reaching her lungs. Maybe she should just apologize for the chest's irrational locking system and hope he wouldn't hold it against her.

"I thought so." This time his smile appeared more genuine.

"Look, I'm really sorry." She made a feeble waving gesture in the chest's direction. "I didn't mean to pry. I mean, I haven't pried. I haven't looked at anything at all." She was gabbling with nerves and sounded as guilty as sin. Because she *was* guilty, but he didn't know about the discovery she'd made in his office.

He shrugged, apparently unconcerned. "It's okay."

Something was very odd about his reaction. She chanced another glance into the chest. Although the toys looked well-loved, they didn't look that old. Doubt surfaced. Had she jumped to the wrong conclusion?

But why would he have a chest full of a child's things if they weren't his daughter's?

She couldn't help herself. "What is it?"

"Work related."

"What is it that you do?" She'd been dying to know but hadn't liked to ask before now.

"I track the missing."

She stared at him, entranced. Now this was more like the myths of old. Wasn't Gabriel the Archangel of Mercy?

"You mean you're like a private investigator?"

Disgust washed over his face. "Do I look like a PI?"

She had to give him that. "No. But it doesn't matter what you call yourself. What's important is what you *do*."

"Don't get too emotional." There was a grim note in his voice. "I don't do it out of the goodness of my heart. My fees are astronomical."

For some reason it hadn't occurred to her that he'd charge a fee. Then again, he had to live, and he'd already told her he amassed fortunes as a hobby. It shouldn't come as that much of a surprise.

"I suppose that's only fair," she conceded. "You need to cover expenses."

"That has nothing to do with it. It's so potential clients are fully aware of the magnitude of their request."

Gabe

"Okay." She sounded completely baffled. "So, what does that mean, exactly?"

Why had he started this conversation? It wasn't something he discussed with anyone.

But then, Aurora wasn't just anyone.

How had it become so complicated between them? He should have kept their association firmly in the zone of savior and victim. Immortal and human. Not let anything else filter through the cracks in his armor.

Too late now. Maybe she'd back off in disgust if he told her the price his clients were prepared to pay. And maybe then she wouldn't distract his every waking thought.

"It means I demand their soul in payment."

"You can't demand a person's *soul*." She sounded incredulous. But she didn't recoil.

"Give me one good reason why not."

"You're telling me souls are *real*?" She pushed herself from the floor and perched on the edge of the chest.

"Yes." What other answer was there?

"But you're an *archangel*." She made him sound like a benevolent god. The literal definition of oxymoron. "I thought the taking of souls was something only the devil did."

"Depends what you classify as a devil." He'd been called that and worse in his time. It was all a matter of perspective.

She gave a little huh, as though she thought he was joking. He resisted the urge to tell her that he was deadly serious. What did it matter what she thought?

It matters.

A haunting reminder that no matter how he denied it to Zad, his attachment to Aurora was far more than spectacular sex.

"But why do you demand their souls?"

"It's the ultimate proof." He owed her nothing, yet the need to tell her everything consumed his reason. "If a potential client is willing to sacrifice the possibility of ever being reborn, just to save the one they love in this life, then maybe the missing one is worth searching for."

"Reborn? Are you saying people really do reincarnate?"

"Only if they possess a soul." He couldn't stop the bitterness in his voice. "Otherwise once you die, that's it. You're gone forever. No second chances."

"Wait." She frowned, oblivious to how astonishing it was for a mere mortal to say such a thing to an archangel. "You return the one they love, and at the same time take away the chance they may have of getting together in a future life?"

That was exactly the conclusion he wanted her to believe. She would retreat, and this strange connection between them would shatter. Their relationship would be based exclusively on sex, and his fascination with her would fade.

Except the suicidal desire to leap to his feet, drag her into his arms, and tell her the truth thundered through his brain. Did she really think so little of him that she could believe he'd demand such a thing?

Despite the price his clients believed they paid, all he did was wipe their minds. They retained only a hazy memory of having approached him, or what he had done for them. But the rumors persisted that he demanded not only his client's soul, but also their life as payment.

And still the desperate sought him out.

He crushed the illogical urge. Let her believe the worst of him.

"That's right." To his disgust, he sounded belligerent.

"But that's *ridiculous*."

His grin was feral. Her lack of respect was breathtaking. Mortals had died for far less. Why, then, did he find her irreverence so damned exhilarating?

"What criteria would you use?" he demanded, as though she

was his equal and her opinion mattered. "How would you prioritize which case to take and which to leave?"

With the right one, sex can heal the soul. But Aurora was not the right one. And his soul was beyond salvation. But curse the gods, he didn't want to lose this fragile thread that had inexplicably woven them together.

She gazed into the chest and trailed her fingers over the contents as though she was clairsentient and could discover secrets from touch alone.

"You'd need harsh criteria." Reluctant acceptance threaded through her words. "Otherwise you'd be swamped."

"That's why I've never suppressed the rumors." To hell with it. He wanted her to know the truth, because she hadn't condemned him. How fucked up was that? "What would I do with a million souls?"

Her smile was soft, accepting, and every reason why he'd convinced himself to put distance between them evaporated like morning mist.

"You're looking for a child, aren't you?" She didn't wait for him to answer. There was no need, when the contents of the chest told its own tale. "How old is she?"

"Four years old."

"Do you," she hesitated, then took a deep breath. "Do you want me to help? I'd like to."

She wanted to *help*?

She had no idea what to look for, and he didn't need her. But despite that logic he acknowledged, with a sense of fatality, that he wanted her help.

Even if all it amounted to was simply keeping him company.

CHAPTER 25

AURORA

Curled up on the sofa, Aurora stifled a yawn. She had no idea what the time was, but it had been dark for what seemed like hours. The remains of another mouth-watering meal Gabe had brought back a while ago was strewn across the coffee table, and he was at the other end of the sofa, focused on his laptop.

Surreptitiously, she indulged her obsession and gazed at him, soaking in the glow of his hair, the sculpted perfection of his face, and his total concentration on the task he'd set himself. Besides loading intel onto her laptop, he had suggested she go online and research.

She sifted through the information Gabe had received from Evalyne's father and uploaded to her laptop. There were a lot of family pictures, and she never would have guessed these people were aliens and not humans from Earth.

She couldn't stop scrolling through the pictures that catalogued the little girl's life, from the celebration of her birth, to what were clearly birthday parties.

It was all so … normal. Nothing like the aliens she'd seen at Eblis' club.

The last picture showed Evalyne cuddling with an older woman. They were both laughing, and the bond between them shone through. Aurora hitched in a ragged sigh, but just as she was about to close the folder, something caught her eye.

Frowning, she enlarged the image, and eerie shivers raced along her arms. She hadn't imagined it. Around the little girl's neck, partly obscured but still recognizable, was a replica of Aurora's own necklace, and the vibrant shimmer of rainbows and gold dust was clearly visible.

Before meeting Gabe, she'd never seen anything exactly the same as her necklace. But in the space of three days she'd come across *three* identical to her own. Belatedly, she remembered she hadn't told him about the one she'd discovered around the throat of a suspected victim of the Guardians, just before Mephisto had turned up.

It couldn't be a coincidence. There had to be a connection between the two abducted girls who had possessed archangelic artifacts.

"I've found something." She turned the laptop around so he could see the screen. Gabe glanced up, a frown of concentration etched across his brow. "Look at her necklace."

Gabe looked, but didn't comment.

"It's the same as mine." Except what she really wanted to say was *it's the same as your daughter's.*

He wrapped his arm around her. She had the strange impression he didn't even realize.

"It's of no significance."

She pressed her palm against his heart.

"It means something, Gabe. My one is a fake, but what are the chances this one is, too?" She cradled his jaw and forced him to look at her. "I'm not suggesting this was made for Evalyne's mother or grandmother. Obviously, we're talking generations ago." Why was she so sure about that? "But the original beloved would have passed it down to her daughter, who would have passed it down in her turn. A continuing chain of endless devotion."

"What?" His voice was hushed, and he looked at her as though he had never seen her before. "How do you know about that?"

Unease whispered through her heart.

"You told me. The other night." When he had first seen her necklace. And yet she had the strongest conviction she had known that fact for so much longer.

"No, I didn't." The words were uncompromising. "I told you your necklace was based on an ancient archangelic design. I didn't say who we gave them to, or the tradition of passing from mother to daughter."

So how did I know?

"Well, it's a reasonable guess that's what happened. And I think it's a strong possibility that's what happened in Evalyne's case. I think … she could be descended from an archangel."

"No." There was a dread finality in his tone, but his gaze was riveted on the image of the child. "There are no Nephilim left, Aurora."

She didn't want to disagree with him. It was obvious who he was thinking of when he looked at Evalyne. But she couldn't let it go. Her hypothesis might be wrong, but it deserved to be investigated.

"How can you be so sure?" Her voice was soft, and once again she pressed her hand against his chest. Against his wounded heart. "You can't know for certain."

Finally, he looked at her, and the sorrow of ages glowed in his eyes.

"I'm certain." Ancient resignation permeated each word. "Gods and mortals had children together from the time the Alphas discovered they were sexually compatible. At our most basic level all of us—gods, archangels, mortals—are made of the same stardust."

"Yes," she whispered, afraid to shatter this glimpse into his extraordinary past, but he had paused, as though he'd expected a response. Would he tell her about his own daughter? She desperately hoped he would. It would mean more to her than he'd ever know.

"Our goddess, for reasons known only to herself, wasn't interested in procreating with her fellow Alphas, let alone mortals. She wanted more than that. She wanted to create her own unique species."

Awe trickled along her spine. "The archangels," she breathed. "She made you in her image."

How twisted the truth had become through millennia.

"No," Gabe said. "Surprisingly, considering the size of her ego. She stole DNA from all of the Alphas for her baseline, found this primitive planet in the backwaters of the universe, and experimented for millennia until she was satisfied with the outcome."

Whoa. DNA from *all* the Alphas? Without their consent?

She bet that hadn't gone down well.

"And created the archangels?"

This time he offered her a crooked smile, and it pierced right through her heart.

"Again, no. She created, for want of a better word, our cousins, the demons. You met one. Eblis."

Eblis was a demon? What had happened to the horns and forked tail of myths?

"There was one problem with the demons, though. They bred like rabbits with the humans on Earth."

"I suppose that would be a problem," she said, but her mind was reeling. Was half the Earth swarming with the descendants of demons?

On second thoughts, that would explain a *lot*.

Gabe grunted. "The *problem* was the demons were spending far too much time indulging in earthly pleasures, and not nearly enough in worshipping at our goddess' feet. And she loathed their offspring with a passion."

His goddess sounded like a nightmare. "It always makes sense to blame the innocent."

A reluctant smile tugged at his mouth. "Demon spawn are many things, but they're never innocent."

She had only the sketchiest idea of what demons were. And that information mostly came from novels and movies.

Probably not the best source of factual evidence. Then again, from what she'd discovered, neither were the myths that populated Earth's histories.

"What happened?"

He gave a heavy sigh. "She banished her demons and as many of their children as she could find. Turned them loose in the universe and began Version II. The archangels. And this time she ensured there would be no messy distractions in the form of offspring."

Wait. Was he telling her …? "She created you sterile?"

But that couldn't be right. Apart from the sheer vileness of such an act, he'd already admitted some archangels had children. *He'd* had a child.

"She thought she did." He leaned his head against the back of the sofa and gazed at the ceiling. She could only guess what he saw in his mind's eye, and her heart ached. "As we matured, we, too, indulged in earthly pleasures. There was a magnificent civilization back then, Aurora. A thriving culture based on science and mathematics that had evolved over ten thousand years or more. We were the immortal ones, and yet we learned so much from them."

Had she missed something? She'd assumed he was talking about Earth, but obviously not. No way was she going to interrupt him by asking. He might never open up to her like this again.

"In time it became apparent that, with the one who claimed our heart, we could have children. But despite the joy they brought us, we were always consumed by guilt."

His pause lengthened. Was he waiting for her to say something? She took a chance.

"Because you were going against the word of your goddess?"

His heavenly gaze clashed with hers. "No. It was because our beloved Nephilim didn't possess souls. Unlike the offspring of gods and mortals, who suffered from no such curse, our children —children we loved with all our hearts—could never be reborn. We were condemned to know that because of us, our precious children were destined for one life. And one life only."

His daughter.

A hard knot of anguish filled the center of her chest. She couldn't even begin to imagine the depth of his despair. How long had he existed, consumed by such misplaced guilt?

"I'm so sorry." They were only well-worn words, but what else could she say? And she meant them, so deeply.

"It happened long ago." He drew in a deep breath, his magnificent chest expanding beneath her. "But that's the reason why Evalyne can't be descended from an archangel. We only ever procreated on Earth, and that was millennia ago."

He *had* been talking about Earth. How was that possible? What great civilization did he mean?

"When we finally left the place of our creation and ventured into the vastness of the universe, we all made a vow. We would never fall again."

His words shouldn't hurt. She knew he didn't love her. Knew, now, why he never could.

It still hurt.

Grow up. He was telling her everything she craved to know, and nothing came without a price.

Except it didn't add up. There was something he still wasn't sharing, apart from the fact he had once had a daughter. A piece of history between the time archangels had children and when they made the decision to never love again.

"Gabe." She kept her voice soft, although it was hard to hide her urgency. She knew he considered the matter of Evalyne's heritage closed, and maybe it was. Or maybe he was blinded by his preconceived notions. "I understand what you're telling me. But there's something I want to show you. I found it earlier today, just before Mephisto turned up."

Had that really been only earlier today? It seemed like a lifetime ago.

He didn't question her, but as the minutes crawled by, panic churned through her. Suppose she couldn't find it again?

And then she hit gold.

"There." She turned to Gabe, who still appeared lost in another world. "Look. She's wearing a necklace identical to Evalyne's."

He took a measured breath before glancing at the screen. And then his focus sharpened, and he took the laptop from her.

"Shit." He ground the word between his teeth. "*Archangel blood. It can't be.*"

"What can't be?" She gripped his arm. He was still transfixed by what she had shown him. "What is it, Gabe?"

There was a wild gleam in his eyes. "Something the pirate said when I interrogated him. 'Faith that the cursed bloodline survives.' I discounted it as the ravings of a miscreant desperate to save his own skin."

"There were others," she whispered. "I found three other victims whose bodies were drained. But they were only suspected to have been abducted by the Guardians. Do you think whoever took Evalyne is responsible for them, too?"

"I can't say without evidence."

Nausea churned in the pit of her stomach. She'd been so fixated on connecting the necklace with an archangelic heritage that she'd overlooked the obvious.

"It doesn't mean they'll kill her though, does it?"

He shoved the laptop onto the sofa and stood up. "I'm going to ask Jaylar about his immortal heritage."

CHAPTER 26

GABE

Gabe contacted Jaylar via the telepathic link he had established, as Aurora pushed the laptop onto the sofa and took his hand.

"Let me come with you, Gabe."

"No. It's too dangerous."

"I know you're trying to protect me. But I want to help."

"You have already." Because without her, it wouldn't have occurred to him to question Jaylar's immortal lineage. "I won't be long."

"But I might perceive something he says in a different way than you."

He wanted to tell her there was no way she could see anything more clearly than he. But he'd just acknowledged that she did.

And it was simply an excuse, in any case. The only reason he didn't want to take her with him was because of the threat of the Guardians.

Why did she always question him?

"Aurora." He ground her name between his teeth, but it didn't change the facts. Her reasoning was sound, even if he wished it wasn't. "Stay close."

He teleported directly into Jaylar's office, his arm wrapped securely around Aurora. The Guardians were sneaky bastards, but they weren't omnipresent. And at the first sign of trouble, he'd get her back to his island faster than a heartbeat.

Jaylar gave a half-bow. "My Lord Gabriel."

He'd barely replied, when Aurora whispered in his ear.

"What is he saying?"

She couldn't understand the Medan language. For the first time, he acknowledged the foresight of the demons' technological advances. Centuries ago they'd developed software to address this problem for their high-ranking half-bloods. Those who, unlike archangels and demons, hadn't inherited the ability to process a multitude of languages from their Alpha forebears.

He should have established a telepathic connection with her. Then he could instantaneously translate the conversation to her. With anyone else, he'd initiate the connection right now. But with her unique brain structure, there was no way he could rush it.

"I'll translate." He turned back to Jaylar. "Where did your daughter get her archangel wings necklace?"

"My Lord?" Jaylar glanced at Aurora, obviously baffled by her presence. "Her what?"

Before he could translate, Aurora pulled her necklace from beneath her top. Jaylar's focus riveted on her outstretched palm.

"Archangel wings?" He sounded confused. "We've never called it this. My mother gave Evalyne a necklace much like this one on her fourth birthday. Just days before she disappeared."

"Where did your mother get the necklace?"

"My Lord, I fail to see how the origin of a necklace can have any bearing on—"

"Answer the question."

Aurora curled her fingers around his arm. "Gabe," she said softly. "Ask him if his ancestors came from Earth."

He relayed the question, even though it was unlikely Jaylar had even heard of the planet.

"No." There was a thread of defiance in Jaylar's tone, as though he expected Gabe to take issue with his denial. Not that he would. How could anyone in the Andromeda Galaxy have ancestors from Earth?

Then Jaylar shot Aurora another glance and appeared to reconsider. "But our family history has always hinted that our esteemed demigoddess ancestor spent time on that far-flung planet before she settled on Medana. The necklace originates from her. We've always believed it was forged by the gods themselves."

As Gabe translated for Aurora, he trawled through ancient memories. In those enlightened days, before the great devastation had ravaged Earth, many resident demigods and goddesses had taken archangels as their lovers.

But it still didn't answer the vital question. How had Jaylar's ancestor been in possession of a such a precious artifact?

"He's almost right about the necklace," Aurora said. "Except it wasn't forged by gods, but by archangels."

"And Jaylar's descended from the gods, not archangels," he reminded her. "It doesn't explain why his mother's lineage was in possession of the wings."

"Yes, it does," Aurora said. "It means an archangel gave that demigoddess the necklace before she left Earth."

He almost laughed. "That would never have happened."

She frowned. "Do you think she might have stolen it?"

That was just as unlikely. While minor deities had never had a problem with taking whatever caught their eye, and the archangelic necklaces were both exquisite and rare—two things all immortals adored—the necklaces were off-limits.

Not because they were designed only for an archangel's beloved. But because they were crafted from the very fabric of their home world. The place of their creation. And no deity of any stripe wanted anything to do with *that* place.

"Absolutely not."

Aurora tilted her head, assessing him, and while it touched him that she wanted to help, he should have left her at home. Where she was safe, and he didn't have to worry about her.

"Yet the fact remains," she said, breaking into his thoughts, "the necklace was handed down for generations. If you're so certain a demigoddess wouldn't have stolen it, that leaves one big possibility. Even though I don't know why you think it would never have happened. It seems pretty obvious to me. An archangel gave it to her because she was his beloved."

"Trust me. No archangel would have fallen for a demigoddess. That's just … inconceivable." As inconceivable as an archangel falling for a demon.

Or a human with a trans-dimensional parentage.

"I don't see why. And it stands to reason she was pregnant with his child before she left Earth, as well."

"She couldn't have been." They would have known of such a liaison. *Surely, they would have known?* "We only conceive with our beloved."

"Yes." She smiled at him and gently brushed her fingers over his chest. "It's making sense now, isn't it?"

It didn't make any kind of sense at all. The offspring of gods were—had always been—exciting and enjoyable lovers. But never anything more.

Because at their core they regarded archangels as anomalies of nature. A freak of creation. They were neither hybrid nor pureblood, but merely the physical manifestation of an Alpha goddess' insatiable ego.

A fuck was one thing. Falling was something else entirely.

It seems pretty obvious to me. And to someone who didn't know the facts, he had to concede it was a reasonable conclusion.

Unease crawled along his spine. Until meeting Aurora, he

would never have considered her dual heritage was possible. What if she was right?

Was he discarding a viable option, simply because of his own ingrained prejudices?

It wasn't a great analysis of his critical thinking. He'd never considered he was blinded by prejudice before. But now she'd planted the seed, he couldn't move past it.

Was it possible a Nephilim had been born in another galaxy, after the great destruction that had decimated Earth? He had no right to assume that bonds of eternal devotion had never existed between an archangel and demigoddess simply because he had never known of it.

Could Jaylar and Evalyne be descendants of an archangel?

He gripped Aurora's fingers, his anchor in a rapidly disintegrating reality. *How fucking warped is that?*

For the second time, he scanned Jaylar's aura. Was that strange, elusive glimmer that he hadn't been able to place when the man had first approached him, the result of an archangel and demigoddess union?

"Do you have your daughter's necklace? I need it."

"No." Anguish flayed the word. "She was wearing it when she disappeared."

There was nothing more to learn here. He inclined his head at Jaylar, tightened his grip on Aurora, and teleported.

Home.

Aurora

As DAWN SLID DELICATE ribbons of pink and peach into the bedroom, Aurora propped her head on her hand and gazed down at Gabe. He was sprawled on his front, the sheets tangled around his hips, and pain twisted through her heart at his ravaged back.

The parallel scars that distorted his flesh, despite their obvious age, looked as if they still caused untold agony.

How had he lost his wings? Why hadn't his powers of regeneration repaired them?

She had so many questions. Maybe one day he would answer them all.

Slowly, she trailed her fingertips along the length of his back, perilously close to the deep gash, yet not quite touching the mangled flesh. Were these injuries linked with the death of his beloved?

A dull pain cradled her heart. It was pathetic to be jealous of a woman who had been dead for thousands of years, and yet here she was. Envious of a love that could never be hers.

She braced her weight on her hand and leaned over him. The juxtaposition of perfectly sculpted muscle and bronzed, unblemished skin contrasted with the brutal slashes that had once ripped open his body. Yet far from detracting from his beauty, the imperfections only enhanced it.

And at the same time made him seem, somehow, more human and less … immortal.

Tenderly, she pressed her lips against the knotted seam of flesh where, millennia ago, his wings had been ripped from him. Her eyes drifted shut, and in her mind, she saw their glorious majesty. Yet the flecks of gold, which highlighted each individual cream feather, had been so pretty. Delicate even.

Not majestic at all.

She was only recalling the image she'd found in his office. But in her heart, it was so much more. As though she could remember his wings herself. The way he wrapped them around her, and how she delighted in the incredible power and deceptive softness imbued in each individual feather.

The exhilaration when he held her as they flew through the skies.

Her head sank lower and she breathed in deep, savoring the

scent of elusive rainforests and the tantalizing hint of ages old familiarity. Was this how it began? The gradual erosion of the memories of her previous existence, until all she recognized was life with Gabe?

No. She would never forget her previous life, no matter how long it took her to return to it.

She wound her arm across his back and pressed her cheek against his scar.

Suppose I never find a way to safely return home?

But what if she did and never saw Gabe again?

He stirred, and she shoved her disquieting thoughts into a dark corner of her mind. This morning they were going to follow up on the information Gabe had extracted from the pirate he'd interrogated, but it wasn't quite morning.

Not yet.

She molded her body to his as he rolled onto his back. His eyes were still closed, his hair tangled, and every shadow of his face was so achingly familiar.

But she'd only known him for a handful of days. She had to remember that. She hadn't known him all her life, no matter how the certainty seeped through her senses.

Still bracing her weight on one hand, she trailed her fingers along his jaw and over his lips, and his cock stirred against her thigh.

With an inelegant wriggle, she trapped his hips between her knees. Palms spread on his chest, she delicately caressed his rapidly thickening length with her damp sex.

Her clit ached with the delicious friction, but it wasn't enough. She wanted him inside her, possessing her, but she also wanted to prolong this moment of anticipation. The heady sensation of having Gabe, her beloved archangel, powerless beneath her while she tormented him with sensual pleasures.

A fantasy, maybe. But it worked for her.

"You finished?" His voice was gravelly, like a rough caress.

"What makes you think that?"

"You stopped." He cracked open one eye, long lashes concealing his expression. "I thought I should check. In case you needed some help."

She smiled, couldn't help herself, even though she had the terrible certainty he would see far more in her eyes than she wanted him to. "I think I can manage."

He cradled her breasts, his gaze meshed with hers, before slowly trailing his hands along her body. Everywhere he touched, ribbons of flames ignited and smoldered beneath her sensitized skin.

"After last night I thought you'd sleep in." His voice was uneven, and he palmed her bottom possessively. "I was counting on you sleeping in."

"You had an ulterior motive?" She gently rubbed the tip of her nose over his. He had done that to her only once, and she never had to him. Yet the gesture seemed so strangely familiar. "I thought maybe you just couldn't get enough of me."

He gave a rumble of laughter. "That too."

After they'd returned from seeing Jaylar, Gabe had told her that he was going to follow up on the pirate's cryptic comments. He hadn't agreed when she'd suggested going with him, but neither had he argued.

They'd hardly slept last night, and her body still glowed from their lovemaking. But she knew his plan had been to leave her so exhausted that she wouldn't be aware when he left this morning.

His plan had failed. She was going with him to the Fornax Galaxy whether he liked it or not, but she had no intention of discussing it with him right now.

She kissed him, long and slow, and his fingers teased her tender flesh. She groaned, the sound vibrating between them, and his grin was a potent aphrodisiac.

Her muscles contracted around him, but he didn't take the

hint. She needed more, and she surged upwards, shuddering with a torturous fusion of pleasure and frustration.

"Are you sure you're not some kind of sex god?"

His grin was feral. "I'll be your sex archangel if you want me to."

"I'm serious." With agonizing deliberation, she sank slowly onto his engorged cock. A whimper escaped her, but she didn't care. "I only have to look at you and I want to shag you senseless."

He laughed and shoved further inside her, stretching and filling her in the way only he could. She squeezed him tight, and thrills pulsed through her when he gritted his teeth as though she pushed him to the very limits of his control.

"The feeling is mutual," he growled.

Slowly she raised her hips, the heavy slide of his cock inside her utterly intoxicating, and then he bucked beneath her, spurring her onward.

The breath rushed from her lungs as his size expanded her tender flesh, as he filled her body and heart and soul. Intermingled, they became one, and she didn't know where she ended and he began, because there was no divide.

There's never been any divide.

As she convulsed around him, he came with brutal ferocity. His arms encircled her waist, and he ground out words in his strange language. Words she couldn't understand but that captured her heart, regardless.

For eternity.

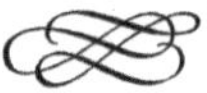

AURORA

Sprawled on Gabe's chest, Aurora listened to the comforting thud of his heart as it gradually slowed its erratic thunder. He held her close, one arm around her waist, his other hand curled around her shoulder.

As though he feared she might try to escape.

She pressed her lips against his damp skin and closed her eyes.

Stop imagining his every gesture means so much more than it does.

Dawn had long broken. Any moment, he would shatter this tranquil interlude and there would be no time for her questions. She snuggled more securely in his embrace and traced her fingertips over his impressive biceps.

"What's that language you sometimes speak?"

She didn't need to be psychic to feel the surprise roll through his body. But he didn't brush her question aside.

"It's unknown on Earth these days." Idly, his fingers played with her hair. "It eventually evolved into what's now referred to as archaic Sumerian."

It *eventually evolved?* Archaic Sumerian was one of the oldest languages ever discovered. But he was referring to a civilization that had existed further back in the past.

A civilization she knew nothing about.

The one he'd mentioned when he had told her how Evalyne couldn't possibly be descended from an archangel.

Excitement and an unformed dread collided in her heart. She had the strange certainty that if she continued this conversation, her life would be irrevocably altered.

And perhaps not for the better.

But in the end, she couldn't help herself.

"What happened?" Her awed whisper drifted between them. Such a simple question, but one that showed how stark the chasm was that divided them. "Why haven't we discovered any archaeological evidence of this civilization?"

His body tensed, and regret flooded through her. Had she pushed him too far? But then he exhaled a long sigh.

"Humans have discovered evidence, Aurora. But they choose to ignore their history. As far as they're concerned, there were no great civilizations on their planet more than five thousand or so years ago."

Shivers raced over her arms. Was he talking about the ancient pyramids that were scattered across the globe?

"What did we ignore, Gabe?"

His smile was sad and touched a place so deep inside her, she wanted to wrap him in her arms and reassure him that everything would be all right.

But the damage had been done long ago, and nothing she did or said would ever make things right for him again.

"Where do I begin?" There was only the faintest trace of bitterness in his voice, and it wasn't directed at her. "Are you sure you want to know?"

"Yes," she whispered, even though a part of her soul screamed *no*, because the knowledge he was about to impart might drive an irreparable wedge between them forever.

But her thirst for knowledge had always outweighed her need for self-preservation.

"We discovered Earth at the end of the last so-called Ice Age. The true golden age of technological advance and enlightenment among humanity."

Riveted, she gazed at him. He was speaking of prehistoric times, ten, eleven—*more*—millennia ago. That couldn't be right. She had misunderstood him.

"But people were hunter-gatherers then, Gabe."

Gently, he cupped her face. As if she was something infinitely precious. This time she didn't try crushing the thought. Because deep in her heart the improbable certainty glowed.

He did care for her.

"Yes, that's true," he said, and it took her a second to recall he was responding to her comment, not her errant hope. "For the most part."

"The most part?" she echoed, enthralled.

"There was a vast continent where the culture was rich and diverse. That's where we made our playground. The scholars of that time were our teachers, our lovers. They taught us about the stars and the celestial cycle of the Earth."

His mesmeric eyes were glazed, as though he recalled living in that far off time, in that fantastical land. She hardly dared breathe, in case she distracted him.

"Our goddess was fine with this. At least we weren't polluting the human gene pool with countless offspring. She'd got some serious shit from the other Alphas over her ..." He paused, clearly debating his choice of words, before continuing, "*experiments*. They would have ripped her apart if they'd been able to. Not only were we created from them all, but she'd given us wings. The ultimate indulgence. Or insult."

"They were jealous?" *Gods* had been jealous of *archangels*?

He shrugged, like it didn't matter. "They rarely deigned to

interact with us. We were content to remain on Earth. And eventually, some of us discovered love."

"And your goddess wasn't fine about *that*." It wasn't a question, and when he shot her a considering glance, she knew she was right.

"She didn't like it." He sounded reluctant to admit it. "But she tolerated it."

"Because as far as she was concerned, the love of an archangel for their beloved was nothing compared to the eternal love you bore for her."

Where did that come from? And why was she so sure she was right?

"Something like that." There was a guarded note in his voice, and he looked at her as though he wasn't quite sure who she was. "We chose not to enlighten her."

A chill inched along her arms, as what he had left unsaid unfolded in her mind.

"But souls are reborn." Her voice was hushed as the implication illuminated dark fragments of long-forgotten dreams ... memories? "She thought the love died when your beloved died. She didn't know you waited for them to come back to you."

His intense gaze roved over her face, searching for something elusive. Something unimaginable. Her breath stalled in her throat as his eyes darkened, and then he slowly blinked, and the moment shattered.

"It never occurred to her we were capable of undying devotion for a mere human. And it certainly never crossed her mind that despite her best manipulations and sacred edict, a few precious Nephilim had been born."

Dread scraped a skeletal claw along her spine. She'd wanted to know the missing segment of his history, to understand what had made archangels decide to never love again. But now that he appeared willing to tell her, she didn't want to know.

I'm afraid to know.

But he was waiting for her to ask the question. Did he believe that by sharing the past with her, the magnitude of his misplaced guilt might diminish?

She was being ridiculous. This wasn't about her.

"What did she do?"

"Why am I telling you all this?" He speared his fingers through her hair and held the back of her head. "I've never told anyone of my past. Why you? Why now?"

"I don't know. Why not?"

Once again, his gaze raked over her face, searching for something he knew he would never find. Because the one he truly wanted in his arms had perished long ago.

Don't weep for something that can never be. He had never promised her anything more than to protect her.

"Our goddess walked the Earth." There was a fatalistic note in his voice that sent warning prickles racing across her skin. "To see for herself why we were so enamored. She found those willing to betray our secrets. They told her how those archangels who fell waited, life after mortal life, until their beloved was reborn. And they told her of our Nephilim."

And the heavens opened, and the seas rose, and escape was denied to all those with tainted blood.

It was more than a random thought. It was what she had always known but been unable to access. Images of tsunamis, erupting volcanoes, and devastating earthquakes saturated her mind in terrifying detail.

Stop.

They weren't memories. She wasn't recalling long ago events.

I'm only imagining how it must have been.

After all, the stories of that catastrophic time had been handed down through the ages, generation after generation, in every major culture across the planet. The reason may have become lost in time, but the terror of the devastation had survived.

"She sent the flood to destroy everything." Her voice was hushed with the horror of it. She already knew the answer.

"No." His stark response was unexpected, and she frowned, uncertain. "She didn't have to. The geophysical upheavals of that time were simply a part of the natural cycle of the celestial clock. The floods came anyway."

That made more sense than the devastation being nothing more than the vindictive actions of a spurned goddess.

But there was still more he hadn't yet told her. He loathed his goddess. And the only reason she could imagine for such hatred was because that Alpha Immortal was responsible for the death of his beloved and their daughter.

"Could she have prevented it, if she'd wanted to?"

"There was originally another planet in this solar system," he said, seemingly oblivious to her question. "Called Nibiru. But it was more than a planet. It was the City of Archangels, where we'd been created and where our goddess occasionally resided. More importantly, it was immune to the natural forces that govern any normal planet."

They would be safe on Nibiru. Although many would perish on Earth, with the exodus, enough would survive to start again. To recreate their society and pass on their knowledge to future generations ...

Where were these thoughts coming from? *What's happening to me?* Or was this how it had started with her mother? Not the gradual fading of her old life, as Aurora had always believed. But the certainty that she had lived *another life* altogether?

"You wanted to save the people," she said, because of course he had. "By taking them to your city."

"We couldn't have saved them all." It was obvious that still razed his soul, even after all this time. "You have to understand something. Their civilization was ancient long before we discovered their continent. They had studied the heavens for millennia, passing on their knowledge from one generation to the next. They'd unearthed the secrets of the past, and with mathematical precision, gained foreknowledge of their future. The celestial body they had charted for so long would slingshot around Earth, and the apocalypse would come."

He said it with such finality. She didn't doubt him for a second.

"But they were trying to find ways to stop it?" It's what any advanced civilization would do.

"No. That was never their design. It was carved into their collective consciousness that they wouldn't all survive. It had been an accepted facet of their future for countless generations." He dragged in a heavy breath. "I'm not saying they were happy about it. But they channeled their energy into preserving what they could pass down through the ages to descendants far in the future."

But nothing had survived. No one had ever heard of this great, doomed, civilization, except perhaps in myths or fairy tales. A strange sorrow pierced her at that forlorn knowledge.

"What happened?" she said softly, even though deep in a shadowy corner of her mind, she could guess.

"We offered the chance of escape for a select few thousand." A trace of bitterness edged his voice. "But the plan leaked, and it was like a dam exploded. While the people had accepted their predestined fate and the odds of perishing, they absolutely weren't ready to accept the kind of intervention we offered. Not when we couldn't offer it to everyone. Their once peaceful society dissolved into anarchy. They sold us out to our goddess and then hunted down the innocent."

He drew in a deep breath. "We didn't discover this until afterwards. If we'd known, we would never have answered her call. Never have returned to Nibiru. And she would never have had the chance to neutralize us, while on Earth tsunamis crashed across continents and the tectonic plates pulled apart. And life as we had known it was all but eradicated."

Silence vibrated in the air, but frantic fragments of disjointed thoughts—*memories?* —tumbled through her mind.

I always knew he had not forsaken us. He didn't willingly sever our telepathic link. One day I will return to him ...

This was crazy. A sign of desperation. Was she really trying to fool herself that in a previous life she had been Gabe's beloved?

Yet how easily she could let herself believe it. But it was a fantasy.

She would *not* allow her reality to blur.

Tenderly, she cradled his face between her palms. He had promised to save the ones he loved and been unable to keep his word. This was the crux of his guilt, and he had never been to blame.

How could he have known the extent of his goddess' wrath?

No wonder he hated her.

Maybe she shouldn't say any more. He had shared so much. Yet she could no sooner stop breathing as hold her tongue.

"And when it was over, she released you?"

"No. We revolted against her. Destroyed our City and annihilated the whole damn planet in our battle for freedom. But we were too late. Earth had reset her clock. And the human gene pool had been cleansed."

"I'm so sorry." It was a useless thing to say, but she had nothing else.

Without releasing her, he rolled onto his side, so they faced each other.

"It was my fault. We'd decided long ago to save our own—our beloved, the Nephilim, and current lovers. But I suggested we try and preserve the nucleus of the civilization as well. If I hadn't done that, there wouldn't have been the uprising. Our goddess wouldn't have discovered our plan until we'd executed it. Until it was too fucking late for her to do anything about it."

"It wasn't your fault." How could she make him believe that?

But after so long, what hope did she have of changing his conviction?

"I've never forgiven humans for how they betrayed us to our goddess. And as the Earth shifted around them, they turned their wrath on our Nephilim and murdered them." Futile rage blazed in his eyes and smoldered her heart.

That vilification of the archangels' beloved children had survived countless ages, twisting something that was pure and beautiful into a monstrous travesty of the truth. No wonder he had never forgiven humans.

"After the destruction of Nibiru, we shunned Earth and explored the universe. We'd never been inclined to do that, before."

"But you live on Earth," she whispered, and even though deep in her heart she knew why he did, she couldn't say it.

"It's our curse. It doesn't matter how far we travel or where we make our homes. The Earth calls to some primitive core deep inside us. Whether we live here or not, few of us can stay away for more than a few decades. Ironic, isn't it?"

It wasn't ironic. She knew why he couldn't stay away. And this time the words came, each one ripping a little more from her aching heart. "It's because you know that one day your beloveds will be reborn."

This time the silence was so profound she thought she'd pushed him beyond his limits. She threaded her fingers through his. It didn't matter that his confession would crush what remained of her fragile hopes that he might one day feel more for her. All that mattered was he speak of his past, and that somehow it would help heal his wounded soul.

He raised their joined hands and focused on their entwined fingers. "We knew it would take millennia for humans to recover from the brink of extinction. We deluded ourselves that, eventually, the odds would once again be in our favor."

Finally, he looked up at her, and the raw despair in his eyes pierced her soul. "But the odds have never been in our favor, Aurora, because we were never meant to exist. Humans were never supposed to fall in love with us. We watched our beloved Nephilim die, knowing our blood in their veins damned them. How could we put the ones we loved through that, life after life? How could we keep going through that, again and again?"

Her throat ached with unshed tears for all that he'd told her. And everything that he hadn't.

And no matter how she tried to ignore it, the insidious certainty that she had known Gabe in another time haunted her.

She was reaching, she knew it. But he'd just told her that, in time, their loved ones would be reborn. If she discounted the possibility that her mind was failing, how else could she explain the flashes of knowledge she'd experienced? The eerie certainty she had once understood the language of the ancients and that once Gabe had wrapped his incomparable wings around her?

Was it possible she was the one he had loved so fiercely, so long ago?

He had irrevocably lost his daughter, but wouldn't he embrace the chance of loving his child's mother, once more?

"But what about you?" She pressed his knuckles against her heart. "Have you never searched for her? For your beloved?"

"No." There was chilling finality in that one word that sent shivers scuttling over her exposed flesh. *Why did I ask him that?* She wasn't ready for the answer. But she couldn't take it back, now. "Eleni—my beloved—wasn't a full-blood human like most of the beloveds. She was part Nephilim—descended from an archangel. Our beloveds were our soul mates, but because of her heritage Eleni didn't possess a soul. If she had, I would have searched for her until the end of time."

Pain crushed her heart, all-encompassing, and fragile hopes and elusive dreams crumbled into dust, as though they had never existed.

Because they had never existed outside of her frighteningly vulnerable mind.

She had never loved Gabe in a previous life. And although he couldn't search for Eleni, he would never stop loving her until the end of time.

And perhaps not even then.

"I know what you're thinking." He stirred restlessly, and panic clawed through her. He couldn't know what she'd been thinking. *Please don't let him have guessed of my stupid hopes.* "Eleni wasn't immortal. She would have died eventually, and there would have been no hope of us ever being together again. I know that. Always knew it. But she was taken before her time."

His fingers tightened around hers, as though willing her to understand. But she did. He didn't have to try and justify his love to her.

"Nephilim, even when their blood is diluted by generations as Eleni's was, still lived longer than pureblood humans. We could have had a thousand years or more together. Not long, not for me, but longer than we had."

She closed her eyes against the bleak expression that clouded his eyes and pressed her lips against his knuckles. This was all he could give her. It wasn't enough, but maybe it was enough to know that once he had been capable of a love she had only ever dreamed could exist.

And maybe it was enough to know that she, too, was capable of such love.

For her beloved, damaged, Archangel of … Mercy.

CHAPTER 28

AURORA

*D*ressed in long black pants, leather boots, and black top, Aurora figured she looked the part for a trip into a pirate's lair. Not that Gabe was any more willing about taking her to the Fornax system than he had been last night, but at least he'd stopped arguing.

They were sitting in the kitchen, facing each other, and he was painstakingly initiating telepathic contact with her.

His touch was delicate and electrifying, nothing like the day they'd met, when his intrusion had been the equivalent of a casual glance.

It was hard to remain perfectly still and relaxed when his mind brushed hers in a sensual caress, as he wove elusive links and connections between them.

Her brain simmered with denied arousal, and she dug her teeth into her lip to keep her focused. Not that he appeared able to read lascivious thoughts, for which she was intensely grateful.

"Am I hurting you?" He ground the words between his teeth, as though he was in physical pain. "I'm going as slow as I can. Your brain is beautiful."

She totally melted. "You say the most wonderful things."

"I don't want to inadvertently damage you. I've no idea how deep inside your brain your protective network penetrates."

Until she'd met Gabe, she'd had no idea she possessed such a thing. Did her mother even know about it? Or was it such a part of her people's biology that it was hardly worth commenting on?

And that reminded her.

"What did my mum say to you when you met her?"

Fierce concentration etched his face. She shouldn't have distracted him. But then he gave a pained grunt and caught her gaze.

"She told me to keep you safe."

Considering the circumstances, she'd been expecting something more profound. "Was that all?"

"No." He sounded reluctant. "She—" He reared back and bit out a curse in that ancient language he favored, and alarm streaked through her.

"What's wrong?" Had he discovered something terrible lurking deep inside her brain?

"Nothing." He withdrew from her mind, and she gave an involuntary sigh. "Just received a message from Zad. Another archangel. He's at the beach and on his way here. Talk about crap timing."

Had Zad turned up to continue what Mephisto had started? From the corner of her eye she saw a figure emerge from the forest, and trepidation snaked through her as she followed Gabe onto the terrace.

He threaded his fingers through hers and pulled her to his side, a blatant gesture of possession. Was he expecting trouble from Zad?

"Zad." Gabe didn't sound overly friendly. "Caught me at a bad time. I'm late for an appointment."

Mesmerized, she gazed at Zad as he came to a halt by the edge of the terrace. His mahogany wings were coated in fine dust and were ragged around the edges. He was dressed casually enough in black jeans and shirt, but understated power radiated from him, as tangible as a living entity.

Why did she find that comforting?

"I was passing," Zad said, his voice deep and melodic, and she still couldn't tear her gaze from his dark eyes. "Thought I'd stop by."

"Like I said." Gabe sounded defensive, although she couldn't think why. "I'm seeing Kala. You know how she is if kept waiting."

Was that the pirate they were scheduled to meet?

"Not personally." Zad shot her another glance. "Don't let me keep you. I'll stay here and entertain your guest."

"No need. Aurora's coming with me."

"You're taking a human to the Fornax Galaxy?" Zad didn't raise his voice, but fury throbbed through each word. Fascinated, she glanced between the two archangels. What was going on? Why did Zad give the impression he was concerned about her welfare when he'd never even met her before?

Equally, why wasn't she irritated by his interference? Especially when she'd fought so hard to accompany Gabe to his meeting.

"She's under my protection." Gabe was obviously irritated enough for them both. "*No one* touches her."

Zad turned to her and held out his right hand, palm up. His gaze meshed with hers and his challenge was blatant.

"Zadkiel," he said.

She placed her left hand on top of Zad's. "Aurora Robinson."

He held her hand longer than was strictly necessary, but there was nothing predatory about it. Even Gabe's death grip on her other hand relaxed.

"I once knew your parents," he said, and she gaped at him, speechless. Before she had time to even process his comment, never mind respond, he took a step back and unfurled his wings. "Look after her, Gabe."

With that, he soared into the sky and she watched, awestruck, until he disappeared over the forest.

She turned to Gabe, who was glowering into the distance.

"What did he mean?" she asked. "How can he know my parents?"

"Beats me. I think your mother thought I was him at first."

"*What?*"

He shrugged, like he didn't care, but she saw the frustration. He really was as clueless as her. "I'll ask him, if you want me to."

"Thank you." She squeezed his hand. "Who *is* he?"

He turned his mesmeric eyes to her. "You know who he is."

Yes, but that wasn't what she meant. She didn't even know why she was so certain there was more, only that there was. "What is the Archangel Zadkiel to *you*?"

For long moments she didn't think he was going to answer. And then he let out a measured breath and focused on their joined hands.

"Zad was the first archangel to fall. Centuries before any other of us did. Zad and his beloved"—Gabe hesitated for a second, and a ghostly finger of presentiment trickled along her spine—"were Eleni's distant ancestors. Eleni was almost the last of Zad's direct bloodline. He adored her."

Gabe

GABE WOUND his arm around Aurora and teleported to Anzu, the largest planet in the Seventh System of Fornax, directly into the outer sanctum of Kala's personal penthouse suite. It wasn't strictly protocol, and only the fact he was an archangel allowed him to bypass the numerous security measures set up to block a multitude of lesser beings from entering the building. The female guard who gave him a piercing once-over was a high-grade half-blood demon and didn't appear impressed by his arrival.

"The Primus is expecting me." He tightened his grip on Aurora's hand and hoped she'd do as he'd asked and keep her mouth shut. Demons weren't the most benevolent of species.

"Wait here." The guard flicked a disinterested glance at Aurora, and her lip curled in clear affront that he'd dared to bring a mere human, uninvited.

That made two of them. He'd had no intention of agreeing to her demands, but then Zad had turned up and he'd committed himself.

As soon as the door shut behind the guard, Aurora let out a ragged breath.

"This is nothing like I was expecting." Her voice was scarcely above a whisper as he completed his third scan of the room since arriving. "I thought the pirates would live in a dodgy dive somewhere."

"Under no circumstances refer to Kala as a pirate." Gods, she'd incinerate Aurora on the spot and only ask questions later. "She's third-generation pureblood demon and doesn't let anyone forget it."

"Oh." For one misguided second, he thought she was going to leave it at that. No such luck. "I don't really understand. What's the connection between the demons and the pirates?"

He swallowed a groan of frustration. He really should have left her at home. But since she was here now, she needed to get a few facts straight.

"When the demons were banished from Earth, many of them ended up in the Fornax Galaxy. Along with a lot of their half-blood descendants—those that survived the initial banishment, that is. But over millennia the chasm between the demons and those they considered unworthy of acknowledging as their descendants widened. Remember I told you they breed indiscriminately? They only claim parentage if the offspring is exceptional. Most of the time demon spawn is left to its own devices."

If demons, like archangels, were able to procreate only with the one they loved, would they also cherish every child? "The crème of the hierarchy spread throughout this Galaxy, conquering worlds populated by primitive mortals. Their abandoned descendants, for the most part, merged in the mortal populations. But a segment carved out lucrative careers in piracy."

"*Oh.*" Her eyes widened in comprehension, but before she could ask another inevitable question, the door to Kala's inner sanctum opened, and the guard beckoned with an autocratic jerk of her head.

Gripping Aurora's hand, he followed the guard inside. Twilight slanted through the glass wall that gave panoramic views over the impressive sky city, bathing the luxuriously appointed room in a surreal glow. Kala, tall, sleek, and demonically beautiful, stood in front of her desk, arms folded, pale gold wings partially extended. She always confronted him that way. Flaunting their haunting beauty, the cream highlights threading through the gold in a perfect inverse of his own long-lost wings.

"Primus Kala." He inclined his head in a gesture of greeting, acknowledging her rank.

"Archangel Gabriel." She glanced at Aurora. "I see the rumors are true. You are ensnared by a human female." Chilly amusement tinged her words. "How quaint that you felt the need to bring it with you."

Gabe refused to rise to the bait, despite the fact Kala had deliberately used the one language in the universe that Aurora could understand. He wanted answers from Kala, and he'd get nothing if he pissed her off.

"I've heard there's a tribe based on Anzu who trade in minors from the Andromeda Galaxy. Heard any of *those* rumors?"

She didn't rise to his bait, either.

"Those who specialize in minors have no need to raid Andromeda. We have plenty of our own ripe for harvesting in the lesser Sectors."

Aurora sucked in a shocked breath and her nails dug into his hand. He tightened his grip, a silent warning. She was under his protection, but they were in Kala's jurisdiction, and if Aurora annoyed the demon it was doubtful Kala would give a shit about protocol.

He hadn't been giving a shit about it either, lately.

"My intel was clear." At least, Eblis had been clear that the pirates from Fornax had been discussing a solar system located in Andromeda. His informant who'd named *this* planet had been virtually incoherent with terror and hadn't categorically stated anything that made much sense.

Fortunately, Kala was unable to penetrate his mind, just as he was unable to penetrate hers.

"Your intel is faulty."

"If the Higher Councils in the Andromeda Galaxy discover the trade, they'll turn Fornax inside out."

"There is no trade, Gabriel." Kala rolled her shoulders and her wings expanded by a fraction. "The dickless wonders who rule Andromeda would stand no chance against Fornax. And they know it."

"Evalyne isn't an ordinary child, though," Aurora said.

Fuck, she just couldn't help herself, could she? Fortunately, Kala took as much notice of her as she would a pet cat stretching.

"If you have any solid evidence, then share it. Otherwise you know what you can do with your *intel*."

He wouldn't give her Eblis' name, but he could tell her about the pirate leader he'd interrogated. It was a long shot that Kala would know of him, but her connections in this Galaxy were legion.

If there was a tribe specializing in such abductions, he needed Kala on side if he had any hope of hunting them down. No matter how much she despised the people of the Andromeda Galaxy, she wouldn't go to war over something in which she had no personal involvement.

Unless the order had come from her direct. He wouldn't put it past her, but his gut feeling was she was as completely in the dark as he was. And beneath that icy exterior she was furious that something of this magnitude might be happening in the Seventh System without her spies having discovered it.

"This child," Aurora said, not even wincing when he gripped her hand tight in warning, "was taken because she has archangelic blood."

Fucking great. She'd now blown to hell any hope of Kala's cooperation. It didn't matter what tenuous suspicions they had. It had been millennia since any mortal had possessed a trace of archangelic blood, and only then on Earth. Kala would conclude he was wasting her time.

If he didn't appease the demon right now, she'd likely liquify Aurora's brain.

"Kala." He didn't get the chance to say anything more. She raised one hand in an imperial gesture, her gaze fixed on Aurora's face.

"The Andromeda minor has *archangelic blood?*"

At least she hadn't thrown them from her domain. "It's one theory we're considering," he said.

"Yes." The conviction in Aurora's voice rang through the room. "She does."

"The Nephilim were obliterated in the Great Cleansing." There was a gleam of malice in Kala's eyes. Most demons considered the genocide of archangelic offspring was something to be celebrated. "They haven't existed for millennia before my time." She paused, and her wings undulated in a sensual play of power. And then she gave a deadly smile. "*Officially.*"

CHAPTER 29

GABE

Officially? Shock ricocheted through him.

"What do you know?" he demanded.

Kala shrugged one shoulder. "Nothing has ever been proved. But there's an underground cult that are obsessed by the notion that Nephilim still survive. Fuck knows why. This cult goes back generations and we've never taken much notice of them. They don't cause us trouble, so we let them wallow in their fantasy world."

Why the fuck hadn't he ever heard of this cult?

"If your minor really does possess archangelic blood and they found out"—Kala paused and exchanged a significant glance with the guard who'd accompanied them—"then it's possible they risked abducting her. And if they have, I'll personally hang them with their own entrails. No filthy pirate tribe goes behind *my* back."

Rage, and a crazy hope that against all the odds Nephilim might have survived the ages, crashed through him. "Not before I've interrogated them. We need the girl back."

Aurora

AFTER KALA GAVE orders for the cult leaders to be rounded up, Aurora stood beside Gabe as an ear-numbing silence descended. It didn't appear to affect either Gabe or the demon, but it screeched along her nerve endings in a never-ending loop.

Kala stood by the windows and regarded the view, although who knew what she was doing in reality? And as for Gabe, he appeared lost in his own world.

Stop fidgeting. Time had a different meaning for immortals. Just because she wasn't used to standing still for hours was no reason to draw attention to the fact.

Especially when Gabe had been so against bringing her here in the first place.

Through the windows the light shifted, and shadows rose in the spectacular sky city. And finally, after what seemed like eternity, the guard reentered the room.

"Primus. The accused have been located." Oddly, she spoke in English, just as Kala had. It appeared the demon wanted Aurora to understand exactly what was going on.

Kala gave Gabe a laser sharp glance. "My jurisdiction, Gabriel. Don't interfere."

She then gave a brief nod to the guard, who handed Gabe what looked like a glittering earpiece.

"For your pet," the guard said with a hint of derision.

Gabe's jaw tightened, but he didn't say anything as he took the earpiece before handing it to her.

"It's a translator."

Awed, she held it between finger and thumb before carefully inserting it into her ear. She had the surreal sensation of delicate tendrils connecting inside her head. If this worked, imagine the difference it could make to the people on Earth.

She highly doubted the demons would ever willingly share their technology, though.

"Bring them in," Kala told the guard.

Ten warriors, male and female, marched in, herding a motley group of six, and arranged themselves between the prisoners and the doors.

Kala strolled towards the one who appeared to be the leader. He sank to his knees and the others followed. Without a word, she kicked him in the face, and blood spurted from his shattered nose.

Aurora sucked in a shocked breath and glanced at Gabe. He appeared unmoved by the demon's methods of interrogation and she swallowed, unnerved.

I'm not on Earth, anymore. As Kala had reminded Gabe, this was her jurisdiction.

"Found any Nephilim lately?" Kala tapped her bloodied boot on the floor.

The man babbled in an unintelligible language and Aurora tapped her earpiece. Wasn't it working?

Kala kicked him again, and Aurora heard the sickening crunch as his cheekbone splintered, and her stomach churned. Somehow, she'd imagined such a technologically advanced race wouldn't need to resort to this kind of torture to gain information.

"Don't address me in your barbaric lexicon."

The man spat blood onto the floor and Aurora glanced away. Clearly, demons didn't believe in being innocent until proven guilty. And if he'd really kidnapped a small child, then he deserved everything Kala dished out.

She just didn't want to witness it.

Hypocrite, much?

"Nuh-nuh Nephilim," the male spluttered between broken teeth and bone. "Leh-legend." The words were muffled but perfectly understandable, even though she'd never before heard the language.

Kala strolled to the next quivering pirate and gripped the

female's hair, lifting her almost off her knees in the process.

"We can do this the easy way," she said, sounding deceptively friendly. "Or I can hand you over to the archangel. If he gets inside your mind there won't be anything left to salvage afterwards."

All the prisoners turned toward Gabe and terror gleamed in their eyes. A shudder inched along her spine. What kind of reputation did an archangel have to cause such a reaction?

"My Lady Primus," gasped the captured female. "It's our life's work to seek out those descended from the cursed Usurpers of our forebears. To ensure justice for the wrongs against our ancestors. To stand up for—"

"If I wanted your manifesto, I'd read your fucking literature." Kala pulled a glinting stiletto from her ankle boot and casually drew the tip across the prisoner's exposed throat. A line of crimson appeared.

Involuntarily, Aurora gripped Gabe's hand and he squeezed her fingers, probably to reassure her that she was safe. But that wasn't her main concern right now. Why couldn't he just slip into their minds and find out what information they had?

Because it's not his jurisdiction.

The prisoner slapped her hand across her throat, eyes bulging with fear, and blood seeped between her fingers. Kala wiped her blade on the woman's worn leather tunic.

"Where's the Andromeda minor?" She released the woman's hair and examined the tip of her stiletto.

"We don't have her, Lady Primus." A third pirate shuffled forward on his knees and held onto the bleeding female. "For seven generations our lineages have searched for a Nephilim descendant. But it was never our intention to keep the creature. We searched by order of another."

"Another?" Kala's blade came within an inch of the male's left eye. "Explain."

He shuddered but didn't back off. "The Guardians."

Gabe, still gripping her hand, was by Kala's side before Aurora had time to take a horrified breath.

"You gave a child of archangelic descend to the Guardians?" Incandescent fury burned each word. "You fucking piece of—"

Kala held up her hand. Incredibly, Gabe shut up. Aurora unclenched her free hand, her chest tight, and it hurt to breathe. How could anyone hand over a child to those terrifying creatures?

"Let me get this straight." Kala sounded perfectly reasonable, but her eyes glowed crimson. "For seven generations your cult has been spewing the word of retribution for our demonic Fall from Grace. Right?" She didn't wait for an answer. "But all the time it was a cover while you searched on behalf of the Guardians?"

"No. We've always believed in our Word. But the blood search, yes, Lady Primus. That was for the Guardians."

Kala turned to Gabe.

"They're yours," she said. "Destroy them now or take them back to Andromeda. I'll issue a hunt. Not one of their followers will remain alive in any of my Sectors. You have my word. Ensure it's conveyed to the Andromeda Higher Councils."

Gabe released her hand. He didn't say a word, but the male who had just spoken collapsed onto his back, writhing in agony and clutching his head. Foam bubbled from between his clenched teeth, and blood trickled from his eyes and ears.

She backed off, arms wrapped around her stomach. The other prisoners appeared frozen, the warriors watched with avid interest, and Kala appeared utterly unmoved by proceedings.

And she'd thought his methods of extracting information would be less brutal than Kala's? More civilized?

He's not human. He was an archangel, and he was seeking vengeance for the abduction of one of his own.

She couldn't watch and turned away. Didn't these pirates

deserve all this and more for taking a small, frightened child and handing her over to those monsters?

"I'll contact the premier of Andromeda," Gabe said, his voice grim. "Can you keep these prisoners secure in the interim?"

"If I must." Kala didn't sound thrilled by the prospect. "There's not a lot left of their brains for the Higher Councils to interrogate."

"There's enough. I made sure of that."

Aurora released a ragged breath. His methods were ruthless but hadn't killed them.

A flash of violet split the room in half. She stumbled back as the jagged scar wrenched open and a familiar silvery arm slid through, enlarging the gap.

Her lungs forgot how to work, and her throat closed in terror as its body appeared, its arm extended. Waves of unadulterated loathing smashed into her, and she staggered at the physical impact.

And then the creature began to retreat.

Instinctively, she darted forward, but there was no mistake. The creature recoiled, spitting mental venom, its language a horrific screech across her psyche.

Adrenaline pumped through her, banishing the last remnants of terror. Something had changed. The Guardians could no longer touch her.

"No." Gabe's roar thundered around the room, and he gripped her arm and pulled her back. She had less than a second before he teleported her to safety and she tugged free, panting as if she'd just run the four-minute mile in full combat gear.

"They backed off." She chanced a glance over her shoulder. The rift had vanished. "They could have got me, Gabe, but it's like they changed their minds at the last moment."

"The Guardians are prohibited in my domain." Kala sounded infuriated by the breach. "That wasn't a random probe. They're searching for your pet, Gabriel."

"What do you mean, they backed off?" Gabe glared at her. "They never back off."

"Yet they did." Kala's wings shimmered in outrage. "The question is, why?"

CHAPTER 30

AURORA

"I don't know." Aurora glanced at the prisoners sprawled on the floor. None of them were moving. "They reached for me, and then they just … stopped."

"I'm taking you home."

And she knew that once he got her there, he'd never allow her to leave the island again.

She backed up another step.

"No. Wait. Don't you see what this means? Your protection is working far more than you thought it would." He'd told her she had negated his protection by breaching dimensions. And although it hadn't been enough to hold back the Guardians on Eta Hyperium, clearly that wasn't the case anymore. She had no idea why the dynamics had shifted, but more to the point it appeared Gabe didn't, either. "It means I can come with you to help rescue Evalyne."

"Is this really a human?" Kala sounded fascinated. "It behaves like a fucking goddess. I've seen the aura of archangels' pets before, but they've never looked like *this* one's."

"You're not going anywhere near the Guardians' Voids," Gabe said, ignoring Kala's remarks. "It's too late for Evalyne."

Ice slithered through her heart. What had he discovered from raiding the pirates' minds?

"They killed her before handing her over?"

"No, they delivered her three months ago."

Three months. She couldn't even begin to imagine what Evalyne had gone through, but why was he so sure they were too late to rescue her?

"But you can't know for sure she's dead."

"A *human* is questioning the word of the Archangel Gabriel and is still in possession of all its faculties? What's going on?"

Gabe shot a toxic glance at Kala but didn't respond to her question.

"The Voids where the Guardians live are devastating to archangels. If Evalyne truly possesses our blood, then she died weeks ago."

She must have misunderstood him. "You don't mean you'd die if you tried to rescue Evalyne? How is that possible?"

He gripped her hand and pulled her close. "Through an agonizing process of disintegration until there's nothing left." He turned to Kala, who looked intrigued by that revelation. "I'll be in contact when I've spoken to the Premier of Andromeda. Let me know when you've exterminated the cell responsible."

And then he teleported them back to his island.

Gabe

GABE HELD onto Aurora after they arrived home, and the way she kept her arms around him with her head against his shoulder was a balm for his outrage against the pirates. But it wasn't enough to calm the frantic thunder in his mind or the ugly fear that gripped his heart.

The Guardians had come for her again. And because he had

been intent on extracting every last fragment of information from the guilty, he hadn't been aware.

Ice shivered through his veins, and one terrifying truth pounded through his brain.

I nearly lost her.

And he would have, if the Guardians hadn't retreated voluntarily.

Yet bound inextricably with the dread was a soul-destroying revelation and it didn't matter how fiercely he tried to deny it.

If she died because of his negligence, the fabric of his existence would unravel. But it wasn't just guilt at having failed to protect her that corroded his soul. It was the horrifying prospect of *losing her* that clawed through his heart.

He didn't need to examine her aura in order to see what had baffled Kala. He knew why the Guardians could no longer touch Aurora.

Kala had seen the glowing halo of love and devotion in Aurora's aura. Something the demon would have never encountered before. Since the beginning, archangels had taken mortals as lovers and given them their protection, but not for millennia before Kala's birth had an archangel ...

Fallen.

The only way Aurora could be safe from the Guardians' clutches outside his island was if she was an Immortal's beloved.

Eleni is my beloved.

There was no decree written in blood, but he'd always believed archangels could have only one beloved. Wasn't that the way it should be?

Archangels didn't fall lightly.

But against all the odds he had fallen again. For Aurora. And by doing so, he had given her the ultimate protection.

His love.

Despite Zad's assurance that by loving Aurora he didn't betray Eleni, guilt scorched through him. He should have seen this coming, should have prevented it. Although how could the inevitable be prevented?

He had told her things he'd never shared with another living being. Because, at primal level, he'd recognized she was his equal. And always had been.

But he couldn't tell her. Not yet. Telling her would force him to face the knowledge she was mortal and he an archangel, and unlike his Eleni, Aurora didn't even have the advantage of archangelic blood to extend her fleeting, fragile, existence.

Vertigo slammed through him, vicious and raw. This was why he'd denied it. Why he hadn't wanted to acknowledge it.

Because Aurora would die, and he would once again have to endure.

Except things had changed.

She possesses a soul.

She could be reborn. And he would search for her, life after life, eternal.

But he still didn't want her to die.

Aurora stirred, and with deep reluctance he loosened his grip on her. She eased back just far enough so she could look at him, and her eyes enslaved, just as they had enslaved him from the first moment he'd seen her.

"How do you know about the Voids, Gabe?" Her voice was soft, as if she knew this was something he'd never spoken of before.

Yet he'd told her so much of his life. As his beloved, she had the right to know everything.

Even if she didn't know who she truly was. Or what she meant to him.

She was the reason for his existence.

But even now, with her, he didn't want to talk about it. Yet knew he must.

"After Eleni and ..." *Helena.* He should tell her about Helena, but her name lodged in his throat. They would talk of his daughter another time. "After she and the others perished, I lost my mind. Rampaged through the universe. Finally ended up on an obscure planet in the Fornax Galaxy just so I could plague the hell out of an obnoxious demon called Eblis."

"Eblis? I thought you were friends."

He guessed they were, even if officially they remained enemies.

"I won't bore you with the details of our decades-long feud. But during this time, he was involved with a mortal who had a small daughter. Eblis was besotted with the kid. Anyone would think she was his own. Except demons aren't known for their great parenting skills."

"What happened?" Trepidation filled her eyes.

"The Guardians abducted her. It was random. They had no idea a first-generation demon watched over her, and even if they did, it would have made no difference. Eblis hadn't given her his formal protection, so in their eyes she was fair game."

"The protocols apply to both archangel *and* demon?"

"Yes. Much as we would all like to deny it, the fact is there isn't much difference between us. Except for archangels, every Nephilim birth was a rare and precious gift. Whereas demons rarely fell in love and the males usually had no idea how many offspring they'd spawned."

"Did Eblis try and get her back?"

"He wasn't there. But I was. Stoned out of my skull as usual. This little kid—I liked her. Seeing her dragged into their world turned my guts. I could barely see straight, but I plunged through that violet split in reality with only one thought in my mangled head."

"To save her," Aurora whispered.

He threaded his fingers through hers. So much of what had happened during those early centuries after he'd failed Eleni and Helena was a drug-and-alcohol-induced blur. But he remembered leaping into the Voids. He'd never forget the time he'd spent in that hell.

"I fought the Guardians for her. Not something I'd recommend. But they finally relinquished their grip and I tossed her through the rapidly shrinking rift. Right into Eblis' arms. Then the rift closed, and I was catapulted into the center of their cursed Voids."

"Christ, Gabe." Horror burned through each word. "You were trapped in there with them? What did they do to you?"

He knew what she was thinking. She was wrong.

"Nothing. They can't touch us, remember? Protocol. They wanted me out. I was polluting their domain, but here's the thing. I refused to leave."

"But what—I thought—"

"Within seconds of entering the Voids my skin started smoldering. But that's nothing to what that place did to my wings. It was like acid seeping into the root of each feather, corroding it from the inside. Agony like nothing I'd ever imagined. And I embraced it."

Her fingers tightened around his. Did she know that just by being here, listening to him, was giving him more comfort than he'd known in millennia?

"With Eblis' help, Zad, Mephisto, and another archangel, Az, finally tracked me down. It's not easy breaking into the Guardians' realm. By the time they found me I was half mad with the pain but still refused to leave. They didn't give up. They've always been stubborn bastards."

"But you recovered." He heard the anguish in her voice. He pressed her hand against his heart and offered her a tired smile.

"Despite how hard my DNA worked on repairing the damage while I was in the Voids, by the time they pulled me out I was a mess. I'd gone beyond anything our archangelic powers of regeneration could handle. In the end, they took me to the astral planes. The ultimate realm of healing and renewal."

"It was the astral planes that healed you." Awe threaded her voice.

"Nothing else had worked. It took decades. My soul in the astral planes, and my physical body here, on this island, absorbing the vibrations through the spiritual connection. Eventually, I healed enough to return to my body, but there'd been an unexpected side effect."

Understanding dawned in her beautiful blue eyes.

"The island's protective shield."

"I was like a nuclear reactor in meltdown. We didn't figure it out until later, but when I returned to my body, the essence of the astral planes couldn't be contained in a physical form. It flooded into the atmosphere, encasing this island. The Guardians can't ascend into the astral planes, and that's why they can't gain access to this island. But equally, it acts as an effective barrier against anyone wanting to ascend into that realm from here." He sighed heavily. "I'm responsible for the force field, but I can't manipulate it. It just is."

Tenderly, she cradled his jaw. Such a light touch, yet he could feel it deep in the heart of his being.

"But your wings ... were beyond repair?"

His wings. Ancient sorrow surfaced, but it was no longer all-consuming.

"They were destroyed long before I was dragged from the Voids. There was nothing left to salvage. When I finally regained my senses, I was bitterly glad they'd gone. They were the one thing our goddess loved above all else about us. Our glorious wings. Her own unique creation."

He rolled his shoulders and felt the phantom tug of long-destroyed muscle and feathers. Yet still the ache did not consume.

"That's how we discovered the Voids aren't archangel friendly."

Her thumb caressed the corner of his mouth, and all he wanted to do was lose himself inside her once again. To try and scrub his soul of the knowledge that he had failed to save a child who was, perhaps, the last Nephilim child in the universe.

"You didn't know before?" Aurora's whisper curled through his jagged thoughts, pulling him back to reality.

"Why would we? We knew of the Guardians, but not through personal experience. And we were protected as the Alphas were protected. Not because we were beloved, but because our DNA was pure first-generation Immortal."

"And now I'm protected through you." She sounded as if she was thinking aloud. "If there was some way to pinpoint where Evalyne's being held … I have an idea. It might work."

"No." His voice was harsh. "Dark Matter doesn't behave in the same way as the rest of the universe. It's not easy entering those vast sectors of space, and even if I did manage it, I'd still have to break into the Guardians' Voids. The chances of finding Evalyne in that endless labyrinth are virtually nonexistent. The only way Zad and the others found me was because the Guardians were so desperate to get rid of me they laid an energy trail. Even then it took years. Evalyne, if she's still alive, doesn't have that kind of time on her side."

"I wasn't suggesting you teleport in and grab her." Oddly, she sounded offended. "I know you can't enter the Voids again."

Then what *was* she suggesting? Because there was no fucking way he'd allow *her* to go into that hell.

"There's no way of discovering where she is. And even if by some miracle we did, teleportation doesn't work in the Voids. Their physics are completely alien to ours."

"I'm not even talking about teleporting, Gabe."

He knew she wasn't, but if one of them had to enter the Voids, it damn well wouldn't be her. Why did she have to be so stubborn? Why could she never accept his word?

Yet if she was any different, she would not have captured what remained of his heart.

"Please, just listen to me." She threaded her fingers through his, and he knew he'd give her anything she asked of him. Except he wouldn't risk her life on a hopeless quest.

"When I tried reaching my mother's dimension, I was in the exact place where she'd entered our world. I had the flower she'd worn on that day, and I focused on that flower *and* the meadow of flowers she used to talk about from her world. I was attempting to psychically connect our two worlds together."

He did understand. Could it be possible to locate Evalyne in a similar way? But even as hope flared, reality crashed through.

"That's different. I assume you succeeded because your DNA is of two dimensions. There was a prior connection, even if you'd never been there before. It's not that easy to cross into a parallel universe."

"But Evalyne isn't in another universe. The connection would be between two points in *this* dimension."

If she could locate the exact position of the child, there had to be a way he could rescue her. *Am I seriously considering this crazy idea?*

"There's no guarantee you could make a connection within the Dark Matter, never mind penetrate the Voids."

"We *have* to try." Her voice was fierce, and her eyes glittered with determination. "We'll never forgive ourselves if we don't."

Pride surged through him at how she didn't flinch from danger.

She was right.

"We need to find something of Evalyne's for you to focus on."

"Yes." She sounded startled, as though she hadn't expected him to realize that.

"We'll look through the chest of her belongings her father gave me."

"I don't think there's anything in that chest that will give me the connection I need." She sounded nervous.

"In that case, we'll visit Jaylar again. See if you connect to something in his home."

"That's not what I mean." She cleared her throat. What was she finding so hard to say? "I need something unique and precious. With my mum, I had the flower that only grows in her dimension. With Evalyne, it's her necklace."

"Her necklace," he echoed. She couldn't know of Helena's, so what was she talking about?

"Please believe me." Guilt dripped from every word. "I'd use mine if I thought it'd work, but we both know it's only a cheap fake."

She does mean Helena's necklace.

But he'd never told her of his daughter. How did she know?

"I'm sorry." Her whisper drifted through his mind, strangely disconnected. "I discovered the picture of you with your family the day I arrived. I saw your daughter wearing her necklace."

Aurora

AURORA HELD her breath as Gabe finally focused on her. She'd never intended letting him know that she'd looked through his things. That she had discovered he'd once had a beloved daughter.

But to have any chance of rescuing Evalyne, they needed that artifact. It was a link across time and the cosmos between two beloved Nephilim.

"She was four years old." The words were bleak, torn from his soul, and pain squeezed her heart. She had been little more than a baby. "We never expected we'd have a child. Nephilim could conceive with mortals, but not easily. What were our chances, Nephilim and archangel, when we were both cursed by the same vindictive goddess? But finally, we held our baby in our arms. *And I couldn't save her.*"

"Because your goddess betrayed you. It's never been your fault."

"I was sworn to protect them." Had he even heard her? Would he ever hear her, when it came to trying to assuage the guilt that corroded him? "I would've torn the universe apart to keep them from danger. They were my beloveds, Aurora. I'd have laid down my immortality for them, but instead …" He gritted his teeth and his eyes glittered like raindrops through a fractured rainbow. "They died and I survived."

A tiny piece of her heart withered. He would never forgive himself, no matter what she said. The necklace was too precious to him. He'd never allow her to use it for something that she couldn't even prove would make a difference.

"Evalyne is four years old." His voice was hushed. Her heart broke a little more.

"Yes." She'd find something else to use. There had to be something that called to her in that chest. Something she could get a psychic grip on. Even if, deep inside, she feared nothing else could work.

"The one I gave Eleni was lost with her," Gabe said, and she caught her breath at his unexpected confidence. "Before I left Earth, that last time I saw them, Helena gave hers to me. So I wouldn't forget her." His smile was sad and so full of love it hurt to look at him. "Her necklace was the one Zad had once given to his beloved, centuries before Helena's birth. It had passed down through the generations to Eleni, and she gave it to our daughter on the day she was born."

Her throat ached with tears she could never allow to fall. She hurt for his loss, but she could never seek comfort from him. Not for this, when he had suffered so greatly already. He was an immortal, but right now she was the one who needed to be strong.

He brushed his lips across her clenched knuckles. "I'll get the necklace."

CHAPTER 31

AURORA

They teleported to Kala's planet and into the underground headquarters of the pirate cell that had abducted Evalyne. The information Gabe had extracted had led them to the exact place where the Guardians had come to collect the child.

The place was wrecked, and Kala's warriors looked pissed at having to cut short their plans of total destruction. But finally, she and Gabe were alone, and with infinite tenderness he removed her necklace and placed his treasured one around her neck.

Awe whispered through her as she curled her fingers around the ancient pendant. Its shape was familiar, but an ethereal vibration emanated, as if it possessed a fragile heartbeat of its own. Her breath caught in her throat, and instinctively her fingers tightened as a surreal glow of tranquility enveloped her.

It was as though she had discovered a long-lost piece of her soul.

"Do you want me to come with you into the astral planes?" Gabe's husky whisper pulled her back to the present. He stood behind her, his arms wrapped around her, and she leaned her head against his shoulder.

She should be able to make the connection without ascending into trance. But the astral planes had been her special place for so long, and this wasn't the time to take chances.

"No." Once she made the connection and located Evalyne, Gabe would reach through the physical gateway she created and rescue the child.

The echoes of chaos that had disturbed the astral planes the last time she'd been there had dissolved. She concentrated on the precious archangelic necklace Gabe had entrusted to her, the token of devotion from an immortal to his beloved. And simultaneously focused on the image of Evalyne in her mind, anchoring her with an identical archangelic wing necklace.

Energy, raw and primal, throbbed from the necklace that she cradled in the palm of her hand. A blazing trail of starlight shot from the necklace and collided with an identical glowing trail that emanated from a place beyond her comprehension.

From Evalyne's own necklace.

It happened so fast. She had barely done anything at all. It was as though whatever magic contained within Evalyne's necklace had been transmitting a celestial SOS.

Waiting for a lightning rod.

Her.

A shimmering darkness unfolded on the physical plane. Something alien and icy that didn't belong in the world she knew. It hung there, hovering above the ground, a rupture in reality. And beyond lay only desolation.

Her mind reeled against the unimaginable vastness that threatened to seep into her psyche and steal her soul. *Concentrate.* She couldn't afford to let terror wrap her in its relentless embrace.

Gabe loosened his hold on her, waiting for the moment her psychic energies connected with Evalyne.

Inky shadows thickened in the darkness and the hideous sensation of nothingness receded. Distortion took on form, and a dull violet illumination emanated from slick rocks glistening in a stark chamber.

And there, in the center, was the child.

Evalyne floated, bound by ethereal smoky restraints.

Wild relief slammed through her chest. They weren't too late. Evalyne was still alive.

Please let her still be alive.

Gabe plunged into the Voids, and Aurora gripped their psychic connection with such fierce concentration her mind trembled on a precipice of self-destruction. Through the veil of the spiritual realm she watched him stagger toward the child.

The Voids rippled like restless water, and Gabe's steps grew slower. Muscles strained and an agonized expression tore across his face as his skin smoldered.

What was happening? Her connection had been tight. He should have passed straight through from their world directly to Evalyne.

Panic twisted through her. He'd assured he would be fine for the few moments it would take to rescue Evalyne. But he was wrong. What did he really know about the Voids? He'd already admitted the physics was a mystery to him.

He wasn't fine. *He isn't going to make it.*

Agonizing seconds stretched into infinity as Gabe wrestled with the diaphanous restraints that appeared to not only hold Evalyne in place but also sank into her arms.

When he tore the last deceptively fragile bonds from Evalyne, he turned and stumbled back toward the fracture Aurora had created. But he was only halfway to freedom when he fell to his knees, his agonized groan flaying her heart. And then he catapulted Evalyne through the rift before falling onto his hands.

God, no. She tumbled back into her body. Disoriented, she lurched toward the rift. Violet, gaseous tendrils snaked through the gap and curled around her, chilling her blood. She battled against the primeval warning that screamed through every molecule to retreat, to escape while she still could, and gritting her teeth, she stepped into the deadly Voids.

Unexpected, acidic heat seared her lungs and the air was thin, but she could still move. She grabbed Gabe's arm with both hands and pulled.

"Move!" she screamed.

"Get out of here." His voice rasped in her head.

"Not without you."

Shadowy creatures swarmed in her peripheral vision, their hideous psychic hisses shredding her brain.

I'm still wearing the demonic earpiece. She could understand them. And their hate-filled venom wasn't directed at her. It was directed at Gabe.

He bared his teeth, gripped her wrist, and shoved her forward. The fracture was shrinking, and the more she tried to focus on it, the further away it seemed. She gasped frantically for elusive oxygen as dizziness whirled through her.

I'm not going to fail.

Gabe grabbed her hand, and together they fell through the rift. The jagged edge slashed her flesh and blood trickled down her arms, but they were out. And the fracture sealed shut with a vindictive screech and vanished.

"What the hell were you doing?" Gabe panted, propping himself up on one hand as he gently brushed Evalyne's tangled hair from her face. "You were meant to stay out of the Voids. Can't you ever do as you're told?"

She watched Evalyne's face and saw the child's eyes flicker. Relief spun through her. Despite being in the Voids for months, it seemed her archangelic heritage was diluted enough to save her from the devastating injuries Gabe had suffered. The little girl was going to be all right.

"You fell down," she whispered, turning to look at him. Her

heart squeezed at his scorched flesh, but at least he didn't seem about to collapse. "I thought you needed some help."

He pushed himself back onto his knees and gripped her shoulders.

"You were helping. Until you jumped through and scared the shit out of me."

"I'm sorry. I was just afraid of losing you. I didn't want you to be trapped in there again, that's all."

Except they'd both almost been trapped inside the Voids because she'd abandoned her post. What would they have done then?

Kala would have ensured Evalyne was returned to her parents, but there wasn't any way she could've saved them, lost deep within the Guardians' domain.

Even if she'd wanted to.

"Gods, Aurora." He pulled her into his arms and buried his face in her hair. "Just promise me you'll never do anything like that again. Don't ever put yourself in danger for my sake. Do you hear me? I'm an archangel. I can take care of myself."

She sniffled into his neck. *Don't cry.* She'd wait until Evalyne was safely reunited with her parents before she indulged and fell into relief-induced shock.

He let out a pained breath, and then lifted Evalyne in his arms.

"Hold on," he said, looking at Aurora. And then he teleported.

Gabe

"MY LORD GABRIEL." Jaylar sank to his knees in the luxurious room where they'd met previously and kissed Gabe's feet. It was a custom of homage, and he'd never thought twice of it before.

But he thought of it now. Because it was wrong, so wrong, for Jaylar to show such subservience to anyone.

Even an archangel.

He glanced at Evalyne, who was wrapped in her mother's arms. The last shred of doubt as to the child's heritage had died in the Voids, when the Guardians hadn't tried to reclaim her. Gods and goddesses might not acknowledge their half-blood descendants or care what happened to them. But no archangel would turn their back on a Nephilim, no matter how diluted their heritage.

And now the Guardians knew that, too.

"Thank you." Tears glittered in Jaylar's eyes. "My soul is yours, my Lord." Again, he bowed his head. Waiting to pay the price.

Jaylar had no idea he was descended from an archangel. Had no idea he didn't possess a soul. Not that Gabe would have taken his soul in any case.

But he couldn't wipe the minds of this small family. He had no rights over Jaylar.

Except to love and protect him and his daughter—as Nephilim.

Who is their archangelic ancestor?

Only one thing was certain. The archangel in question had no idea.

He drew back, dragging Aurora with him.

"Stand up." His voice was hoarse. Evalyne's mother flinched, clearly expecting dire recompense now the mission was completed.

Jaylar stood and looked him fearlessly in the eye. He would give whatever Gabe demanded because he would do anything to save his daughter.

As it should be.

"She was taken by the Guardians." He waited and saw dread comprehension dawn in Jaylar's eyes. "They wanted her for her diluted archangel blood." He recalled the other victim Aurora had discovered. The one who been wearing an archangelic wing necklace.

How many other Nephilim were scattered throughout the

universe? While archangels had blindly believed all their beloved children had perished in the Great Cleansing and its immediate aftermath, the Guardians had discovered differently.

And were hunting them.

Guardians abducted mortals so they could feed on their terrors. Did an archangelic heritage give an added edge? Or was there another reason?

Jaylar gripped Gabe's arm, as an equal might.

They had always been equals.

"They'll return for her, is that what you're saying? How can we protect her, my Lord? What must we do?"

He doubted they'd be back for her. But in the distant future they might well return for one of Evalyne's descendants, unless the protocols were once again resurrected. "We'll let you know what you must do to ensure continued immunity from them."

"Archangel blood?" Evalyne's mother said, looking at Jaylar. "You're descended from the *archangels?*"

The fact that Evalyne had a drop of immortal blood in her veins should have been protection enough against the Guardians in the first place. But, just as the ritual to affect an archangel's protection over a mortal required the spilling of blood, a similar ritual was needed before the descendants of immune immortals were also granted the same invulnerability.

The gods, like the demons, had never experienced any problems with procreating, and only acknowledged their offspring when it pleased them to do so. If Jaylar's demigoddess ancestor hadn't bestowed the protection on her own child, or told anyone else on Medana of it, then the knowledge hadn't been lost.

It had never been shared in the first place.

Mephisto needed to be informed and the archangel responsible for Jaylar and Evalyne's protection found. But right now, he needed to heal Aurora's injuries.

"My payment is this." Instantly, their attention returned to him. "Keep your child safe. She is more precious than either of you can imagine."

With that, he teleported home.

Back in his kitchen, he healed the bloodied gashes on her arms. His blood ran cold at the memory of her leaping into the Voids.

To save him.

"How's that feel?" He looked up at her, and her blue gaze caught his.

"Amazing." But she didn't check her arms. "Thanks."

"It's the least I can do, when you insist on putting yourself in danger for me." He attempted a sardonic smile. He wasn't sure he succeeded.

Because one thing kept pounding through his head. She was his beloved, and therefore she was immune from the Guardians' wrath. There was no need for her to remain on his island anymore.

"I can't help myself." Her smile seemed kind of sad, too. Then she gingerly removed the earpiece and placed it on the table. "This is impressive. I don't suppose I'd be allowed to examine it and find out how it works?"

"Not unless you want the Demonic Council on your case. And trust me. You don't."

She sighed. "That's a shame. It would make an incredible subject for my doctorate."

"Or your government would lock you up."

"Good point. Humans probably aren't ready for demon technology in their lives."

He threaded his fingers through hers, and silence wrapped around them, a deceptive cocoon of warmth and familiarity. She had been in his life for such a short time, yet he couldn't imagine an existence without her.

But he couldn't keep her here, isolated on his island. *I have to let her go.*

Phantom claws scraped through his chest, an insignificant precursor of the rank emptiness that crouched on his horizon. A future without Aurora.

She cleared her throat. She only did that when she was nervous. Was she going to ask him to take her home? It was all she'd wanted, from the moment he'd brought her here.

But far from keeping her safe as he'd promised, he'd exposed her to the wrath of Mephisto, the continued evil of the Guardians, and taken her into the heart of demon territory.

No wonder she wanted to get back to her normal life as soon as she could.

"Have you always lived here on this island? Since, uh, discovering Earth, I mean?"

And yet again, she said the last thing he had expected. A small reprieve from the inevitable, but he'd take it.

"This island didn't even exist back then. I found it a couple of decades before I became the uninvited guest of the Guardians. That's why the others brought me here afterwards."

"I thought maybe you'd always lived here. The villa ..." Her voice trailed off, and she focused on their entwined fingers as a faint blush heated her cheeks.

He understood.

"The picture you found." In a twisted way, he was happy she'd found it. That she knew of the life he had once had. "That was where I lived with Eleni and Helena. I built a replica here after I recovered from the Voids. I told you once I never brought women here. It was the truth. You're the first."

And you'll be the last.

She blinked, but her eyes glittered with what looked suspiciously like tears.

"Did I ever thank you for rescuing me from the Guardians?" Her voice was husky, and it took every shred of self-control he possessed not to pull her into his arms and bury his face in her hair.

If he did, he'd never let her go. And while she couldn't leave his island unless he allowed it, what good was it if she remained here against her will?

"Yeah." He sounded tired. Defeated. And he didn't even care if she heard it. "Did I ever tell you that you're welcome?"

She smiled, but her bottom lip trembled, and she didn't say anything.

She didn't have to.

Do I have to hurt you? Her teasing words floated in his mind.

I'd like to see you try. He'd been so sure she never could.

Be careful what you wish for.

He'd feared the time when Aurora would grow old and die, and he would be left behind. But that had been a fool's dream, because he didn't even have those few blissful years ahead.

I'm not fucking ready to say goodbye.

He never would be.

She wanted him. She desired him.

But it wasn't enough.

She was his beloved, and he would give her anything that was within his power to make her happy. And she wanted her freedom.

Something cracked deep inside his chest. His heart, maybe. He'd always thought he no longer possessed a heart, but Aurora had proved him wrong.

She'd proved him wrong about so many things. Gods, how could he let her go?

How could he not?

How the hell am I going to survive?

"Oh." There was a choked note in her voice as she tugged her fingers free from his and unclasped the necklace from around her neck. "This is yours." She dropped it onto his hand. Eternal silence spun between them, and he couldn't break it. Because the inevitable was so very near. Finally, she let out a ragged sigh. "What happens now?"

Now, it ends.

"I'll take you home."

She swallowed. "Yes. Thanks." She stood and wrapped her arms around her waist, and it killed him not to take back his promise. To tell her she wasn't going anywhere if he wasn't by her side. "I'll collect my things."

After she left the room, he followed her upstairs, but she had gone into the bathroom. He pulled her necklace from the pocket of his shirt, and then transferred his gaze to the one Eleni had given to their daughter, so many centuries ago.

He loved Eleni. Would always love her. But now he also loved Aurora. And his love for Aurora didn't diminish his devotion for Eleni. The one love enhanced the other, as if they were entwined.

Tenderly, he kissed the ancient archangel wings before tucking it into Aurora's bag. He hadn't created this necklace, but in the end it was merely a symbol for the unending love of an archangel. Maybe when she discovered what he'd given her she'd understand how he felt.

Understand why he'd let her go.

She came into the bedroom and he dropped her necklace back into his pocket. Against his heart.

It was a poor substitute for her love, but it was the only piece of her he could keep with him for all time.

CHAPTER 32

AURORA

It had been twenty-four hours since Gabe had brought her home. His last kiss before he'd disappeared would haunt her forever.

She should have told him she loved him. But what good would that have done? He had never asked for her love. All that confession would do would make him feel guilty for being unable to return it.

A clean break was better for her heart. How could a human and an archangel ever have anything together? She'd cherish their memories, and not fall apart over their inevitable goodbye.

He'd shown her a hidden side of the world to the one that she'd always known. And while there might not be another trans-dimensional child in the universe, at least she no longer felt as isolated.

But my heart will never recover.

Curled up on her bed, she clutched her pillow tighter. She'd always love him. There was nothing she could do about that. But she still had to get on with her life, even if her driving force—to discover who she was and where she came from—had smashed into an impenetrable blockade.

I know who I am.

A shiver rippled through her. She had always known who she was. Just because she could never visit her mother's world didn't mean all her research and years of study had been in vain.

Gabe had told her the humans he had once loved *had* left evidence of their magnificent civilization. Beneath the surface of all the great archaeological sites on Earth, was there another, secret, world waiting to be rediscovered?

She sat up, still hugging the pillow, as ideas swirled in her mind. She'd switch her focus to biomolecular archaeology, and even if it took the rest of her life, she'd hunt down and find that ancient DNA that would prove the great civilization, where Gabe and Eleni had found love, had once existed.

It was the least she could do, as a lasting testament for the man who had broken ancient covenants to save her life.

AN HOUR later she was sifting through research on her laptop. It was so strange how quickly she'd become used to Gabe's technology. Navigating the web, something she'd done her whole life, seemed so limiting, now.

"Aurora." Her mum's voice floated up the stairs. "Can you come down for a moment?"

She bit her lip and glanced at her bedroom door. When she'd arrived home, she had fully intended to tell her parents the truth. But it was harder than she'd thought, especially when her dad was convinced she'd been staying with friends and her mum didn't give any indication that she even remembered Gabe's visit.

Was it really worth upsetting them with the truth?

I once knew your parents. Zad's voice whispered through her mind. How had they known an archangel? One day, she'd ask them.

Maybe…

She sighed heavily and tugged her hand through her tangled hair. That happened, when you forgot to brush it.

"Be right there." She injected a cheerful note in her voice. How long would she have to pretend everything was just fine?

She scraped her hair back into a ponytail. It was easier than tackling the tangles, and she made her way downstairs to the living room.

What the fuck?

She clutched the doorframe. Standing in the middle of the room, flanked by her parents, was the Archangel Zadkiel.

"Hi, Aurora." His voice was calm and soothing, but it didn't calm or soothe her in the least. She was about to vomit.

"Is Gabe all right?"

"He's fine." Zad's welcoming smile faded and his gaze sharpened, as though he was seeing far more than he'd first anticipated. "Are you?"

Relief flooded through her, but she still didn't trust herself to let go of the doorframe.

"Yes," she croaked. She didn't sound very convincing.

Her mum came over to her and took her hand. "We should have told you the whole truth. But we were sworn to secrecy."

"You can blame me," Zad said.

"We weren't supposed to let you know where your mum really came from," her dad added as he came to her side. "But we couldn't do that, could we, Aria?"

Her mum smiled at her dad, and their love glowed from them, a shining aura that seemed to enclose them in a translucent sphere.

Aurora blinked, and the illusion vanished. Except it wasn't an illusion. Her parents' love was a magical thing, and pain engulfed her heart.

It was the kind of love she so desperately craved with Gabe.

"We believed you had the right to know your heritage," her mum said. There was no faraway haze in her eyes or dreamlike quality to her voice, and Aurora caught her breath as hope raced through her.

Had her mum returned to them?

"But we should either have done what Zad said or told you why it was so dangerous to try and cross dimensions." Her dad sighed. "All we've ever wanted was to keep you safe."

She glanced at Zad. "Why didn't I meet you here before?"

"I haven't visited your parents in twenty-five years. I thought a catch up was overdue." Zad's gaze lingered on her, and she had the strangest sensation it wasn't her parents he was here for this time, at all.

"If not for Zad, I would have been trapped between dimensions," her mum said. "He saved me."

"He saved both of us," her dad said. "I was trapped too, remember?"

"I remember." There was certainty in her mum's voice that Aurora hadn't heard in years. Then she turned to her. "When the other one collected your things, I recognized him as an archangel. He forced me to face the truth of my past. I won't hide from it anymore."

"Another archangel?" Her dad gazed at her before frowning at Zad. "You stayed away because you didn't want to draw any possible attention to us from malignant entities. Did this other archangel put Aurora in danger?"

"No, Tom." Her mum shook her head. "He saved her, the way Zad saved us. I think it's time we told her everything."

"I'll see you in a few days," Zad said, and she heard the simmering rage beneath his words, but it wasn't directed at her, or her parents.

And then he teleported.

Gabe

"WHAT IS THIS, A FUCKING ARCHANGEL RETREAT?" Eblis sounded disgusted, and Gabe glowered across the club as Zad and Azrael strode toward the dimly lit alcove.

As far as he was aware, neither of them had set foot on Eta Hyperion before.

"Gabe's not the only one who can manipulate your security systems," Zad said, but his gaze was fixed on Gabe and it wasn't friendly. He took another long swallow from his tankard. For two days he'd been hanging out with the demon, and the hard knot in his chest was as suffocating as the moment he'd left Aurora.

He didn't expect that to ease, but he'd hoped for some measure of oblivion.

Eblis cursed in the language that had once flourished on Earth. "You're not welcome here."

Zad gave a wintery grin. "Tough."

"Are you here to drink? Because I'm not in the mood to talk." To underscore his point, Gabe finished the last drop from his tankard. Eblis slammed another bottle of alcohol onto the table. Unfortunately, it wasn't the stuff Mephisto had shared last week.

Zad gripped the edge of the chair opposite him and loomed over the table. He must be more wrecked than he realized, since the other archangel looked murderous and Zad never let his feelings show. And even if Zad was furious, why was he taking it out on *him*?

"I told you to look after her. Not fucking break her heart."

Gabe choked on a mouthful of alcohol. "*What?*"

"Seventy or eighty years. That's all the time you had to invest to ensure her happiness. But you just couldn't fucking do it, could you?"

"What the fuck?" Az sounded shocked, which sure as hell made two of them. "We came here to make sure Gabe was okay. What are you doing?"

"All you archangels are the same," Eblis said, but despite the derision in his voice, he sounded intrigued. "As crazy as our shit-faced goddess."

Gabe surged to his feet. Zad was questioning his integrity and that stung.

"Whatever happened between Aurora and me is none of your fucking business." Maybe the alcohol was stronger than he realized and this was a hallucination?

"It is when you just discard her without a second thought the moment you had enough."

Had enough? If his entire chest wasn't burning from the loss of her, he would have laughed in Zad's face.

"What's wrong with you?" Az glared at Zad. "Why would Gabe stay with a mortal if he didn't want to? That's never been our way. A clean break. It's kinder."

"Aurora isn't just any other mortal." Zad ground the words between his teeth.

"Sounds like you're attached to this female yourself." Eblis gave a mirthless laugh. "So much for the bonds of protection."

Raw, primitive, possessiveness slammed through Gabe. It hadn't even occurred to him that Zad might want Aurora himself.

"You touch her …" The words lodged in his throat, choking him. He hadn't allowed himself to think of the future, but some day Aurora would find a man. Fall in love.

Bear his children.

His splintered soul corroded with the knowledge. But the possibility of another archangel having her destroyed him.

Wouldn't happen. *Couldn't happen.* He'd never allow it.

The hostility on Zad's face faded.

"You care for her." He sounded both thunderstruck and horrified. "*You fell.*"

It was the last thing he wanted to discuss. But he couldn't deny the truth.

"Gabe." Azrael's tone was urgent. "She's only a human. Nothing special. Right?"

Nothing special? She was his everything. And he'd let her go without telling her.

"When I said she could heal your soul, I didn't expect you to fall."

"Make up your mind, archangel." Eblis sounded macabrely entertained. "You want Gabe to hook up with this woman until she dies, but only if he doesn't *want* to. I fucking love your logic."

Finally, Gabe found his voice. "Mind your own business, Zad. This has nothing to do with you."

"You can't have fallen. Not again." Az glared at him. "Gods, Gabe. If it's a human you want, there are plenty of them to choose from. And most of them don't try and destroy the astral planes."

So Az had figured out Aurora's connection with the disruption in that realm. Not that it mattered.

"I don't want another human." He hadn't wanted a human at all, had believed he could never love again, but it seemed he had no control over his heart. "Aurora is the only woman I want."

"Then why did she leave?" Zad demanded.

"Don't you understand?" Az grabbed his shoulders. "She's mortal. She's destined to die. No matter how many times you find her in the future, she'll always fucking *die*. And each time your heart will die as well."

It was the reason he'd fought his love for her. But it made no difference if he acknowledged it or not. He loved her, whether or not she loved him back. And he was a deluded fool if he thought he could have stayed away from her for the rest of her life.

He'd let her go because he was so sure they had no future together.

No. Brutal honesty forced him to face the truth. He'd let her go because he hadn't wanted to risk hearing her say she wanted her old life back—without him.

Hadn't wanted to risk rejection. From a mortal.

From Aurora. The only woman since Eleni who had managed to intrigue and bewitch him with everything she said and did.

The only woman he wanted to share his life with. Even if her existence was as brief as the flame of a candle.

"It's a small price to pay, Az." Yes, it would destroy a piece of him every time she died. But the love would survive.

And he would find her again.

"How can a few fleeting years possibly compensate for that kind of heartache?" Az demanded.

"Shut your mouth, archangel." Eblis stood and unfurled his wings. "Before any more shit comes out of it."

"What the hell do you know?" Az said. "You're a fucking demon."

Eblis curled his lip. "And you have never fallen."

CHAPTER 33

AURORA

$\mathcal{A}$urora was on her bed researching when her mum came into her room. It had been a whole day since Zad had visited, and her parents had shared the truth of how they'd met.

They hadn't encountered the Guardians. But it hadn't been as simple as her mum walking from her world straight into her dad's arms, the way they'd always told her.

If not for Zad, her parents would have been crushed between realities.

Not that it mattered. She'd never try breaching dimensions again. And not just because it was too dangerous.

It was because her mum no longer denied her true heritage.

Her mum sat at the end of her bed and smiled at her. She'd given her parents an edited version of her missing week. One day she'd tell them the truth about Gabe, the archangel she loved, but she wasn't up for that heart-to-heart just yet.

"Why aren't you wearing your necklace?"

Instinctively, her fingers went to her throat. She hadn't worn it since leaving Gabe. The urgency to feel it next to her skin had died. After touching the real archangelic token of devotion, she couldn't bear the thought of an inferior, human-crafted imitation.

"I don't know." She shrugged, then wondered if her mum thought she had lost it. "It's in my bag."

Her mum picked her bag up from the floor and pulled out the glittering jewelry, and frowned, as though she'd never seen it before.

"What's *this?*" She dangled the chain from her finger, and the wings sparkled in the early afternoon sunlight that spilled through the window. "It looks like yours, but it isn't."

"What?" She shoved her laptop onto the bed and went to her mum's side. Her breath hitched as she stroked a shaky finger over the wings, and the ethereal pulse echoed through her blood. The magical rainbows and gold dust originated from a long-destroyed City of Archangels.

Gabe had given her his beloved daughter's necklace. And kept hers for himself.

There was only one reason why he would have given her something so precious. Why hadn't he said anything?

Why didn't I?

"Gabe didn't just save your life, did he?" Her mum's voice was soft, and Aurora slumped against her. She guessed today was the day, after all.

"No."

"I could feel how much he loved you, Aurora."

Bittersweet pain squeezed her heart.

"I don't know—" The words locked in her throat and she caught her mum's steady gaze. *"You felt it?"* But she didn't speak out loud. Her mum hadn't spoken aloud, just now, either.

"Yes," her mum said. *"And that's when I remembered everything. I'm sorry I left you for so long."*

"It wasn't your fault." Her voice was husky, and she cleared her throat. "I'm just glad you're back."

"I was always so afraid." Her mum's voice was barely above a whisper. "That one day you'd find someone the way I did. That you'd leave this world, the way I left mine, and we'd never see you again. My mind tried to convince me none of it was real. Because if it wasn't real, you could never leave, could you?"

"Why didn't you tell me?" Guilt gnawed through her. By trying to help her mum regain her memories, she'd attempted to do the one thing her mother had feared above all else.

"You were too young. And then it was too late." Her mum took her hand and dropped the necklace onto her palm. "You need to find him. However impossible you think this love is, it's real."

"How am I supposed to find an archangel?"

"The same way you did before," her mum said, which didn't make a lot of sense. And then she whispered with her mind. *"He's in your heart."*

THE BEST CHANCE of Gabe hearing her call was if she was in the exact same spot as when they'd first met.

She made her way to the other end of the village and halted just before the woods. She wasn't going into trance or entering the astral planes. Gabe had initiated telepathic contact, and that was how she was going to try and reach him.

There were a few tourists wandering about, but she couldn't worry about them right now. She took a deep breath and prepared her mind.

"What the hell are you doing?" Mephisto's incredulous voice blasted through her head and her eyes sprung open. He towered over her, his moonlit streaked midnight wings fully extended like an avenging archangel of death. And instead of terror whipping through her, all she could think was *why isn't everyone staring at him?*

"I wasn't trying to cross dimensions." Obviously, he was invisible to everyone but her. Which meant it looked as though she was talking to herself. Great. "I was just trying to contact Gabe."

A tortured expression flashed over his face.

"If you love him, E, set him free. Don't let him find out who you really are."

"E?" Her whole body froze. He raked his gaze over her. But it wasn't condemning, and there was nothing threatening in his manner, the way there had the first time he'd seen her in Gabe's villa.

It was almost as though he was fighting an internal battle as to how, exactly, he should treat her.

"You really don't know, do you?" He folded his wings, but she had the feeling he didn't expect an answer to his question. Not that she had one, anyway. "What a fucking mess."

A shiver trickled along her spine and she curled her fingers around the necklace, drawing comfort from the ethereal pulse within it. There was nothing benevolent about him, the way there was with Gabe. Yet she wasn't afraid of him.

He had called her E. Did that stand for Eleni?

Had her fragile hope been true?

Before she could untangle her thoughts to ask him, the earth rumbled, and she staggered. An earthquake in Cornwall?

Except it wasn't anything as ordinary as that. A violet streak of lightning ripped reality apart, and a dozen nightmarish Guardians emerged.

No ...

Mephisto gripped her arm and slung her behind him. Terror snaked through her. Why were the Guardians still after her?

"Explain." Mephisto's voice was low. Deadly. He did not speak in English.

He spoke the language of the ancients.

And I can understand him.

A screeching hiss scraped through her nerves, but deep in her brain dormant synapses reconnected and primal pathways reactivated. And then the hisses and shrieks formed substance and cohesion and the most ancient words of all clawed through her mind.

It belongs to us—

Anomaly of nature—

Outside of your jurisdiction—

"No matter what the parentage," Mephisto said. "You touch the beloved of an archangel and you risk war against all Immortals."

The beloved?

Gabe had elevated her to the status of a beloved. *That* was why the Guardians had backed away in Kala's suite.

Why he had given her his precious archangelic necklace.

So why the hell were they back?

Section 188, Sub-Section 52, paragraph nine point three hundred of the—

"Don't quote the protocols at me," Mephisto snarled.

We have the right to take all anomalies in order to maintain the integrity of the universe—

Such abominations cannot be allowed to survive—

The anomaly must be given to us for neutralization—

Slowly, he turned and looked at her, his wings outstretched, protecting her from the Guardians' sight. Awe radiated from him in lethal waves.

"You didn't just come back. You came back as the one thing outside of an Immortal's protection. A trans-dimensional being."

How had the Guardians discovered her dual heritage? And then she remembered. She'd torn her arms and left traces of her blood in the Voids when they'd rescued Evalyne.

Terror hammered through her. "I'm condemned because of my *parentage?*"

Mephisto's eyes turned crimson with rage. But it wasn't directed at her.

"Aren't we fucking always?"

. . .

Gabe

GABE PULLED on a fresh shirt and ignored the trepidation that washed through him. He was an archangel. Trepidation was something mortals suffered from.

It didn't change the facts. Apprehension snaked through him at his planned confrontation with Aurora.

The outcome wouldn't change the way he felt. He'd always love her. But he had to find out if Zad was right. He'd rather his heart shattered into a million pieces a thousand times over, than have broken hers a single time.

He picked up her necklace and dropped it into his shirt pocket. Without warning, vertigo slammed through him, so violent that he staggered against the wall for support.

The oxygen burned his lungs, and a formless, primal, terror struck him, twisting his gut and squeezing his heart as the image of Aurora filled his mind. For a split second he saw the repellent shadows of the Guardians looming over her and denial crashed through him.

It wasn't possible. His love protected her. Yet the dread ground through him that it wasn't over. It would never be over.

Aurora, his beloved, was in deadly danger.

CHAPTER 34

AURORA

"There must be something you can do." Aurora took an involuntary step closer to Mephisto as the Guardians began to fan out around him. "You're the top archangel and you're powerless against them?"

"Did I say that?"

"You mean you *can* help me?"

There was a crazy gleam in his eyes. "Nephilim were always flesh and blood. But you're Eleni. I don't understand you. You shouldn't exist, yet you do."

She briefly touched his arm, and he didn't incinerate her for her presumption.

"So, what now?"

He cursed in the language of the ancients. She understood every word, and it was breathtaking in its imagery.

"If I twist enough of the sub-sections, dig deep enough into the protocols, there'll be something I can use. There's nothing that specifically cites Nephilim can't return as trans-dimensional."

He didn't need to finish that thought because she already

understood. No provision had been made because Nephilim never returned.

He swung around, wings fully extended, to face the enemy. She hitched in a breath and then, from the corner of her eye, saw a lone Guardian beyond Mephisto's peripheral vision.

And it was pointing a gleaming, cylindrical weapon directly at her.

Gabe

GABE ARRIVED at the exact place where he'd first met Aurora. In a nanosecond he saw the Guardians surrounding her, saw Mephisto turn his back on her—and the weapon aimed at her.

No ...

He didn't think. Just reacted and teleported directly in front of her to deflect the beam. Regret burned through him that he couldn't ask her, couldn't give her the choice. Because there was no longer any option. For her to live, he had to take her back to his island.

Their gazes collided, and fear and endless love reflected in her eyes. Then she shoved at him with her mind, a psychic punch, trying to push him from the path of danger, just as she'd tried to physically protect him from the Guardians on the day they'd met.

Time stood still, balanced on the precipice of eternity. Her psychic barriers opened for him, and their minds linked together in a way he had never imagined. Vivid images smashed through him, *memories* saturated with Eleni.

Her eyes, her laughter. Her fragrance.

Vibrant visions of their life together. Flashes of memory that were familiar, but they weren't his.

They were Eleni's.

The memories he'd lost last week came flooding back. When

she had breached dimensions, the psychic core that forever bound him to his beloved had burst into life.

Instinctively, he'd connected with the pure essence of Eleni —*of Aurora*—on the astral planes. And against all laws of physics he'd crashed through them, with only one thought thundering through his being.

Eleni was in danger. *And this time I can save her.*

The knowledge seared through him, and as he wrapped his arms around her, a cosmic blast from the Guardian's weapon smashed into his back and arrowed through his chest.

What the fuck ...

It shouldn't hurt like this. But their technology was alien, and the very air they breathed within the Voids was corrosive to archangels. Who knew what damage their weapons might inflict? He'd forgotten that, when he'd leaped in front of Aurora. Not that it would have made any difference.

He glanced down and saw her necklace glow from inside his shirt pocket. *How the hell is that happening?*

She sagged in his arms, her head falling back and eyes flickering shut. He clasped her tight against his chest, acidic fear scorching through his heart.

She couldn't die. He should have been able to save her.

I failed.

As blackness descended, the glow from her necklace expanded, connecting to an identical white-blue beacon of light that radiated from the archangelic wings around Aurora's throat.

Despair consumed him, and then there was nothing.

A RED-HOT PSYCHIC flame seared through Gabe's brain and he shot upward, heart pounding, mouth dry. Every bone in his body ached, and through his blurred vision, he could make out only two things.

He was attached to a drip. And Mephisto, whose primitive psychic prod had slammed him awake, was glowering down at him.

Wait. *A drip?* He grasped the needle with uncoordinated fingers and pulled. It hurt like shit and he collapsed back onto the bed. He was in his own bedroom, on his own bed—and Aurora was by his side.

He shoved himself up and leaned over her, fear spiking through his chest. Why was she hooked up to a drip and all those monitors?

"Don't touch her needles." Mephisto sounded rabid. "I need to talk to you."

Fuck that. Gabe began to unwrap the dressing around her hand. He could heal her in a heartbeat without all this primitive junk surrounding her.

Zad appeared from nowhere and gripped his wrist. The fear punched deeper and he glared at the other archangel.

"What's the matter with her? Why can't you just heal her?"

"She's no longer injured," Zad said. "We were simply keeping her unconscious. Same as you."

"*What?*" He pulled his wrist free, and damn if it didn't feel like he cracked a couple of bones in the process. Disjointed fragments of memory surfaced.

Aurora was Eleni.

Somehow, that wasn't important right now. The only thing that mattered was that Aurora was okay.

"If she's no longer injured, why are you still keeping her unconscious?"

Mephisto unfurled his wings.

"Forget about E for just two seconds, will you?" He loomed over Gabe, and his eyes flickered crimson. "The Guardians fired on an archangel. According to the protocols, that gives us the right to decimate their ranks. But since they claim this fucking archangel appeared from nowhere after the beam was fired, the case is not clear cut."

"Aurora's not being sacrificed to the Guardians." Gabe glared at Mephisto and ignored the worrying fatigue that snaked through his body. "If Armageddon is what they want, then Armageddon is what they'll get."

Mephisto offered him a feral grin. "I've spent the last six weeks negotiating with those bastards. Six weeks while you lay here, oblivious. And I finally managed to broker a deal."

Gabe reared off the bed and grasped Mephisto's shirt.

"Six weeks?" He'd been unconscious for that long? It was the only thing his bruised mind could latch onto. And then the rest of Meph's comment thudded through his brain, and that didn't make any sense either. No one negotiated with the Guardians.

"The blast from the Guardians went straight through you and hit Aurora," Zad said. "You were knocked out and she almost died. She *would* have died. There was nothing we could have done to save her, Gabe. Except—we're not sure how—your souls entwined. You kept her alive. Gave her time to heal."

A shudder crawled along his spine. Souls didn't entwine. It wasn't possible.

He released Mephisto, who hadn't retaliated, and looked down at Aurora. Since the moment they'd met, so many of his long-held convictions had crumbled.

Just because he'd never believed souls could entwine, didn't make it so.

Once, he had believed Nephilim could never be reborn.

"Yes, you kept her alive." Mephisto glanced at Aurora before turning his blazing gaze back to Gabe. "But at what cost? Your fucking *immortality*."

"*What?*" His immortality? He'd given up his immortality so Aurora could live?

"Do you really think I would have let the Guardians take her? She's one of *ours*."

So Mephisto knew. But he hadn't seen the threat of that lone Guardian.

"We don't know how it happened." Zad gripped his shoulder. "We tried to separate you, but it wasn't just a case of you keeping Aurora alive. The connection went both ways. Your life forces were as one."

I'm mortal. The concept was too alien, too immense.

Except …

If he was mortal, he wouldn't have to exist for countless centuries without her. Their souls were entwined. Neither could live, nor die, without the other.

Wild hope flared, illuminating the dark abyss of his no-longer endless future. Aurora would be reborn, and so would he. And they would find each other, two halves of the whole, life after life.

For eternity.

"In exchange for holding off your Armageddon—and let's face it, as a mortal you'd be fucking useless in that battle—the Guardians have agreed to relinquish all rights over Aurora and her direct bloodline."

She's safe.

Mephisto folded his wings before continuing. "I told them I made you a mortal because of your actions. Couldn't have them suspecting we had no fucking idea how it happened. I thought it'd take a lot to convince them, but they accepted it right away."

Zad tore his gaze from Aurora. "Her parents are safe too. Meph constructed a magnificent defense. He argued that they were immune from the Guardians' jurisdiction because it was love alone that had allowed her mother to breach dimensions. Since the Guardians have no concept of love, they had no rebuttal."

Gabe gave a hoarse laugh. For millennia he'd cursed the fates that he couldn't turn back time so he could hold his beloved once again. That, somehow, given a second chance, he'd be able to thwart his goddess and save the lives of those he loved.

He would have sacrificed anything, *everything*, to change the past.

And then he met Aurora, and for the first time in forever found someone worth surviving for.

Someone worth sacrificing everything for.

He had craved redemption, never believing it could be possible.

Yet in a paradoxical twist, the universe, for once, had got things right.

Aurora

Aurora stirred, and strong arms tightened around her. She smiled against Gabe's shoulder and a comforting sense of floating on clouds filled her mind.

Where was she?

Slowly she opened her eyes. She was lying on top of Gabe, near the woods on the outskirts of her village, and the early dawn glow gave everything a mystic haze.

For endless seconds she basked in the warmth of Gabe's embrace, inhaling his unique scent as unformed images drifted like feathers through her languid psyche.

And became solid.

The Guardians.

Where had they gone? What had *happened*?

She raised her head and her gaze locked with Gabe's. And she remembered.

"You saved my life. *Again*. You're making a bit of a habit of it."

"You saved mine first. A long time ago. I just never knew it."

Memories flooded through her mind, of another life, another time. Memories of Gabe, of Helena, and Zad.

Eleni's memories.

Mine.

"I came back." Her voice was awed. And then she linked to him telepathically. *"And you found me."*

"If I'd known, I would have searched for you, Aurora." Millennia of guilt and regret seeped through every word. *"I would have found you years ago. You would never have put yourself in danger with the Guardians, if only I'd found you."*

"Stop it." She speared her fingers through his glorious hair. "How were you to know? We always believed the legends were true. And maybe they were. Maybe Nephilim and their descendants can only be reborn with an extraordinary pairing of trans-dimensional DNA. Something that even the ancients, with all their knowledge, had no concept of."

"Or my fucked-up goddess lied to us, and the demons, right from the start. That sounds more likely."

She had to admit to the truth of that.

"It's possible we might never know." She gave a shaky sigh. "But I'm going to dedicate the rest of my life in trying to find out. If it's happened once, it can happen again. Helena could come back too. It's possible. You know it is."

She saw the hope, the longing, glitter in his eyes as he struggled to overcome millennia of ingrained inevitability. Finally, he rolled onto his side, still holding her, so they faced each other.

"Yes." So much heartache echoed in that one simple word. "It's possible. Anything's possible." His mesmeric gaze ensnared her, the way it had so many years ago. The way it had, once again, just one week ago. "I'm no longer an immortal."

"What?" She pressed her hand against his heart, and something grazed her palm through the material of his shirt. "But you're an archangel." A different kind of fear spiked through her. "Did the Guardians' weapon destroy your immortality?"

"No." There was a smile on his face. Why wasn't he totally freaking out? "It was the price of having my wish granted."

Her heart ached with all he had lost. "It's a high price to pay, Gabe."

"It really isn't." He tugged her closer. "All that matters is we're together. Remember I told you I'd accumulated several fortunes over the centuries? You can have a state-of-the-art lab on every continent on the planet, if you want."

"Excessive." She gave him a watery smile. Was it her necklace he kept next to his heart? She slipped her hand into his pocket and pulled out the delicate chain.

And gasped.

"Shit." Gabe stared at the shard of fossilized charcoal that vaguely resembled her substitute archangel wings. "What the hell?"

She curled her fingers around the necklace at her throat. No ethereal pulse warmed her flesh. A small, silent grief washed through her. *It's dead.*

He unclasped the necklace from around her neck. The rainbows were scorched, the gold destroyed. The magical, beautiful life that had survived for millennia had been extinguished.

"Gods." He sounded awed, shaken. "It was the archangel wings. That was the conduit between us. When the blast went through me and hit you, your Earth created necklace and this one fused our life forces together. The spark of eternity within the wings reversed. It sucked out my immortality in order to save you."

He looked at her, and she didn't need a piece of archangelic jewelry, because eternity glowed in his beautiful eyes. "My beloved," he whispered.

"I love you." The words filled her soul. A soul she had once believed could never be hers. "I always have. And I always will."

He tangled his fingers in her hair. "I fell in love with you, Aurora. Before I ever knew you were Eleni. It was *you* I wanted to save from the Guardians. I don't even know what that means."

She cradled his jaw and sighed softly. He had fallen for her, believing he betrayed Eleni. Her beautiful, loyal, beloved archangel.

"It means you can let go of the past. Unburden the guilt that was never yours to carry."

He brushed the tip of his nose across hers, and deep in her ancient memories she recalled all the other times they had touched like this. How could it have been so long ago?

She remembered their life together so clearly, now.

"This mortal thing might take some getting used to. I can't heal myself anymore." He flexed his fingers that were still buried in her hair. "I think I've cracked a couple of bones in my wrist."

She threaded her fingers through his. "You do know you could ask Zad? He'd heal you without a second thought."

Gabe grunted. "And you do know that's never going to happen, don't you? I'm a mortal. I need to get used to it."

She gave a soft laugh. "You'll always be the Archangel Gabriel. Nothing's ever going to change that. But that was never why I fell in love with you."

"Just as well. Otherwise this would be a real problem. There's no escaping our destinies. We're bound to each other for all of eternity." His wicked grin suggested he couldn't wait.

A fierce, protective love surged through her. "It's about time. And there's something you should know." She brushed a tender kiss across his lips. "Eternity is just the beginning."

NEMESIS

A REALM OF FLAME AND SHADOW NOVEL
BOOK 2

Falling for his nemesis is the most dangerous thing he's ever done...

One thousand years ago, the Archangel Azrael made a pledge to wipe dhampirs from the face of the earth.

No exceptions.

Then he meets the enigmatic Rowan. She's keeping secrets and he's determined to uncover them.

Until he discovers the truth. And his whole damn world implodes...

"A sexy, fast-paced paranormal/urban fantasy read containing secrets, danger and betrayal plus *oodles* of passion and hotness!" Tina, A Readers Review blog

SALVATION

A REALM OF FLAME AND SHADOW NOVEL
BOOK 3

I just spent the best night of my life with the hottest guy I've ever met. Too bad he turns out to be my deadliest enemy – the Archangel Nathanael…

Half-demon Isabella has dreamed of bringing archangels to justice and there's no way she'll forgive Nate for his deception. Except it turns out he has no idea who she is… can this be the chance for retribution she's been searching for?

There's only one rule I live by. Never trust a demon.

Close to finding a rogue demon he's been hunting for millennia, Nate's not looking for any distractions. Until Isabella turns his world inside out and leaves him wanting so much more. But when he uncovers her true heritage, her betrayal rocks him, and he faces the choice of leaving her to her fate or breaking the only rule in his book.

With dark secrets threatening their survival, there's no way an archangel and a half-demon can work together. But with the clock ticking, and danger stalking every move they make, the only way to save themselves might just be to save each other.

ACKNOWLEDGMENTS

I first got the idea for Gabe and Aurora's romance many years ago, and have lost count how many times I've rewritten this story. But even when it was published, it never quite matched the vision I had in my mind, and I was so happy to receive the rights back. It took me a few years before I was able to return to this world, and I owe a huge debt of gratitude to my amazing editor, Amanda Ashby, who encouraged me to rip the book apart and start over!

Huge thanks also to Sally Rigby for your invaluable insights and all the times you've talked me down from the ledge!

Cathleen Ross, your support and encouragement over the years has meant so much to me. Thank you!

Big thank you to Amy Hart for your fantastic proofreading. I'll never get the hang of those pesky commas!

And, of course, love and thanks to Mark and our family. Big squishy hugs!

ABOUT THE AUTHOR

Christina Phillips is an ex-pat Brit who now lives in sunny Western Australia with her high school sweetheart and their family. She enjoys writing paranormal, historical and contemporary romance where the stories sizzle and the heroine brings her hero to his knees.

She is addicted to good coffee, expensive chocolate and bad boy heroes. She is also owned by three gorgeous cats who are convinced the universe revolves around their needs. They are not wrong.

Christinaphillips.com